MAGIC IN DISGUISE

AGENTS OF A.S.S.E.T.

KATIE SALIDAS

BOOKS BY KATIE SALIDAS

Agents of A.S.S.E.T.
A Weapon of Magical Destruction
A Taste of Your Own Magic
Magic in Disguise

Chronicles of the Uprising
Dissension
Complication
Revolution
Transition
Retribution
Annihilation

Little Werewolf
Pretty Little Werewolf
Curious Little Werewolf
Fearless Little Werewolf

Immortalis
Carpe Noctem
Hunters & Prey
Pandora's Box
Soustone
Dark Salvation

Olde Town Pack
Moonlight
Mated
Being Alpha

Autographed Editions of all Katie Salidas books may be purchased at
www.KatieSalidas.com

The world is full of magical creatures and artifacts. That's
where the A.S.S.E.T. agency comes in:
Anonymous Supernatural Security and Elimination
Taskforce.

The front line, maintaining the balance of power,
ensur-ing humans remain safely oblivious to the
dangerous magic around them.

Acknowledgments

This book was a product of tough love, and I want to thank the team of readers who really put me through my paces. Anne Loshuk, Jacob Devlin, Jason LaVelle & J.E. Taylor!

Thank you for going over multiple drafts, giving me all of your honest feedback, and really paying attention to the small details. You're honesty and critical eye have shaped this story into something special.

Beyond the critical, thank you as well for the enthusiasm you've had for this book series. You guys jumped on this project the moment I announced it and devoured each section faster than I could produce them. The late night chats, encouragement, & feedback was just the encouragement I needed to keep this project moving, even when I felt it was all for naught.

And last but not least, thank you to my readers!
You are the reason I keep writing!

ONE

How did I get here?

Deep within her hand, the twinges began. Sage stared at the ugly blemish blackening her palm. A few days earlier, the only deformity she could claim was the birthmark that labeled her a Terra: The Tree of Life.

The Great Mother had bestowed innate magical protection upon those who bore her mark. But all magic comes with a price. Especially for Terras. If only she'd read the fine print, she'd have been more careful with her gift.

Sage had been tasked with protecting the greatest weapon known to the magical community, The Seed of Destruction; daring to use its magic, however, earned her this penance. And if the ever-growing black mark on her palm was any indication of the consequences, she too, would ultimately be destroyed by the seed's need to consume power.

Pain was fast becoming her constant companion. Living in a house with vampires, she was never too far from magic. Dark or light, it didn't matter. The seed burned with insatiable hunger for power. She clenched her fist tight, but it did nothing to silence the throbbing.

A knock at her front door provided a perfect distraction from all the negative thoughts that came to her during the lonely hours of isolation.

She jumped to her feet, happy to have any kind of company. Well, any kind of non-magical company. What she wouldn't give for a pair of missionaries to drop by. She'd endure whatever religion they wanted to peddle as long as they would sit and have a cup of coffee with her.

"What's the password?" Sage called playfully as she clicked the door lock.

"Coffee," Grey responded mechanically.

"That was last week's password." She yanked the door open, and met him with an impish smirk. "Try again."

Grey stood, arms crossed, that silly fedora ever present on top of his head. She was tempted to knock it off, just to continue her playful greeting, but he beat her to the punch with an annoyed, "Grow up."

Mercurial as ever, she never knew if he was going to play along with her jokes or throw a wet blanket on her good mood. Still, she had to try. He was the only person who visited her since she'd earned the scarlet letter at ASSET. Administrative leave, they called it. Sage had other words. Cabin fever, a slow decent into madness.

"Don't you want to know the new password?" She stood her ground, hands on her hips, a flimsy barricade, more playful than purpose, but enough to prevent Grey from entering her home.

"You're either going to let me in, or find a new way to get to work."

After nearly a week without news, his words renewed her spirit. Her blockade crumbled. She reached out and yanked Grey into the apartment.

"Do we have a case?" *Thank the Goddess! Real human...er...Terra interaction. Non-bloodsucker company.* Vampires didn't make the best of roommates. "Fill me in. Shifters, witches, trolls? Who needs our help?"

"Slow your roll there, newbie." Grey cracked a smile. He had to know how much she needed this. How desperate she was for something useful to do.

She closed the door behind him and ushered Grey to the kitchen table. "Easy for you to say. You're not on house arrest. I'd willingly jump on the back of your bike and ride across the country and back if it means getting out of this house."

"Careful what you wish for," he teased.

She pressed him down into one of the dining chairs and rounded the table to take the one opposite him. "I might be a newbie, but I'm not messing with wishes and djinn again. Hell no!" She crossed her fingers behind her back. Luke's fate had been a need-to-know basis kind of thing, and even though Grey was her partner, she hadn't quite let him in on that secret yet.

Luke was still very much alive and living across the walkway from her apartment too. Though he couldn't possibly have retained his magic after what she'd done to him.

"All right, there's this kid." Grey folded his arms on the table and leaned in closely. "Poor, pitiful little thing." He whispered the words like a secret none but the two of them should share. "She got herself into a lot of trouble. Mixing with the wrong sort."

"Really? Do we need to rescue her?" Chills prickled at the back of Sage's neck. She bristled with excitement. This was her chance to make amends. Anticipation had her salivating for more information. She wouldn't fail. "Who has her?"

"Oh yeah. She needs rescuing, all right. If I had my way the minute I brought her in, I'd have her locked up. For her own protection." He snickered, breaking just long enough for Sage to catch the cruelty of his joke.

"Jerk." She reached across the table and swatted the hat off his head. Too bad she'd been aiming for his cheek.

Grey laughed all the way to the ground as he ducked under the table to retrieve his fedora. His amusement vanished as he came back up. Eyes widened with fearful curiosity. He stared silently as if seeing Sage for the first time, only he hadn't looked her in the eye. The target of his concern fell much lower than her face.

"You sure you're up for working in your current condition?"

Sage hid her ruined hand behind her back, but it was too late. He'd already taken in the new damage. "I'm fine. I can still work."

He stood and dusted off the hat before placing it back on his head. "I'd rather we get you sorted before hitting the field again, but Ava's ordered you in for a meeting."

She cringed at the prospect of another lecture from Queen High Bitch herself. "Should I be scared?"

Grey gave a noncommittal shrug. "Whatever it is, we're partners, so we'll take our lumps together."

She stood and grabbed her keys off the wall hook. "Speaking of… How come I got sent home while you were still allowed to work?"

"I didn't get anything stuck in my hand on our last mission,"—he pointed an accusing finger at her—"but don't think I got off easy. Ava's had me tied to her desk all week."

Her mind instantly sank into the gutter, conjuring up a naughty vision of Grey bound at the wrist and ankles across Ava's mahogany desk. Ava certainly fit the dominatrix persona, but Grey as a submissive? *Nope. Can't have thoughts like those. Bad Sage!* Where was the mental bleach when she needed it?

"You're right. Administrative leave is so much better. But I'm still ready to get back to work." A sharp shock jolted through her palm quick as a strike of lightning. She winced, hissing as she clenched her fist tight enough to send her nails into her skin. The seed never failed to make its desire known. Even the prospect of being near magic was enough to awaken its insatiable hunger.

Grey was at her side before she opened her eyes, taking her hand in his. "You're getting worse." Carefully, he inspected the damage. Blackening skin spread out from the center where the seed had made its home, its darkness reaching out in all directions, devouring her slowly. He tiptoed the pads of his fingers across each of the lines in her palms.

The shocking tenderness of his touch took the edge off her pain. Tickled a bit too. Sage fought against the smile it brought to her face. It wasn't like Grey to be so... Had he numbed her mind as well? What new magic was this? His gesture was stirring something else within her.

"Fine... I'm... Good. Can I have my hand back?"

He let go as if she'd burned him. "Does it hurt?"

So much! "A little. More when I'm around magic."

"I don't doubt that. You're like a lightning rod caught in a thunderstorm. All the magic around you, right there for the taking."

"To put it mildly." She scrubbed her hands, trying to stop the tingling left in the wake of his grip.

"You sure you're going to be okay?"

"I'm fine."

"Good, because I don't need my partner getting all weird on me when we're out there dealing with whatever shitstorm Ava assigns us."

Snarky tone. Condescension. Teasing. That she could handle. That didn't send butterflies buzzing around her stomach. She reached for a pair of silver-lined gloves on the counter and slipped them on. Ava had suggested she wear them. She hadn't tested whether or not it blocked the seed's power, but better safe than sorry.

"Me, weird?" She waggled her silver-coated fingers at him. "Don't know what you mean."

"Maybe keep those in your pocket."

"You think, Captain Obvious? Gloves in the desert, in the middle of summer. Might as well walk around with a neon sign on my head." Looking weird was the least of her worries. It was the very real risk she could accidentally kill someone with a single touch that weighed heaviest on her mind.

"I know this is difficult. I'm proud of how brave you are being. You're handling this so well."

What the hell was that tone? He'd gone from snarking to simpering in a blink, talking to her like she was some fragile creature moments from shattering into a thousand pieces should he utter a negative word. Come to think of it, he'd been noticeably less Grey since she'd been cursed.

"Don't talk to me like a lost cause."

Grey stepped back as if she'd took a swing at him. "What?"

"You're being too nice!"

His brow crinkled. Grey opened his mouth but no words came.

"You know something you're not telling me, *partner*." Sage threw her hands on her hips. He wasn't going to weasel out of giving her an answer. He wasn't a soft and gentle kind of guy. The new case was a charade. Sage was dying. Or worse. If there was a worse. That thought sent a whole different kind of chill slithering down her spine.

"As long as I've lived, I've pissed off my fair share of women," – Grey stared at her in disbelief – "but not once has any girl ever yelled at me for being nice."

"You know what I mean." She narrowed her eyes, daring him to blow more smoke up her ass. "You're not being you. What world-altering devastation are you hiding from me?"

"Woah. Hold on there, Drama Queen." Grey threw his hands up in the air, taking yet another step away from her. Any further and he'd plaster himself against the front door. "You jumped right onto the crazy train."

"You're an insufferable asshole, and that's on a good day. But since this whole thing happened." She pulled the glove off and shoved her blackening hand in his face. "You've been distant. And when I finally do see you, you're speaking to me like…I'm some sort of…cancer patient who's been given two weeks to live."

"Put that away." He swatted at her hand.

"No." She held it firmly in his face. "Not until you tell me why you're acting so weird."

"Stop this now!" He took hold of her hand with a growl that made him sound part wolf. His grip was iron, tightening when she resisted, preventing her from pulling away.

"Let me go," she demanded.

"You can't hurt me. I'm not afraid of you. Probably the only person in your current circle of friends that can say that right now." His breath came slowly as he moved her hand to his chest. Grey fixed the ruin of her palm directly over his heart.

Stubbornly, she gave one final attempt to pull free before resigning herself to his will.

His heart knocked against her wounded hand. The steady rhythm vibrated powerfully through his chest, but it was the warmth that radiated from him that worked true magic. Each pulse of his heartbeat fought against the ache, absorbing it, neutralizing it, and steadily gaining ground against her pain.

He loosened his iron grip, letting the choice to continue their physical connection fall to her. Sage found herself floating somewhere in the neutral zone between pain and something much more intense. His thumb ghosted over the back of her hand, so tender, so intimate. She sucked in a frightened breath, realizing how much his touch had kindled within her. A wonderful distraction from the pain in her hand but sure to leave lasting scars on her heart. She wasn't ready to let him past her defenses. This wasn't the time for those thoughts anyway.

She let her hand fall, instantly regretting the loss of his warmth, and released her breath in an attempt to force with it all the stress she could expel from her body. Their physical connection had said what words couldn't, and that scared her more than the meeting she would soon have with Ava.

"You paid a high price for your service to the gods." Grey's voice cracked. He cleared his throat to cover the sound and leaned in, their noses almost touching. The silent way his eyes had begged her to come closer could not be unseen.

"It's only temporary." Her legs went soft like warm jelly. She backed away awkwardly, struggling to stay upright. "I'm sure ASSET had a way to fix this."

"One way or another, we'll set things right." Grey mopped his face with his hands, wiping disappointment away as he replaced it with a stony mask of indifference. She'd have much rather he kept the smile, but ultimately his game face was what she needed.

"Yeah." She chuckled nervously. "Because I'm not wearing these gloves for the rest of my life." She turned away, her cheeks burning with raw emotions she wasn't ready to process. Her focus had to be on removing the stone.

"Sage," he called to her.

"What?"

"You're not going to die, okay? We will fix you."

"Of course we will. I'd hate to inconvenience you with my death." Sage found snarky comebacks flowed much more freely than heavy emotions.

"You know how much I hate paperwork," Grey responded in kind.

"Good, because the alternative is the Luke Skywalker approach, and prosthetic hands are not that advanced yet."

"You have a movie to reference for every situation, don't you?"

"Pop culture is my second language." She fit the glove back over her bad hand. "But I do draw the line at the Michael Jackson references."

"He only wore one glove."

She snorted at his attempted humor. "You think I could get away with that?"

"Better safe than sorry. But if you're itching to test the theory, I could hold Zack down for you."

That was more like it. Grey was beginning to sound like himself. Dumb jokes and playful condescension she could deal with.

"Don't tempt me. He's been nearly as insufferable as you this last week."

Grey's lips twisted into a sneer. "Something you haven't told me?"

Was that jealousy she detected? Sage nearly took the bait, but inciting another testosterone war wouldn't help matters. "It's just difficult having him live here at the apartment while he trains Matt, that's all."

"Better than the alternative."

"You don't have to listen to him. The one saving grace about my new little…affliction." She wiggled her fingers again as if casting a magic spell. "He can't come anywhere near me."

"He'd only make that mistake once."

"And I'd have more blood on my hands. First month on the job… What's my tally?"

"You do have an impressive kill count for a newbie." The wink he gave her held a little too much flirt in its wake.

Sage turned to the door before things got awkward again. "Let's go see if I'm up for any awards, then."

"Promise not to kill me?" Grey shoved her aside as he rushed to open the door. Yet another oddly un-Grey-like gesture.

"We're meeting with Ava," she reminded him. "Are you sure it's not my head on the chopping block?"

TWO

All the eagerness she'd had to get back to work evaporated the moment Sage breached the threshold of Ava's office. Her boss sat, busy as ever, behind the wall of her laptop, shuffling piles of paper from her overflowing inbox to another stack of documents towering on the other side of her desk. Ava either had not noticed them come in, or as Sage suspected, was playing a game of dominance.

"You wanted to see us?" Sage called out.

Ava's head popped up. Her turquoise eyes narrowed as she inspected Sage from head to toe. If only Terras had been gifted with mind reading. Ava Masters had a poker face better than anyone Sage had ever seen. Mouth set in a hard flat line. No hints of a smile or smirk. No body language to signal intentions. Ava kept her posture neutral as her gaze traveled toward their target, Sage's gloved hand.

"Shut the door and sit." Ava barked the order, and Sage found herself jumping from sudden shock. Ava set down her pages and closed the laptop, then folded her arms and waited for Sage to do as she was told. Every movement felt calculated and controlled, more so than usual. Almost as if Ava had some apprehension about being in the room with Sage. But that couldn't be possible.

Ava didn't strike her as the type who feared anything, and even if she did, no one would ever see it.

All the posturing left a bitter taste in Sage's throat. Tests. That's what this was. But what were they testing? How was she supposed to act?

Some days she regretted telling Mark she couldn't work with him. Back home in Phoenix, he'd been a surrogate father. Never too busy to stop what he was doing, he'd always greeted her with warmth. He made her feel comfortable to come to him with anything. Ava held the same top-level position in the Vegas office, but her approach to being the head honcho was more despot than director.

"Enjoying your vacation, Miss Cynwrig?" Ava's tone was anything but casual.

"I wouldn't exactly call it a vacation." Sage struggled to control the tremble in her voice. This felt too much like a trap. She turned sideways looking for Grey, but he hadn't taken the other seat.

"It wasn't meant to be." Ava's shrill reply worked like a slap to the face, refocusing Sage's attention back on her boss. "Have you sorted out your domestic situation?"

"Do you need me in here?" Grey hovered near a chair as if expecting to be told to vacate it the moment his cheeks hit the cushion. "I can wait outside."

"Sit, Mr. Maddox." Ava pointed to the other chair with her perfectly manicured finger. "I'll get to you in a moment."

He responded immediately, like a well-trained pup, taking the chair and leaving Sage to wonder exactly how bad his week with Ava had been. Maybe she had gotten the better punishment after all.

Ava cleared her throat, and Sage snapped to attention.

"My domestic situation is…uh…being managed," Sage answered. "I believe I'm ready to return to work."

"You'll return when I say." Ava held out her hand. "Show me your palm, please?"

At least she asked nicely. Sage pulled off her gloves and held her damaged hand out for inspection.

Ava snapped it up with the speed of a viper and yanked her forward with such strength Sage nearly came out of her seat.

The poker face faltered. Ava's expression shifted between curiosity and concern the longer she scrutinized Sage's palm. She knew it was bad, but for her boss to let slip the control she had over her expression was truly telling.

Darkness, that had started as a small spot marking the place where the seed had embedded itself, had grown, slowly stretching out in all directions as it claimed new territory across her hand. The epicenter remained black as pitch, lightening a little across the recently deadened skin. Like bruises, her hand was splotched purple and blue. The outer areas of the seed's reach had turned yellow, not quite succumbing to the darkness but clearly losing the fight. All of it a stark contrast to the creamy color of her undamaged skin. Her hand was dying. Slowly, but dying all the same. A truth Sage did not want to admit aloud. The black mark had grown from nothing in the space of a week, and she felt the scream of every nerve before being silenced. How long would it be before her whole body was covered by this cursed black mark? What would become of her when it did?

"I'm assuming there is pain to match the outward symptoms," Ava said without an ounce of sympathy in her voice. "Manageable, I expect?"

"Better when I am clear of magic, not so much at other times."

"I'd like to run a few tests." Ava dropped Sage's hand, letting it crash on her desk.

Grey leaned in, resting his chin on his hands. He could have warned her this was going to happen. At least give her a heads-up she was becoming a lab rat.

Falling into the trap of self-pity was too easy. Temptation she'd been struggling with for the last week. But maybe she'd been looking at it wrong. Maybe Ava didn't know all. Maybe she needed to be the lab rat. *Yes.* Sage nodded to herself. *Work toward a cure. Stay positive.*

Ava reached to open the topmost drawer in her desk. "We need to see how that thing responds to stimulus." She pulled out a crystal sphere, the kind of mystical see-into-the-future equipment that would be used in a fortune teller's tent.

Sage almost made a Great Zoltar joke to lighten the mood, but caught herself before she stuck her foot in her mouth. Boss lady wasn't the joking type, and Sage was already on the 'problem child' list.

Ava held it up, letting the light hit it, awakening an inner light within the sphere. Deep within the center, a tiny glowing ember of blue light pulsed. Magic. Hidden from mortal eyes, but clearly visible to the Terra. The seed pulsed within Sage's palm, sensing the magic, burning with hunger. Even before Ava's prompt for her to, "Touch it," Sage felt the pull. As if the seed had already reached out and lassoed the orb, it drew her hand upwards to take hold of it.

She cringed, fighting against the tractor beam guiding her. The wrath of disobeying would be nothing compared to the pain in her hand, but still she struggled to willingly reach out and cause herself pain. Slow, deep breaths, in and out. Sage closed her eyes and gave in.

Zap!

Electricity jolted through her body. She yelped, yanking her hand back, and cradled it against her chest.

Ava picked up the crystal orb to inspect. She held it up in the light. The blue ember was no longer visible. "Let me see your hand now."

Sage complied, holding out her palm for inspection. Residual echoes of the electricity still throbbed, sending pulses all the way up her arm.

"Not enough." Tiny creases appeared on Ava's brow. She pursed her lips as she closed in for a better look at Sage's aching hand. "We need something more powerful." Again, she dropped Sage's hand, letting it smash down onto the desk.

"What are you hoping to find?" Sage asked.

Ava ducked down, opening the bottom drawer in her desk. "When I need you to speak, I will ask the questions, Miss Cynwrig."

A snarky retort nearly leapt off the end of Sage's tongue, but she held it back, turning her confusion toward Grey.

He looked just as uncertain as Sage. They exchanged confused glances and shrugs, further confirming that no one in the room had a clue what to do about her hand.

Ava popped back up from the drawer holding an ornately carved wooden stick in her hand. "Let's run the test again."

Sage wanted to refuse. She didn't have a masochistic bone in her body, despite what everyone said about her always trying to kill herself, but knew her boss would only force her hand if she did. She took a moment to steel her courage, telling herself *this is being done in the name of breaking the curse*, though she didn't doubt Ava was taking some pleasure in punishing Sage for her disobedience.

She sucked in a deep breath and readied herself for the pain that was sure to come.

Ava held out the wand. "Take hold of it, please, with your injured hand."

The seed had already locked onto the magic. Like a magnet, it drew Sage's hand. If she struggled, she could avoid touching it, but all she had to do was let go of control and the seed would guide her there. It throbbed hungrily, burning with an insatiable fire the moment she came close to the wood. Then it struck, the fiery stab like a white hot knife sliced through her palm the moment she made contact with it. Controlled by the seed's desire, she gripped the wand tightly, her fingers wrapping around it, closing the connection. Invisible flames danced up from her hand, consuming her arm, her chest, spreading all across her body. She bit back a cry threatening to burst from her throat. Time distorted. Seconds felt like minutes. The seed lazily savored the power within the magical artifact. Sage was the conduit, feeling the magic flow through her and be incinerated. The seed was in control. She couldn't release her grip if she wanted to.

Tears watered in her eyes. She held back from voicing her agony as long as she could, holding out until the power finally ebbed. She collapsed on Ava's desk. The wand, finally free of her grip, clattered against wood.

"Are you okay?" Grey's hand rested on her back. "You look like you're about to puke."

If he only knew how right he was, but the worst was over. She clutched her injured hand tightly to her chest, allowing small whimpers to escape as she panted through the remaining waves of pain and sat up again.

"Do not mess up my office. If you're going to be sick, use a bin." Ava reached around her desk and pulled a trash can out.

"I'm fine. I'll be fine. Just need a little air." She took the trash can all the same.

"What you just… let's call it neutralized, for lack of a better word, was The Wand of Wailing. It has been around for over a thousand years, wielded by many an Elemental druid."

"Wait. Aren't all elementals magic people?" Sage asked.

"Yes, dear, but wands are for focusing magic. After a time, they retain bits of power. They themselves become quite magical in their own right. We recovered this one last week. No need to put it in the archives now."

Had Ava tried to make a joke? Sage couldn't tell. Either way, she wasn't in the laughing mood. Her body felt like an open wound, raw and tender.

"Let's see that hand again, shall we?" Ava held her own out, waiting.

Sage allowed her boss to inspect it again, praying there would be no more tests.

"Very interesting." Ava's lip curled into an approving grin. "You see the black mark has reduced in size."

Sage and Grey both leaned in to get a better look. Ava was right. The mark had not gone completely, but it had shrunk.

"What does this mean?" Sage asked, afraid to jump to a hopeful conclusion just yet.

"It would seem to indicate that the seed requires a certain level of magic to avoid drawing from your own."

"But I have no magic." Sage knew she'd said something stupid the moment the words left her lips. And Ava looked all too happy to be able to correct her.

"No active magic, no. You are by nature a creature of magic, Miss Cynwrig. Your power is in neutralizing. A very potent form of magic."

"So it's taking from me when it can't take from another source?"

"It would appear so," Ava answered.

"So we need to cut it out of her, then?" Grey jumped to his feet. "She's had that thing in her palm for a week now, and look what it's done."

"And by feeding it magic, we have reduced the effect it has had on her," Ava answered. "She's in no immediate danger. However, as fond as you are of your blades, Mr. Maddox, we do not just slice people open on a whim. There may be consequences. This is unknown magic we are working with."

"Do I get a say in any of this?" Sage asked, feeling as if she were being talked over rather than talked to.

"Only if your words add value to the conversation," Ava replied sharply. "We already understand the impact this is having on you, as well as your ability to work. So if all you wish to add to the conversation is your desire to have it removed quickly, you need not speak."

Sage slumped back in her chair.

"We do need to move quickly," Grey said in her defense.

"I will take that into consideration. For now, Miss Cynwrig is to return home until further notice. See that she gets there safely. And when you have returned, Mr. Maddox, you will assist me in the records room. Dismissed."

THREE

Grey dropped her by the gate to her apartment complex and sped away. She wasn't sure if she should envy or
feel sorry for the guy. Sage might be on house arrest, but
Grey was truly in prison. Being tethered to Ava wasn't
something she'd wish on her worst enemy.

Though her fate hadn't been much better. She unlocked the gate, silently praying her domestic situation – as
Ava had called it – would be drama free, and took the path
toward her building.

A small win – after the crushing defeat she'd had back
at ASSET – would be a welcome change. Her day had not
gone as planned at all.

Sage looked down at her palm. The black mark had
grown again. She nearly made a cardinal sin of asking
"How could things get worse?" but stopped before the
words tripped off her tongue. Still, just thinking of tempting fate was enough.

Right on cue, Sage spotted Josh banging on the door
as if he meant to bring it down. She sprinted to the apartment, cursing her luck.

"Matt! Open this door!" Josh demanded.

"You can't go in there right now." Anxiety kicked her heart into overdrive, testing her Terra immortality. A normal human might have stroked out. She wasn't that lucky.

Josh had never looked so angry and scared. A vein throbbed near his temple. He glared at her, eyes glistening on the edge of tears, and gnashed his teeth so hard Sage could hear the soft grinding.

She had his attention, but words caught in her throat, refusing to pass the safety of her lips. How the hell does someone tell a regular *human* guy that his boyfriend has been turned into a vampire? The phrase sounded ludicrous. The truth, not so much.

The harsh reality of those words had far-reaching implications neither Sage nor Matt had had time enough to comprehend. Why did it have to fall to her, then, to be the messenger? *Damn it!* Sage could hardly stand to be in the room with Matt in her current condition. The seed painfully craved the magic animating their bodies. And Josh… Humans and newly turned vampires don't exactly mix well.

"I'm losing my patience, Sage."

"I know. I'm…okay. He's fine." *Understatement of the year there.* "I'm fine. We're all fine." She'd have struggled less for breath if she'd run a marathon. Her chest ached as her heart threatened to punch its way out. "How are you?"

"Either step aside, or I go through you." Josh balled his fist. He wouldn't strike her. Even if he did, she kind of deserved it. More than likely he'd beat his fist bloody trying to take down the door. "I want to see my boyfriend." His voice cracked with strained emotions.

"Let me explain. No. Wait. Let me sum up." Sage took hold of the handle, placing herself between the door and her very psychotic-looking friend. "He had an accident.

But he's alive-ish. Probably not ready for visitors at the moment."

"What are you trying to say?" Tears began to trickle from the edges of his puffy eyes. "Spit it out. Truth."

"You can't handle the truth."

"Stop it with the stupid movie quotes!" He reared back with his fist balled tight.

"I don't know what else to do." She faced him head-on. If he wanted to let loose his fury, so be it. "I can't let you see him right now. For your own safety."

"Zack?" Josh dropped his hand and let out a growl. Sage knew the sound well as she'd made it plenty of times herself – defeated anguish. "It was that damn vampire you invited into our home, wasn't it? You promised you'd keep Matt safe from your new…crazy! Where's a stake? I'll kill the bastard myself!"

"Okay. First of all, keep your voice down." She looked to the apartments across from her building. No lights in the windows yet, but they were bound to earn a few noise complaints if he kept this up. "Second…that's my job, and a stake isn't going to solve your problems. Third… Zack saved him when I failed to do it. You owe him. If you want to be mad at someone, take it out on me. Go ahead. Rail away. I deserve it!"

Josh's breath came in stuttering waves. He balled his fist again and sent it straight at the door with all the power of his rage, bloodying his knuckles against the wood.

"I'm sorry." She couldn't blame him for acting out. She'd been beating herself up for days since it had all gone horribly wrong. "I truly am. I don't know how to make things better. But we're trying to get him through this."

"Is he in there, with Matt?"

The door opened behind Sage. She nearly toppled backwards but caught herself in the doorframe.

"Unless you would like to make a donation, listen to killer here." Zack kept his voice low enough to avoid the neighbors hearing, but quiet did not diminish the seriousness of his words. "Your man is safe and under my care. Should you choose to enter this apartment, you do so at your own peril. Baby vampires aren't trustworthy around humans."

"You…violated my boyfriend, monster!"

"Yes," Zack replied with unusual calm. "You next?"

Of course Zack couldn't be the adult here and calm Josh's fears. That task again fell on Sage. And she'd already failed once at diffusing the situation. "Stop it, both of you!" She maneuvered within the doorframe so she could give both men the stink eye for acting like jerks. "You want someone to hate, Josh? I'm right here. It's my fault what happened, and I'm doing my best to make it up to everyone."

"How did this happen?" Josh's nostrils flared like an angry bull, ready to charge.

"I was the target of a power-hungry kitsune with a djinn in her pocket," she admitted. "Matt was the bait."

"And Killer went in guns blazing with no backup," Zack said, eagerly throwing her further under the bus.

"Thanks. Didn't feel crappy enough. Why not drive the knife deeper before you twist it," she grumbled.

"As you wish," Zack replied with a devilish smirk she'd love to smack clean off his smug face.

"And the kitsune creature thing?" Josh asked. "Whatever the hell that is? What did you do to it?"

"She's been neutralized. Along with the djinn," she replied confidently. If nothing else, she got that part right. "They will not be a problem again."

"And you?" Anger still tightened Josh's jaw, but his words came out with a surprisingly softer tone. "Are you okay?"

Sage lifted her hand to show him the consequences she'd endured. "Had a bit of an accident myself."

Josh gasped.

"Don't worry. ASSET is helping me sort it out," she reassured him.

"Does it hurt?"

"A lot." She refused to sugarcoat that fact. He wouldn't take her admission as weakness like the other guys.

"And she can't touch anyone magical now without killing them. Something of a backfire with that amulet she broke," Zack filled in the gaps Sage had intentionally avoided revealing.

"Not funny." She'd only told the vampire enough to prevent further questioning, never once admitting it was the Weapon of Magical Destruction she'd been carrying. Per ASSET, that was strictly classified information. Still, she had a sneaking suspicion he knew the truth. Zack's currency had always been information.

"Poetic, though, isn't it?" Zack giggled mischievously.

She'd have words with him in private later. Sage hadn't been home five minutes, and already he was pushing her buttons. "I know you've always wanted me to put my hands on you." Sage pointed a finger at his crotch. "How about now?"

"Rain check?" His impish smile never faltered as he quick-stepped backwards into the apartment, putting himself just out of harm's way. "Would you look at the time? Junior should be waking from his nap, and he'll want a snack. They throw such temper tantrums when they're hungry."

Josh cleared his throat. "How long do I have to wait to see Matt?"

"Let me make sure he is fed and washed and cleaned his room," Zack answered. "Maybe, if he's been a very good boy, we can arrange a little play date for you two kids. How's the tenth of never?"

"Keep with the baby talk, and I swear I'll smack that stupid grin right off your face," Sage grumbled at Zack's over-the-top impression of a doting parent.

"You owe me, remember?" Zack waggled a finger at her.

"One swift kick in the butt," Sage snarked at him.

"Yep. And I'm ready to pay up."

"She loves me. It's just all this stress getting to her," Zack assured Josh. "New parent troubles and all. She's busy all day, and I'm here slaving away with the newborn. We'll work through these issues, I'm sure. Love will out, as they say."

"One more word, Zack. Just one." She narrowed her eyes threateningly at him.

"Love you, too, baby!" Zack blew her a kiss as he backed away and closed the door before she could stop him.

As annoyed as she was at Zack's antics, Josh matched her with anguish. He didn't need to say anything; it was there etched into the lines across his forehead and the slight quiver of his lips.

"I'm truly sorry. Hate me if you need to, but please understand I tried to save him. You know how much I love Matt. He's family."

"I don't know what to do." Josh hung his head and turned away. "How can I have a relationship with him this way? What if he…? What if I…?" Hunched over with defeat, he paced the small patio in front of her door. "I don't know how to deal with this."

"You have love." She reached out and took Josh's shoulder, reeling him in to face her.

They were both in pain. She desperately wanted to hug him, so they could share in a good ugly cry, but she was responsible for his anguish. She had no right to pretend her pain equaled his.

She swallowed her emotions. Brave face time. Make him feel all will be well. That's what Josh needed. "There is no reason to make rash decisions right now. He needs time to adjust, and so do you. Think of it like one of your business trips. You're gone for months sometimes. Now the shoe is on the other foot. You can still call him. Talk to him when he's up and moving. You'll see. He's still the same Matt you love."

"How long do I have to wait to see him? To hold him?" Josh shrugged free of her grip and turned to kick the concrete staircase that led to the upstairs apartments. "I miss him so much already."

"Remember that. Remember how much you love him. Because no matter what has changed him, he is still the same guy. He will still love you."

"But he'll love blood more." Zack's voice came muffled through the thin walls.

Sage growled loud enough for the neighbors to hear. She definitely owed Zack a swift kick in the pants for that ill-timed comment.

"Don't listen to him," she assured Josh. "Love is powerful. You'll see. He's just got to learn control."

"What if he doesn't?"

It broke her heart to see Josh in such pain. They were all helpless to do anything but wait and see how Matt managed his newly enhanced state.

"If that jerk in there can manage to control his urges, so can Matt." She put as much conviction in her voice as she could. "He's ten times the man Zack is."

"I want to believe you." His chin quivered as he took a steadying breath and gulped down the air.

Sage admired his control. Even if Josh didn't feel he was controlling himself, she recognized the immense strength he was employing. She'd been a blubbering mess for days after it all went down.

"A week ago, I didn't know vampires existed. A week ago, you said you'd keep your work away from our home. And now…" Josh jabbed a finger toward her apartment. "This."

He had her there. "I got nothing. I failed us all. I have apologized, and I will continue to apologize for all eternity. But, even if you have lost faith in me, don't lose faith in Matt."

"Faith," Josh scoffed and turned on his heel. "I don't know what that word means anymore." He walked away without another look back, leaving the fate of his relationship in the air.

As if Sage didn't have enough to deal with. No way was she telling Matt his boyfriend might not want to continue dating him as a vampire. So much for the power of love.

FOUR

Sage stormed into her apartment. Her palm burned with the seed's hunger for magic, adding heat to her simmering anger. Her eyes landed on the source of her rage, and for a moment, she entertained unleashing everything she had on Zack. "Give me one good reason why I shouldn't slap you."

Zack matched the scorching glare, blowing a teasing kiss in the air back at her. "Because if you did, you'd probably kill me. And what would become of Junior?"

A door opened in the hallway. Sage held her breath. Matt was there, no doubt, listening to them argue like the new parents Zack had pretended they were. Not far from the truth in reality. Only most newborns weren't prone to killing people with their temper tantrums. Tension had been building between them for days. They'd all been trapped together, bound by the inability to interact with society, magical or not, and it wasn't just Sage feeling the cabin fever. She kept her distance. Matt needed time to come around. He'd had no choice. Zack turning him had been a last resort to keep him alive. In the days that followed, Matt had told Sage he forgave her, but a lingering sense of uncertainty still hung in the air. She waited, letting

Matt decide whether or not he'd emerge from the darkness of the hallway.

"That got your attention." Zack held no such reverence for her roommate's mental state. He smirked as if his words had summoned the beast to punctuate the arrogant point of their conversation. "What would become of poor Matt if I wasn't there to help him keep his cool?"

That man knew every damn button to press to get under her skin. She held her tongue and turned to see Matt casually stepping into the living room, his hair wet and shaggy around his face. Fresh from a shower, he wore a towel around his waist and another like a cloak across his shoulders.

"Everything okay, Sage?"

"I could ask you the same." Sage wanted to give him a great big hug. He looked more himself in that moment than he had for the past week. A good sign for sure. Only the otherworldly edge of his icy blue eyes gave him away as a vampire. It took all her strength to force herself to stand still.

Matt stiffened suddenly. His nostrils flared as if smelling something of interest. "Josh was outside, wasn't he?"

"Yes." She perked up with a renewed sense of hope. Not only did he look better, his voice remained calm despite the stressful nature of the subject. Seeing him like that was worth the constant pain she felt as the seed continued to make its hungry demands for their power. She clenched her fist, trying to shut it out, and focused on Matt. His wonderful progress. He'd be able to see his boyfriend soon. That was definitely something to celebrate. "Josh is going to give you a call so you guys can talk."

Matt's fangs poked out from his lips, more evidence of his new predatory nature. "I'm glad. I miss him." His words came slowly, his tone pleasant and free of the strain she had heard from him all week long.

Sage beamed with pride, absolutely impressed with this new level of control he'd mastered.

"Baby steps," Zack cautioned.

Could he not see how good Matt was doing?

"Shut it, fang boy." Sage turned on him, the seed burning in her palm, souring her mood, losing her own battle for control. She could appreciate a little of what Matt was going through.

"Why loose your venom on me?" Zack quipped with a stolen movie quote.

"Because you mock our pain," she answered in kind.

"Life is pain. Anyone who says differently…"

"Is selling something. I know." Annoying as Zack was, he did speak her language – geek. Employed with tact, it had a disarming effect on her. Zack had failed that part miserably. "You're not going to win me over with movie quotes."

"Even when they are so on point?"

"You have no power over me." She clenched her fist tight and shoved it in her pocket, hoping that might dampen the pain.

Zack eyed her movements with suspicion. "Come now. My ability to match every situation with pop culture quotes is impressive, right?" He'd crossed the line this time. What made it worse was the fact he didn't even realize how badly he'd messed up.

"This hasn't been easy for any of us," Sage shot back at him. "And Josh has no basis of comparison. You didn't have to be a dick to him."

"What did you do to Josh?" Matt growled, turning his otherworldly gaze on Zack.

"The human demanded entry into a house filled with vampires, one of which is new and untested around temptation." Zack matched his accuser's angry glare. "Pardon me for utilizing a little tough love to keep all parties safely at arm's length. Next time, I'll just let him in and grab some popcorn for the show."

"I can handle Josh." All of the calm evaporated from Matt's tone, souring, turning even the simplest of phrases sinister. "Just watch."

"No, you can't," Zack insisted. "One whiff of his blood and you'd drain him dry."

"Who said anything about blood?" Concern for Matt and Josh's well-being worked like a charm, providing the distraction Sage needed to focus past her own physical discomfort.

"No one had to. It comes with the territory," Zack replied.

"I can handle it," Matt assured them. He sounded so confident she believed he could actually do it.

"Do I really have to do this?" Zack pressed his forehead into his hand. A sigh escaped his lips, and Sage swore she heard, "you'll be sorry," floating in the air.

"No." She clenched her fist in her pocket, driving her nails through the skin. Why did she always have to be the voice of reason when she was clearly the least qualified to do so? "Whatever stupid idea you're cooking up. No!"

"You both are operating under the false assumption that Junior here is his good old self. Let me burst that bubble before it explodes very messily in your faces." Zack's eyes darkened, his fun-loving Doctor Jekyll persona fading behind his inner Mr. Hyde.

She'd only seen Zack let his beast out a few times and knew to be on guard. She kept her damaged hand clenched tightly in her pocket, sending the other to locate the folding knife at her belt. Just in case.

"Matty here is only appearing so calm because of my carful training," Zack said.

"No one is training me." Matt scoffed defiantly, proving he deserved the title Zack had so lovingly bestowed on him – Junior.

In a blink, Zack appeared at the refrigerator door. Sage pulled her knife, holding it at the ready. When she realized she hadn't been the intended target, she relaxed, dropping her hand, and watched in confusion as Zack opened the fridge and rummaged through the crisper drawers.

There was only one reason a vampire might need to use a refrigerator. She hadn't seen any severed body parts the last time she reached in for coffee creamer, so what the hell was he after in there? The moment the thought wandered through her mind she realized there was another equally disgusting alternative.

"Please tell me you're not keeping–" She stopped short when Zack stood holding a medical collection bag filled with blood. "For real? Come on. That's where I keep food."

"Exactly." Zack's eyebrow lifted, a silent challenge for her to continue that argument to its natural end.

"Can you at least keep your…" – she struggled to force the words past chunks rising in her throat – "juice boxes…in the drawer…covered…or something out of sight?"

"What an excellent word." Zack turned to Matt holding up the adult-sized sippy. "Tell me you don't want a…juice box."

Matt's nostrils flared. His jaw tightened as if he were struggling to fight against the tempting aroma. To his credit, Junior remained where he stood. His Adam's apple bounced hard as he gulped, but the only move he made was a stiff shake of his head.

Sage couldn't have been more proud, and doubly so for making Zack look like a melodramatic helicopter parent. Her roommate was made of tougher stuff. And now he'd proved it.

Zack moved a little closer to Matt, but remained firmly on the linoleum in the kitchen. He waved the blood bag in the air, level with Matt's face. "2018. Excellent year. A positive, full bodied." He sniffed the plastic casing like a fine vintage wine. "With a slight nutty finish."

The corner of Matt's lips twitched. He stood noticeably stiffer as if all the muscles in his body had been strung taut as a bow string. The struggle was more than real. No doubt about that. But Sage kept faith he'd be strong enough.

"I'll give him credit." Zack surprised her by praising Matt's control. "He's trying very hard. I myself couldn't have stood there as long as he has with a…juice box…tempting me."

Matt's eyes had begun to darken, their gorgeous blue taking on the feral blackness that signaled the beast was coming. Zack wasn't playing fair. But he still remained where he stood, fighting the good fight.

"See. He will be able to deal with Josh," Sage replied confidently.

"You think so?" Zack cocked his head sideways, his eyebrows arched sharply as if to say *challenge accepted.*

Before she could backpedal, he slashed the bag with the nail on his pinkie finger. A gush of cold blood poured out like a morbid waterfall, painting her linoleum floor red.

Matt flew across the room and landed at Zack's feet before Sage could even let out an indignant shriek. All that control she had praised him for moments earlier had gone. The monster had replaced her roommate. It lay at Zack's feet, lapping up the mess like a hungry dog.

"You were saying?" Zack smirked.

Sage simmered where she stood, nails biting into her ruined palm. She was long past the point of feeling that pain. The seed felt like a white hot poker running straight through her hand. Tears flooded her vision but not from her own torment. Witnessing her best friend made so vulnerable and embarrassed like that broke her heart into pieces. All other pains paled in comparison. She hadn't allowed herself to admit that Matt was truly a changed man. But Zack had been all too eager to rub it in their faces. Poor Matt. But, as usual, in the most insufferable way possible, Zack had proven he was not ready to be in the same room as Josh.

"Dammit!" She sent her frustration skyward, then settled on Zack's smug face. "You will clean every last drop up."

"Matt will. He can't help it right now." Zack taunted her with the truth. If only he knew how dangerous a game that was. How close Sage was to the edge. A person can only take so much torture before they snap, and he continued to skirt that edge with every smug comment. "I guarantee he will not waste a single drop."

"This is all funny to you, isn't it?" She couldn't bear to look at the pair of them, turning away and hoping to find something distracting.

"No. It's not. Matt is not in control yet. And no amount of wishing it to be true will make him develop this skill." Zack eased off on his cocky attitude. "I've been very serious with you about Matt's care. He is not ready to be around humans. We need to test him slowly. Build up his endurance and control. Having you around has been extremely helpful. Frankly, it's probably the reason he lasted so long, but he still needs more training before you unleash him on that boyfriend."

"That I believe. But you could have just said all that to me," Sage replied with as much calm as she could muster. "You didn't have to be a dick about it."

"Yes I did." His reply came swiftly. "You refused to listen to any of my friendly warnings. You think the power of a boner will overcome bloodlust." Again, Zack taunted her with the truth, all while Matt continued to slurp noisily at his feet.

Between her inflamed hand, Zack's arrogance, and Matt's disgusting noises, Sage was losing her own battle for control. She needed an escape before her own beast came roaring to the surface. The route to her bedroom would put her straight into the vampire's path. She could go for a walk outside, but what she really wanted was to lie down and put an end to this whole dreadful day.

"Matt knows one love above all right now." Zack switched back to his friendlier tone, continuing to rub his *I told you so* lesson on her. "Let me have the time I need to ease him back into the real world. Because I don't want to see you crying over another lost friend."

"Bit of a low blow there, friend." She wasn't sure if his words were meant to strike an emotional chord with her, or had been meant to egg her into another argument. Either way, it had confirmed her need to get away from both of the vampires. Sooner rather than later.

"Look. I know if anything happens to your people, you'll Midas touch me into oblivion. All joking aside, I'm trying to avoid that happening. Please trust me to do my job, okay?"

She chanced a glance over her shoulder, keeping her eyes level to avoid getting sick. "Can you do it without being a dick about it?"

"I never make promises I can't keep." He could have just said yes, and Sage would have been happy to end it there, but Zack always had to have the last quip.

That man was so insufferable!

FIVE

Ava wants you in the office first thing in the morning. Prepare for surgery!

Grey's text message was just the kind of distraction she needed from the vision of Matt slurping blood from her kitchen floor.

Spirits high, Sage wasted no time leaving the house, and even enjoyed the two-hour bus ride downtown. If all went well, she'd be free, and never have to see that stupid seed ever again.

Grey met her at the elevator, his brow furrowed with worry. "You okay?"

"Like I could take on the world," she chirped. Nothing was going to ruin her good mood. "Where are we headed? Infirmary?"

"No." He glanced over his shoulder cautiously and lowered his voice. "Ava needs to see you in her office."

"Okay," Sage replied suspiciously. "You did say surgery, right?"

"Something like that."

The unexpected cloak-and-dagger act threatened to sour her mood, but Sage had already decided to cling to the hope of a good outcome rather than focusing on the journey. "Bring it."

"You sound surprisingly calm."

"Do I have a choice?"

"Not really." Grey's lip quirked on the edge of a smile, but not fully committing to it. "This is you we're talking about. 'No choice' often ends with dead bodies."

"The day is still young," she joked.

"Just remember your gag order. Don't need another black mark on your record." Grey's gaze flitted over to the receptionist desk again. No one occupied the seat, but by the way he kept looking, Sage wondered if he suspected something.

"I know. Shut up, Sage," she mocked him. "You really should get that tattooed on your forehead or something."

"I'm going to enjoy this." The smile that had been teasing at the corner of Grey's lips turned sinister.

Despite her promise to herself to stay positive, worry slithered its way into the back of Sage's mind. Maybe she had overdone the cocky a bit.

"Can I have that last comment stricken from the record?" she asked sheepishly.

Grey pulled her by the hand. "Dead woman walking."

They came round the corner to find Ava standing, axe in hand, staring out of her office window.

"Oh shit!" Sage's heart nearly leapt out of her throat. "I really am going Luke Skywalker."

"Don't be so dramatic, Miss Cynwrig." Ava turned, resting the axe handle on her shoulder. "This was for my last meeting."

Her words did nothing to quell Sage's fear. At least there was no blood dripping from the blade.

"The appearance of a threat is often enough to motivate. Something you should remember in the future." Ava set the imposing weapon down on its head, leaning the handle against the side of her desk.

"Thank you." Sage spoke the words, not really knowing what else to say. Ava was a threatening presence without the weapon. As many times as she had pissed off her boss, the head of Vegas ASSET had never resorted to a weapon to invoke fear. Whomever she had met with prior had to have been truly evil.

"I've been looking into your little problem, Miss Cynwrig. We're going to try a manual extraction."

She'd figured as much. Hell, she'd thought to do it herself but wasn't sure she could. She'd pierced her own ears in high school with a safety pin. But then she had a little liquid courage to numb the pain. Since her awakening, no amount of tequila could give her the slightest buzz, a theory she'd tested many times. Sage let out a resigned sigh and nodded.

"Mr. Maddox, the surgical tray," Ava ordered and began to clear away the items on her desk.

Grey picked up a lidded metal tray from the credenza against the wall. A roll of towels sat next to it.

Ava snatched those and laid one across her desk. "Do try to remain calm, Miss Cynwrig."

Grey set down the tray and opened the lid. Inside were all manner of torturous implements. Scissors, knives, clamps – those she recognized, but this kit contained more sharp pointy things than even she knew how to categorize.

"Hand, please," Ava requested.

Sage took a steadying breath. Her arm trembled as she lifted it.

Ava took Sage's hand in her own, inspecting the bruised appearance of her palm before letting it rest on the towel. She opened a large whitish bottle of rubbing alcohol.

Sage flinched, expecting pain, instantly regretting her stupidity. Ava's angry glare smacked her harder than words could have.

"Sorry. Just jumpy."

Ava turned her attention toward the tray and selected a slender blade.

Sage held her breath, mentally preparing for the pain to come, as Ava brought the scalpel toward her skin.

"Breathe," Ava demanded. "I don't need you passing out and getting blood all over my office."

Sage nodded and released the breath she had been holding.

"Big baby." Grey snickered.

"Easy for you to say. You don't have a knife pointed at you."

"Scalpel," he corrected.

"Whatever. It's sharp and pointy and about to cut me." Sage defended her fear.

"Miss Cynwrig, if this is how you act in the field, we may have to reassess your status as an active duty agent."

"Sorry, ma'am. I'm fine. Just do it."

Ava nodded to Grey, and he took hold of Sage's wrist, pinning it to the desk.

Sage looked away. The blade sliced through her palm quickly, and by the time she hissed in response, Ava had traded the scalpel for a pair of tweezers.

The pain of the incision was nothing, but the blunt metal instrument digging into her palm was pure torture. Every tiny movement amplified, as if Ava were pushing the tweezers through her hand, ripping open the muscles as she worked her way to the wood desk underneath Sage's knuckles.

"Hold her still," Ava barked at Grey. "I need to work quickly before she heals."

Sage clamped her free hand over her mouth, muffling her embarrassing squeals of pain.

"There's too much blood." Ava roughly mopped the incision with gauze pads. "She's healing too quickly. I'm going to have to go in with the scalpel again."

Sweat beaded across Sage's forehead. Her cheeks flushed with the heated blush of anxiety. Why did this hurt so much? Nothing but a little cut, and yet somehow every nerve in her body was firing off as if she were under the guillotine. Her heart sped as Ava sliced into her palm once more. Sage couldn't stifle the cry that came racing up her throat.

"Don't be so dramatic, Miss Cynwrig." The scalpel clattered on the metal tray, and again Ava prodded the angry wound with her tweezers. "I can't see… Mr. Maddox, irrigation, please."

From the corner of her eye, Sage watched Grey pour liquid on her palm. Cold at first but far from soothing, its icy burn only added to the torture. Sage fought with all the strength she had left to stay her instinct to pull away.

"I think I see… Hold her still!" Ava demanded.

Sage braced for the worst. Like a strike of lightning, she felt the white hot stab of pain, and her world blinked out of existence.

***

Her eyes slammed open, and Sage gasped for as much air as she could to fill her starving lungs. The world had turned sideways. No. Not the world. Sage blinked as her mind struggled to reboot. Feet. Two pair of them. They were upright. It was she who had somehow ended up sideways, splayed out on the ground. What had she missed? How long had she been lying there?

The seed!

"Did you get it?" Sage looked up, finding her answer reflected in Ava's face.

The reproachful look took her straight back to memories of her childhood, her mother staring down at her. Miranda never needed to yell. All it took was *that look*, and no matter how big she was, Sage would feel no more than an inch tall. The silent weight of her mother's disappointment was enough to elicit tears and a full confession, though in this case, Sage had nothing to admit to. Unless being a great big baby counted. Sage whispered a prayer, begging the Goddess to spare her from being sent to the reception desk, seeing as she was clearly unfit for duty.

"I'm afraid we were unable to retrieve the artifact." Ava wiped her hands and tossed a stained towel at the metal tray. It landed on top of a pile of bloody gauze and used towels Sage did not remember being there before her world had gone black. How long had she been unconscious? "The outcome might have been different if there had been a little less squirming, but we're past that point now."

"You passed out." Grey filled in the blanks as he handed her a glass of water. "Drink up. You need your strength."

"I'm going to take you off of administrative leave." Ava placed her laptop back on the desk and started typing. "However, given the circumstances, you are no longer fit for active duty, Miss Cynwrig."

"Wait. No. I promise I'm not usually this squeamish," Sage protested. How could Ava be so cruel? One little mistake. It wasn't fair. She hadn't intended to pass out. She could do it. "Tell her, Grey. Please! I took on vampires. I'm a fighter. Give me another chance." She held her hand out. "Go ahead, try again. I can do this. I won't pass out. I promise."

"I can vouch for her abilities in the field," Grey added. "I have personally witnessed the beatings she's taken. Sage is an asset in the field."

He could have left out the word 'beatings.' No need to reveal to Ava how expert Sage was at getting her ass handed to her. Backhanded compliments aside, Grey's quick jump to her defense gave her hope.

"When I want your input, I will ask for it." Ava's reply came as sharp as the blade she'd used to open Sage's hand. Her fingernails clicked rapidly against the laptop keyboard, the only sound daring to break the silence of the room.

Sage found herself matching the rhythm, drumming her fingers against her thigh.

Her marching orders would come. She'd be lashed to the reception desk, Ava's punching bag for as long as it took to make her soft and malleable. Maybe if she were lucky, the seed would kill her first.

The chair in front of her sat empty. She hovered between taking a seat or sprinting to the door. Why hadn't Ava dismissed her already? Her gaze flitted to the metal tray with surgical implements, still lying on the desk next to the mountain of bloody gauze piled almost as tall as the laptop screen they sat next to. No wonder she'd passed out. So much blood. And yet, her palm looked as if it had never been cut. The darkness consuming her skin, however, had clearly gained new ground.

"Please, Ava…"

"Mrs. Masters," Ava corrected her. "You have not earned the right to speak so informally to me."

"Please, Mrs. Masters," Sage begged. "Don't bench me. I can do the job. I need to –"

"What you need to do is swallow that pride. I need agents fit for duty. Your current injury poses a serious risk to any mission I might send you on. Until we can remove that thing, you are a liability."

"Please. Try again. I'll hold still." She held her hand out, nearly knocking the screen of Ava's laptop.

"Put that away," Ava snarled as she jerked her head backwards.

Sage knew she'd been tested and failed, miserably, but the look on her boss's face spoke to a deeper level of annoyance. If only she knew what had happened during the blackout.

"We're done for today." Ava swatted at her like an annoying fly. "I do not believe we can simply cut it out. We could perhaps take the whole hand."

Sage gasped and yanked her hand back, fearing her boss might make good on that threat. Ava's battle axe still rested against the edge of her desk. One good swing would do it.

"But not today."

Sage released her breath, but kept her hand close to her chest, just in case.

From the corner of her eye, she caught Grey shaking his head. He probably had something snarky he wanted to say, but thankfully he kept it to himself. Whatever it was would most certainly come out later, when they were clear of Ava's wrath. He never missed an opportunity to pick on her.

"You are officially being moved to the disabled list, Miss Cynwrig. You'll be assigned to Devon during your rehabilitation time."

"Won't that be putting him at risk?" Sage asked.

"Don't touch him," Ava barked at her. "He's a trusted source for information, and that is what we need at the moment."

Sage lowered her head, letting her gaze sink to the ground. "How much of my situation is he aware of?"

"Finally, something smart comes out of your mouth." Ava sounded as if she were amused, but Sage didn't look up at her boss for confirmation. "Devon has been briefed by me. He is aware of your physical limitations. He understands the sensitivity of your affliction. At this point in time, you are to refer to this as a cursed artifact. You may reveal the consequences of its power, but under no circumstances are you to reveal its true name, nature, and origin. As of now, we have categorized this as an unknown parasitic cursed artifact."

"Yes, ma'am." Sage nodded, still keeping her eyes on the carpet.

"He, Mr. Maddox, and I are the only three privy to the nature of your condition. I don't need to tell you how important it is that this secret remain such. Each person that is made aware becomes a liability. As far as ASSET is concerned, the true nature of your affliction is a secret more important than the lives of those who know about it. I don't need to remind you of what happened to your mother. That thing in your palm is of great value. The rest of the world believes ASSET has it under lock and key. Should the truth get out, your life and the lives of those you have revealed this secret to will be forfeited to ensure containment."

Delivered without feeling, Ava's words landed heavily on Sage's shoulders. Her knees threatened to buckle under the weight of all the lives she could become responsible for with one slip of the tongue.

"I understand." Sage tried to put confidence behind her words, but fear dried them in her throat. Her voice broke as she forced them out. "I will not slip up."

"See that you don't," Ava replied.

"I'll make sure she keeps quiet," Grey added.

"You and I need to have a word privately, Mr. Maddox." Ava speared Sage with one final, frightening glare. "Miss Cynwrig. Report to Devon for rehabilitation immediately. You are dismissed."

SIX

Sage wandered through the halls feeling as if everyone who passed her was staring at her deformity, whispering rumors that might lead to her death. She'd barely had time to make a name for herself at ASSET, and in a blink, she'd been labeled a pariah. Secret agency or not, all offices operated on the same social level. They didn't need truth. Rumor alone was enough to blacklist a person. Sage was the problem child, the trouble maker, *that* girl. And the worst of it was she was bound by a death oath to keep the explanation to herself.

Rina was dead because Sage had outed her as a fraud bent on revenge. The attack on their office might have been because of Sage, but she had no clue the necklace her mother had given her contained the weapon everyone was after. And she hadn't started that war. Again, Rina was to blame, but dead girls tell no tales. They could be mad at Sage for causing the lockdown a week earlier. That one was unavoidable. But Sage did destroy the amulet, so better that than have things go the other way round. Still, all of her involvement had to be kept quiet, and the results were clear.

Sage rounded the corner and nearly collided with a pair of men. Before she could utter the word "sorry," they jumped back as if she would burn them. Eyes wide with fear, they gave her a wide berth and scooted around the corner to make their escape.

Sage tried to shake off the embarrassment as she entered the training room.

Devon stood on one leg, his vision focused on the mirror ahead of him. Slowly, he lifted his back leg and extended his arm, creating a perfect t with his body.

"I come in peace. I mean you no harm," she called out to him.

At her interruption, Devon's muscles tensed. He turned his head to face her, maintaining his balance and perfect posture. "Well, I'm glad you warned me." His brow creased with the effort it took to hold his position, but to his credit, the ogre did not collapse. He slowly released his hand and his leg in time, coming to the ground with control. "Anything else I need to know?"

"I've got a magical restraining order," she quipped. "Might want to stay back at least ten feet."

"Ahh yes." Devon picked up a towel and mopped the sweat from his brow. "Trouble maker you are."

"So much for being a superhero." She hadn't intended to sound so negative, but the moment the words came out, she felt every sour note down to her bones.

"Most of them are," Devon replied with a chuckle.

How could he think to laugh? Maybe he hadn't been told just how serious her condition was. "Looks like you're my boss until further notice. Rehabilitation." She air quoted with no small amount of snark.

"I've been informed." He squared up to her, arms crossed, sizing her up, perhaps, or maybe just wondering how close he could get. What would be a safe enough distance to avoid her little affliction? "I take it you are still cursed?"

"Operation cut-and-run failed miserably."

His eyebrow lifted sharply. "Have you been taking lessons from Grey? Your attitude has darkened quite a bit."

"Do you blame me?" she retorted.

"I do. You're still acting like a victim. Have I taught you nothing?"

"Does how to get my ass kicked count?"

His brow furrowed, and Sage realized she'd taken her pity party a little too far.

"Victims give up and let bad things happen to them. I train fighters. You need to decide right now what you are, because I'm not about to waste my time on victims."

"I've been assigned to you by Ava," Sage grumbled.

"Is that all? Then go sit in the corner and wait to die."

He was right, as always. Responding to the negativity all around her rather than working against it. This might not have been a physical battle, but it was a battle all the same.

She didn't want to admit it, but the blunt edge of his truth was exactly the kind of nudge she needed. "Captain Trainwreck reporting for duty." She mock saluted him.

"Better." The corner of his lip quirked with amusement. "What have you tried to mitigate symptoms?"

"Silver gloves." Sage wiggled her fingers, realizing she had forgotten to put the gloves on.

"That might shield the outward effects, but I doubt it will do much else."

Even with Ava giving her the okay to work with Devon, Sage felt as if she had to watch her words carefully. What if the walls had ears? What if she slipped and said more than he knew? They were dealing with magic that was not only ancient but also valuable to those of less scrupulous nature. And as she'd already learned with Rina, sometimes traitors were hidden in plain sight.

"I'm not sure what I can say." Sage hoped her clumsy warning would make sense to Devon. "Ava just read me my rights. Standard death threats. My value to the organization, or lack thereof. You know."

"Your value is in how you deal with this." Devon looked as if he were about to send her to the corner again.

Staying positive in the face of such uncertainty felt impossible. But she'd get less quarter from Devon than she did from Ava. Sage kept that in the back of her mind as Devon continued to preach.

"Ava allowed you to come to me to help solve this puzzle. We can start by discussing symptoms."

"I have to admit I was shocked when she sent me to you."

"I've been around a long time, Sage." He strolled over to the bench and picked up his bottle of water. "I've worked with every agent that has come through these doors in some capacity or another."

"Super spy," she whispered under her breath.

Devon downed the entire bottle in one go then crushed the empty plastic in his hand as he pulled it away from his mouth. "Don't tarnish my reputation with words like that. True, I hold a special level of security, but that is not because I'm here to simply spy."

"I didn't mean it like that."

"Sure you did. You heard my words and interpreted them to mean I am somehow using what I see to make reports."

He had her there. That was exactly the impression she'd gotten the moment she realized Ava had him in her confidence. Sage opened her mouth to refute it, but Devon beat her to the punch.

"My people are revered for their minds as well as their strengths. Information is only part of the equation. What one does with that information is where its value lies. Deduction, understanding, assimilating. A spy reports what they see." He lobbed the crushed plastic bottle across the room and sank it straight into the trash. "I am not a spy."

"Sorry. Please. What can you tell me, wise master?"

Her quip earned a scowling glare, but Devon held his tongue. He reached out as if to grab her arm and bring it closer for inspection, but his fingers missed their connection. Pain sliced through her hand. Sage hissed and clenched her fist tight, bringing her hand up to cradle it against her chest.

Had he done that on purpose? What had Ava revealed to him? The seed's hunger awakened, and aware of the magic within reach, it made its desire known, throbbing in time with her racing heartbeat.

"Everything I have been told points to either a curse or Godly magic." Devon pulled his hand away, but his calculating gaze remained fixed on her. "Since you're a Terra and immune to any magic from this world, I have to assume it is Godly magic affecting you. And that is more than just power. It has a sentient nature about it."

"You mean the…" – she stopped herself before naming the artifact, and dropped her gaze to the black spot on her palm – "curse…knows what it is doing?"

"Not in the literal sense of the word. I don't believe it actively invokes its will. But if my guess is correct, it can sense magic, an attraction, like magnetism, nearby. Its purpose being to absorb that magic, acts like hunger, for lack of a better word, and draws closer so it can consume."

"Then why not kill me?" Sage asked, inspecting how much of her hand the seed had blackened.

"Good point. You possess magical blood, but yours is of a passive nature. Protective, if you will. So the, ah, curse may not act actively to consume it. But being what you are, magic surrounds you at all times. You are aware of it because you can see through the veil. And the nature of your occupation puts you in direct contact with it. In effect, you have become a conduit. Larger surface area for it to feed with."

"And yet, I feel as if it is killing me. Slowly." She fingered the black mark on her palm.

"That is troublesome." Devon stroked his chin thoughtfully.

This was the moment he was supposed to be her Master Yoda. She'd had enough unanswered questions. She'd endure being called a noob or any other admonishment thrown at her if someone would just have the answer to her problem.

"Seems I can't cut it out." Sage let her shoulders slump as she dropped her hand to her side. "Tried that already. I passed out like a great big baby."

"And your hand?"

"Well, it's still there."

"The black mark?" His inquisitive tone quickly shifted to annoyance. "Is that when it appeared?"

"No, it was there already. Smaller though," she replied. "It's growing."

"So we know that didn't cause it. How fast did your hand heal?"

"Instantly, I guess. I didn't see any marks when I came to."

"There is definitely a sentient element at play here. It made sure to keep you, the host, in perfect condition." Fear glinted in Devon's eyes. Not a pretty sight on any man, least of all an ogre.

"So what do I do? If it keeps this up, it will eventually kill me."

"That is the question to ask."

That's all anyone seemed to have was questions. How was it that with all the resources at ASSET, no one had a single answer? In all of history, not a single person had come across this magic? Or was she just a special kind of stupid to be the only person since the dawn of time to have used the seed?

"You don't sound like you know the answer," Sage said.

"I don't," Devon replied, employing his trademark blunt honesty. "But we will figure it out."

"Try, anyway." She didn't bother to hide the defeat in her voice. The odds were certainly not in her favor.

"A bit early for doom and gloom. Where's your spunk?"

She shrugged. "Lost about the same time Matt nearly died, I guess."

"But he didn't."

"He hates me for what happened."

"I doubt that. He's going through an extremely difficult change."

"Because —"

"Before you start with the poor me attitude, remember this. We cannot control everything around us. Bad things happen. Bad choices are made. You can't predict the outcome of any situation. The only thing you can do is respond to it."

"I'm trying."

"You're moping. What you should be doing is hitting the library and looking for books related to godly magic, curses, and the origins of your people."

Leave it to Devon to always find a way to turn every interaction into a lesson. "I've read the story of The Great Tree already. I know it was the fruit from the tree of life that stripped our powers."

"And who gave you protection against magic?"

"The Mother."

"So perhaps more research on her. You can't be mopey when your mind is busy problem solving."

"You really think the answers will be in a book?" Sage asked, immediately regretting the question. Of course she'd find answers there. Maybe not in the right order. But the pieces that make up the puzzle would be there for her to assemble. "Don't. Before you even say it, yes, I know."

"Good. I was beginning to think that thing in your hand had rotted your brain."

"I'm not feeling like myself, okay?"

"Really, Captain Obvious."

"Train wreck!" She puffed out her chest proudly.

"Keep asking stupid questions like that, and we may have to demote you to private second class." He smirked. "I've got the beginnings of a library in my office. I'll bring in a few more books from home tomorrow. Plenty of material to keep your mind occupied."

"What about that one guy we talked to before. The water priest... Aqua Man?"

"Quarn? Yes, he's always a good resource on the gods. I will check in with him to see if he has anything. Will Grey be helping us?"

"Not sure. I've been benched. Not fit for active duty pending probation. He's still awaiting sentencing." She hadn't given a thought to whether or not Grey would still be assigned as her partner. He had to be. He was one of the few people in the secret circle.

"Ava's got to make it sound good. Keep your secret safe enough." Devon seemed to be on the same wavelength. "Soon as he's available, we'll need him on task too."

She had her fingers, toes, and eyes crossed, hoping Devon was right. Sage needed Grey more than she was willing to admit out loud. "I'm sure he'll be a big help."

Devon's confidence gave her strength. If anyone could help her figure this out, he was the guy. Zack had called him Yoda. A snarky insult, but more true than she had realized. He had more than just combat knowledge in that big head of his. Ogres were the true tacticians of the magical world.

"Off you go," Devon said. "Grab some books to take home and start reading!"

SEVEN

Getting home on the bus took longer than Sage had expected. The afternoon heat had been brutal, and before she had made her way home, Sage stopped to refuel at her favorite pub. By the time she hit the gate to her apartment complex, the sun had sunk low in the sky. Her roommates would be awake.

The long ride home had given her plenty of time to reflect on what Devon had said to her.

Bad things happen. Bad choices are made. You cannot predict the outcome of any situation. The only thing you can do is respond to it.

Her interactions with both Matt and Zack had not been very good. And despite the hard time Matt was having with the change, she hadn't been reacting well either. This was as good a time as any to start being more positive.

"Matty, I'm home," Sage called out as she crossed the threshold of her apartment.

Zack stood from his spot on the couch, surprising her with such a gentlemanly gesture. He met her eyes with a flirtatious wink. "Dinner is served."

As usual, he had to throw out his personal brand of vampire creepiness to ruin a nice moment. At least he hadn't tried to move in closer.

She pretended to ignore his cheesy line. "Where's Matt?"

"Right here." Matt's voice came from the recliner. He stood slowly as if each movement took an extraordinary amount of thought and care.

After what had happened the previous night, she understood. If it had been her, she wouldn't have been able to show her face again for a very long time. She wondered if she should offer him some encouragement, maybe tell him it was no big deal. But that might make things worse, drawing attention to it. Better just to keep her mouth shut and pretend nothing happened. She put on a smile, all the while holding her breath, praying she would see the old Matty as he turned to face her.

She wanted so badly to rush over and hug him. Even without the stone's curse, she couldn't make a move like that. Zack had warned her. Baby vampires were like feral kittens. They might appear cute and cuddly, but they're unable to control their claws, nor do they want to, most days. She stood still as death, not wanting to trigger his prey drive.

Matt lifted his gaze as he came around to face her.

Blue eyes, good. Breathing, slow but normal-ish. Lips, covering his fangs. Thank goodness for that.

"How's it going today, buddy?" she asked, keeping her tone light.

"Work in progress." Matt's answer came on a hurried breath.

"You talk to Josh yet?"

"We spoke on the phone." His nostrils flared as if he'd caught scent of something distracting. "It was…" – his voice broke, but he still pushed the words out – "a good conversation."

"He's doing so well. I couldn't be prouder," Zack praised him, a sharp contrast from the previous evening where he'd done everything in his power to taunt the beast. "Our little baby is ready for a field test."

Zack's fangs were on full display, and there was no mistaking the eagerness in his voice.

"You sure? Is that…safe?" Blood bags in the refrigerator was bad enough. Sage couldn't allow her mind to go down the rabbit hole of imagining her best friend sucking someone's neck. The last time she had been around a bunch of vampires, they were openly feeding from people. No amount of bleach could burn away that memory. "Can't you just –"

"Get takeout?" Zack finished the sentence for her. "We've been doing that for the last few days. But juice boxes, as you so eloquently labeled them, will only hold a newbie for a little while. If he doesn't get a home-cooked meal every now and again, he'll lose what little ability he has to control his urges."

Even now as they stood in close proximity, Mat's struggle to keep his cool was evident. Bloodlust or not, her roommate was still in there. Sweet, loveable Matty.

Will he lose himself completely if he kills someone?

He was a vampire with needs Sage couldn't possibly understand.

Did Zack understand? He'd shown hints of humanity every now and again. He'd also killed for his supper. A fact he'd boasted about on many occasions. As nice as Zack pretended to be, Sage had seen the demon lying in wait just below the surface. She hadn't come to terms with the reality that the same demon might reside in her best friend.

"Relax, Agent Sage." Zack mock saluted. "We'll keep it within the limits of the law. Scout's honor."

His words failed to reassure her. Their laws didn't always protect human life, only the secrecy of the magical world from humans.

"Sage." Matt's voice warbled. "I have to do this. I…have to…" – his nostrils flared again – "figure out what I am. How to exist."

Something was tempting him. His eyes sparkled with eagerness, as if he'd caught the scent of something as distracting as the blood bag Zack had waved in his face the previous evening. Was this another test? She looked to Zack for answers, but he too, seemed preoccupied by something. She followed the direction of his eyes. Not quite meeting her gaze head-on, Zack was staring lower.

Shit. Of course! Her hand. The failed surgery. But her wounds had healed. She glanced down at her clothes, and it all made sense. Tiny spots of blood speckled her jeans. Probably from when she'd passed out. Too small for her to pick up, but a newborn vampire would smell each and every drop from a mile away. She should have changed before she came home.

"Give me a minute, and I can change out of these clothes before he loses it," she said.

"No. Don't." Zack held his hands up to stop her. "He's doing exceptionally well right now. Stay. Talk."

"All evidence to the contrary," she replied.

The look on Matt's face was anything but well. The pain etched across his features trumped any she felt from the seed burning its way through her hand. Standing in front of temptation like that had to be excruciating for him to endure. She'd caused him enough pain already. His body practically vibrated as he worked to maintain composure.

"Are you okay?" she asked. "Seriously, Matty. Tell me."

"I am dealing with this as best as I can." His tone said otherwise.

"He's very strong," Zack praised. "Couldn't have chosen a better man myself for the transition."

"I will get through this, Sage." Matt's mechanical words spoke volumes.

Guilt threatened to drown her under its oppressive weight. Tears flooded Sages vision. She wanted to be positive, to be strong for him, but watching him go through so much torment was enough to break what little remained of her spirit.

"How's your curse?" Zack asked, swiftly moving the conversation. "Was the operation a success?"

"How did you know about that?"

"You went to work today. You smell of blood... Your blood," he added with a sinister smile as he licked his lips.

Sage swallowed hard as a cold chill froze the tears in her eyes and slithered down her spine.

"And there is a very large black blemish on your left hand." Zack tilted his head as if trying to get a better look.

Sage moved her hand behind her back, not wanting him to see the true extent of the damage. The less he knew, the better.

"One can assume you had the *powers that be* look into your newfound death touch. The verdict was?"

She clenched her ruined hand tightly into a fist. "Still untouchable."

"Damn." Zack sighed. "We'll have to postpone date night yet again, then?"

"Don't," she snarled, not in the mood for his flirting or jokes.

"After all we've been through, you still have such animosity toward me." Zack feigned pain in his chest.

"You saved my friend from death, and for that, I will be eternally grateful," Sage admitted. "But you've threatened my life more times than I care to count. I know who you truly are and what you're capable of. I'm not about to let my guard down again."

"Somedays I regret having to teach you that lesson." Zack's smile faltered.

Matt balled his fist. "He did what?" Anger clouded the blue of his eyes.

Sage instantly regretted her choice of words. Bringing up old fights, out of context, always made them sound so much worse than they were. The truth was in there, buried under subtext she didn't have the time to explain fully. But seeing how quickly Matt was losing his cool, she struggled to come up with an acceptable explanation.

"Steady now, Junior," Zack warned. "Don't do something you'll regret, Matt."

Having seen his darker side firsthand, Sage stepped back a few paces, leaving a wide berth between herself and the two aggressive vampires. "Relax, Matt. We're cool."

"All this time, I thought you two were flirting." Matt faced Zack. Rising up to his full height, he stood a bit taller than his sire. A serious gym habit gave him the edge on muscle mass as well. Matt had never looked so intimidating.

Sage felt herself shrinking as she crept another tiny step away from the two vampires.

"You've been threatening her life?" Matt's lips pulled back in a razor-sharp sneer. "My Sage?"

"In my defense, I've saved her life as many times as I've threatened it," Zack replied casually, and by all appearances unintimidated by Matt's aggressive stance.

Muscles strung taut as a bow string, Matt lumbered forward, closing the gap between himself and Zack.

Zack stood his ground. "Control yourself before I put you down." Darkness devoured the otherworldly blue of his eyes, announcing his inner demon was beginning to rise to the surface, ready to play.

She couldn't let them come to blows. "Matt!" she pleaded, but he had already given himself over to rage.

His fist moved with such speed Sage barely registered the movement.

Zack hadn't missed it. He snatched Matt's fist a hair's breadth before it collided with his jaw, and held it firmly.

"Fine." Zack jerked Matt's arm up and to the side, forcing him to spin around with ballroom-like grace. "We do this the hard way." He pinned Matt's arm behind his back. "Submit now or I will end you."

Matt roared loud enough for the neighbors to hear and threw his head back, crashing into Zack's forehead.

Both men grunted, echoing the pain of their collision. Matt escaped Zack's hold and spun around, swinging his fist wildly.

Sage recognized the tactic. His strikes wouldn't connect. He was clearing the air, giving himself time to back up and reposition for his next attack. A hopeful sign he hadn't lost himself completely. She prayed Zack could subdue him quickly. Snap her roommate back into reality, rather than end him as he'd just promised.

She almost said as much, but before she could get the words out, the old recliner in the living room came flying across the floor. She jumped away, before it took her out, on its collision course with the dining room table.

"Kill each other, fine, but leave the furniture out of it, okay?" she yelled.

She might as well have been invisible. Her words were drowned out by the snarls and grunts as the two continued to fight.

Matt hammered hard with his fist. Zack blocked easily, but he failed to take control of the arm before Matt had it cocked and ready for another strike. Zack dodged one punch and pivoted away from another, placing the coffee table between them, prevented Matt from landing his next strike. A flimsy barrier, Matt kicked the wooden table hard. It shot across the room and careened into the TV cabinet. Someone was buying new furniture after this was over.

That should have snapped him out of it. Matt loved the TV nearly as much as he loved Josh, but despite the inevitable destruction of his prized possessions, his punches were only getting wilder. He sent his leg out low to sweep Zack's feet and opened himself to a throat strike.

Sage had trained with Devon enough times to spot the mistake. She covered her eyes, not wanting to see, but couldn't resist peeking through the gaps of her fingers, all the while praying her best friend would still be alive-ish after the dust cleared. Matt fought with mounting rage, but if he pushed his luck too hard, Zack really might have to put him down.

In her current condition, Sage couldn't intervene without hurting either of them.

Zack appeared to be blocking most strikes rather than attacking. But the longer they struggled, the more feral her best friend became. Matt snarled like a rabid dog, spraying Zack's face with spittle. His next strike found its mark. The thump of Matt's fist connecting with muscles was so loud it had Sage cringing with sympathy.

Zack gave no verbal indication of pain, but it was there, in his watering eyes.

Rage, revenge, a desire to dole out death.

Sage gasped, and before she could expel the air from her lungs, Zack retaliated with viper-like speed, snatching Matt's head between his hands.

A quick jerk, snap, and Matt dropped lifelessly to the floor.

Tears flooded her vision as she rushed to Matt's side. This couldn't be happening. After all she had gone through to keep him alive. The curse. The sacrifice. She'd just promised Josh she'd take care of him. Her throat dried as she tried to choke out his name. *He can't be dead!* She reached out to search for a pulse and hesitated, her fingertips hovered over Matt's still body, one thought ran clearly through her mind.

Zack has to die.

EIGHT

"Don't touch him!" Zack shouted. "Stand up slowly and back away!"

How dare he bark orders at her like that, after what he had just done. He had no authority over her. After what he'd just done, he was nothing to her. Why was he still speaking? She held her trembling hand hovering over Matt's body. Frozen in place with rage that needed an outlet.

He was right about one thing. She shouldn't touch Matt's body. All she needed to do was lay a single finger on Zack, and he'd join her dearly departed roommate. Didn't matter where. Any bit of skin would do. Maybe she'd poke him in the eye just to make sure he suffered before he was reduced to dust. Sage slowly turned her head up, letting her gaze travel the length of Zack's body, searching for just the right place to employ her deadly touch.

"Are you listening to me?" Zack didn't even have the decency to look sorry for what he'd just done. If anything, his casual posture and the tilt of his head added to his air of arrogance.

Bastard. A quick death was too good for him!

"You dare to speak after what you just did?" Anger turned her voice demonic. The seed burned within her palm fanned by the fire of her rage, with only one way to quench it. Sage understood in that moment the desire to end someone's life. Beyond revenge, she lusted for the exquisite pleasure of being an instrument of divine retribution. "Murderer!"

Her target in sight, Sage rose slowly to her feet, enjoying the way Zack's eyes shifted fearfully.

The predator had become the prey.

"He's a vampire." Zack threw his hands up submissively, and took a quick step backwards, placing himself just out of reach.

"You arrogant asshole." She cracked her knuckles, still deciding on just how she wanted to punish him. "I'm going to enjoy ending you."

Zack took another unsteady step backwards, butting up against the couch. "He's a vampire, Sage," he repeated, more urgently.

And they called her Captain Obvious. "He *was* a vampire!" she shot back at him. "That lasted, what? A week?" So much for immortality. Matt lay lifeless on the floor in nearly the same spot the kitsune had left him to die when this whole mess started. His chest wasn't moving. She didn't dare check for a pulse. Zack was supposed to have saved him. He had one job!

"Calm down, please," Zack pleaded. "You need to listen to me before you do something you will truly regret."

"What the hell are you playing at?" Every impulse she had screamed for her to end the weasel's life before he found a way to escape, but against her better judgement, Sage hesitated. "Speak quickly and simply, before I send you into the next life after him!"

"He's only mostly dead!" Zack's voice cracked.

"Don't you pull that shit on me. Real answers…now!" She jabbed a finger at him.

"He's a vampire. His body will heal quickly. Matt is fine, I promise." He tried again to move back, away from her. "Though I do not envy him the headache he'll have when he wakes." Nowhere left to go, Zack collapsed on the couch.

"Why should I believe you?"

"Would I make such a classic blunder…when death is on the line?" His expression was hopeful, relying on his nerdy charm to get him out of trouble.

Was he being truthful? Could Matt still live?

Sage clenched her fist, refusing to move until she had proof either way.

The room fell silent. Neither of them spoke nor moved. All eyes focused on Matt, waiting, watching. Sage's heart thundered in her chest. She'd lost so much in the last few months. She could not lose him now. She prayed, wished, and willed Matt to move. Her sanity hung on a slender thread of hope.

"Sage?" Zack spoke her name tenderly.

"Don't!" she snarled in reply. The only thing keeping him alive at the moment was Matt. She stared down at his body. *Please wake up. Please. Don't be dead.*

His head twitched. The sudden snapping motion almost sent her climbing the walls. But as she stood watch, Matt's chest began to rise and fall with slow breaths.

A wave of relief crashed over her and nearly sent her collapsing to the ground next to Matt.

Zack sighed loudly with relief. "You see? All good. Junior just needed a little nap to sleep off his temper tantrum."

"I can't talk to you right now." Rage still simmered within her, needing an outlet, but he had spoken truth. Matt was alive. And would still need to be taught the finer points of managing bloodlust. She couldn't take out her anger on Zack. Nor could she stand to look at him. She walked toward the kitchen, needing a distraction. *Matt is alive,* she reminded herself. Her heart raced painfully, her chest on fire. And the seed within her palm still demanded to be fed.

Matt is alive! It became her mantra, breaking free of her inner monologue, reaching out through her voice. "Matt is still alive." The more she repeated it, the better she felt. Calmer.

"Yes, he's alive!" Zack replied. "But this thing between us needs work if we're going to continue cohabitating."

"Let me be perfectly clear! There is *nothing* between us."

"You can't hate me forever," Zack snarked, unrepentant from the couch.

"I don't hate you." Hate was too simple a word for the emotions she was still struggling to get under control. "But I sure as hell am not dropping my guard around you ever again."

"Say what you want. I know the truth. You'd have welcomed me into your bed if I hadn't made you see the darker side. Much as I hated to ruin my chances with you, I had to do it. You're too naïve. I don't want to see someone truly evil take advantage of you."

Why was he still talking? Did he not realize how close he'd come to being a pile of dust? The arrogance.

"Will you just shut up?" Sage growled and slammed her fist into the kitchen counter. "I don't have the patience for your bullshit right now."

"I'm trying to help you. Have I not proven where my loyalty lies?" he asked. "Why do you think I saved him?" Zack pointed to Matt. "I don't need to train another newbie. For what it's worth, there are too many of my kind here already."

"You want a cookie or something? You must because you keep bringing that up. How many times do I need to thank you for saving him? You think that gives you license to be a jerk to us both?" She needed to vent this rage before she really did kill him. Jerk or not, he was the only one who could help Matt. They both needed him.

"I'm sorry I snapped his neck. I did not see another way to calm him quickly. Okay?"

She hadn't expected him to apologize or sound so sincere.

"I don't know how to say this nicely. You change gears so fast it makes my head spin. And your motivation is always based on what *you* will get out of a deal. So, tell me…What did you think you'd earn here?"

"Your trust." Zack lifted his eyebrows and stared her down from across the room.

Sage opened her mouth, but no words came. Hot and cold. Angel and asshole. He swung so hard, so fast between extremes, that dealing with him left her dizzy. They stared in awkward silence, neither of them knowing what to say.

Matt gasped and sat upright. "What the hell?" He rubbed his neck and stared around the room as if not sure where he was.

"Next time, Junior, listen to Papa when he speaks," Zack replied.

"Matty? You going to be okay?" Sage asked.

"Did he just snap my neck?" Matt stood, still rubbing the soreness from the base of his skull. "That hurt."

"You can either follow my instructions, or you will be put down." Zack stood, towering over Matt as he spoke. "We have a code. As your sire, I am responsible for you until you are able to function on your own. You screw up, I get blamed. I get punished right along with you. And if you get ASSET involved, we're all dead. Got it?"

Matt balled his fist, looking as if he were ready for round two. The two men stared at each other like wolves vying for dominance. Sage worried another fight would break out, but the moment passed.

Matt released his fist, lowering his head, and submitted. "I have no other choice, do I?"

"It's not so bad once you get the hang of it." Zack extended a hand, a surprising gesture of good will. "Controlling your temper is lesson one. You let the beast out for one moment, and you could lose everything."

Matt's brow furrowed. He hesitated before accepting the offered hand. "I'm not sure I can do this."

"I have faith in you," she called from across the room. "And so does Josh." If only she could run up and give him a great big hug. He looked like he needed one. And after what they had just gone through, she needed it too. But she kept her distance, staying put in the kitchen where they were both safe from her touch. "Soon as you can get some control, you and he can have some quality time. Get a nice dose of happy."

Her words put a smile on his face. "I miss him," Matt whispered as if it were his own personal mantra.

"First, you have to learn how not to kill him." Zack's snarky tone ruined the moment. "Time to get Junior a happy meal."

"How long is this going to take?" Matt asked.

"As long as you need to become a fully functioning member of society again." Zack helped him to his feet.

"Speaking of. How am I going to work? Still have rent to pay."

"Baby steps." Sage had the answer this time. "We'll get you registered with Sortilage Staffing Solutions once you're up and running."

"The where?"

"Magical human resources." Sage laughed, realizing that for once, she was not the newbie. She had had the answer before anyone else.

"That's a thing?" Matt's gaze shifted between Sage and Zack. "Clearly, I have a lot to learn."

"You and me both," Sage agreed.

"Let's go, Junior. You're my charge." Zack waved as he walked to the door. "Sage already has Yoda and the Grumpy Avenger teaching her."

Sage stepped back, giving them a wide berth as they passed through the kitchen. She didn't like the idea of Matt going out with Zack, especially after what he'd just done. But he was the only teacher her roommate had. And if Zack had proved anything, it was how desperately Matt needed to learn control.

"You truly want to earn my trust?" She stopped Zack with her words before he closed the door.

Zack nodded eagerly, awaiting her demand.

"Take care of him. Teach him right. And above all else, do not let him kill." She put all the authority she could into her voice as she gave the decree.

"As you wish." Zack bowed with a flourish as he crossed the threshold and closed the door behind him.

Could he do as she'd requested? Sage had her doubts, but she welcomed the opportunity to be proved wrong.

"Have fun stormin' the castle, boys!" she whispered as she watched them head into the night from her kitchen window.

NINE

With the guys out for the night getting takeout, Sage realized how quiet her home was – intolerably silent. Nothing to distract her from her inner demons, frayed nerves, guilt, and self-loathing. She'd had it up to here with negativity. She needed noise, people, real human interaction, anything non-magical to turn off her inner monologue before she let it drag her down into madness.

One place came to mind. Sage took to the night air and set her sights on the pub just down the road. Her home away from home. Julie's shift would be starting soon, and that was reason enough to pop in, even if she'd already had her dinner. She could have some normal, human conversation.

No sooner had she locked her apartment door than the all too familiar feeling of eyes prickled on the back of her neck. She would have feared that sensation a mere week earlier. Her palm throbbed, the stone aching to be fed. Sage welcomed someone fool enough to try and attack her. They'd learn a very dangerous lesson.

The thought stopped her in her tracks. She'd never enjoyed hurting people. This wasn't her. It was that damn seed. She clenched her fist tight, determined to get rid of that thing once and for all.

But first, she needed to figure out who was watching her. She peered into the shadowy spaces where the pathway lights didn't reach, and caught sight of a tiny glowing ember under a set of stairs belonging to the apartment across from hers.

"How did you do it?" Luke's voice came from the shadow.

"You're still around?" Of course it would be him. She blew out a breath, letting her muscles relax. "I thought you'd have cleared out the moment you were free of your kitsune master."

"No need. You took care of her well enough." Luke emerged and flicked his cigarette on the pavement. He squashed the burning ember under the heel of his shoe. "Can I join you?"

"Never given me a choice before." Silence wasn't her friend, but hanging with djinn wasn't exactly an upgrade. Would it be too much to ask for her to have normal human interaction? Clearly it was.

"I wasn't completely in control of my mind then." Luke closed the gap between them and fell in step with Sage.

"And you are now?" She continued on toward the gate.

"I have to know how you did it. Terras have no active magic."

"I didn't use any." Sage shrugged, hoping to give off an air of casual indifference.

Djinn were known to be cunning tricksters. Luke had proven himself just that under the control of Thalia. He'd seen her take out his previous master and use magic that didn't belong to her. But like all the others, he couldn't know the truth. Ava's dire warning hung heavy in her mind.

"I saw you siphon power." Luke fumbled with his lighter, igniting the flame and putting it out just as quickly. "I have to know."

"Neutralize it."

"So you admit it. You did –"

"No. I was merely correcting you. I do not have magic. I can't use magic." She shoved her hand deep into her pocket, and continued down the path.

"But I saw you. Felt you pulling the magic from me. I've never experienced anything like that before."

Why is he so insistent? What is he after? Does he have a motive? Everyone lately had some kind of motive. Information was the most valuable currency out there. But the knowledge she carried was priceless.

"Maybe you just haven't run into many Terras, then," she said.

"That wasn't Terra magic. I've been around many of your kind. You, Sage, are something truly unique." He took her by the arm.

She gasped, expecting the pain again, stopping in her tracks. Her hand throbbed, but the seed did not awaken. "What the hell are you doing?"

Luke twisted her arm, pulling her hand from the depths of her pocket to see the mark on her wrist. "I had to be sure." His eyes moved from the Tree of Life to the black spot at her palm.

"Don't you ever touch me again." She jerked free of his grasp, shocked that he'd had the gall, and clutched her hand to her chest. "How did you –" She stopped herself before finishing the thought out loud.

"That's new, isn't it?" Luke baited her with the question, daring her to lie.

"It's nothing. Are you okay?"

"Should I not be?"

Luke knew more than he was letting on, but she couldn't risk adding to her body count with the truth. Ava's warning echoed in her mind.

"Most people who touch me aren't." She rubbed the black spot on her hand, though it did nothing to lessen the constant ache.

"So it was not your magic, then?"

Damn him, he wasn't letting up. She had to give him something convincing enough to satisfy his inquisition, but what?

"I told you I don't have magic."

Luke's eyes locked on to her hand. Even under the curtain of night, there was no hiding how much of her hand had gone black. "You have something."

"What about you? Still a djinn?" Sage tried shifting the subject to his change.

"That remains to be seen." He showed her the back of his hand. Circling his third finger was the ring she thought she had destroyed, his djinn talisman.

"Searching for a new master?"

"You want the job?" he teased.

"I prefer to keep my soul, thanks."

"A test, then?"

He couldn't possibly have retained his magic. Could he? She'd touched both him and the ring during the battle with Thalia. Surely the seed had absorbed everything? Or had it? djinn magic wasn't exactly attached to their person. Tricksy little djinn he was. That's what Luke was after.

"You're not sure of your own magic, are you?" she asked.

"Since my curse, I have never been able to use my magic willingly." He pulled the ring off his finger and held it out to her. "Call it a freebie."

"Remember, you asked for this." She hesitated, afraid of both the pain and the truth coming out. If it still held any power, one touch would destroy it. But curiosity got the better of her. "Here goes." She winced as she took the ring from his hand.

Nothing.

She released a breath. *Just a ring. Nothing more.* Sage slipped it over her thumb and flashed a smile at Luke. "I wish you to remove the mark from my palm."

"As you wish." Luke bowed his head respectfully and placed his hand over her damaged palm. He closed his eyes and mumbled something under his breath.

Silence passed between them. Sage expected as much after the ring had not awakened the seed. She tapped her foot, waiting for Luke to admit defeat.

He mumbled again and pressed his hand on top of hers. Confusion creased his brow as he lifted his eyes to face her. The truth was far worse than he probably knew, but she couldn't say.

Small creases formed between his brows. "Nothing. It's gone." His words came on the edge of a defeated sigh.

"I'm sorry." She returned his ring.

"I have to know… How?"

"Get used to disappointment."

"Please?"

"Can't you just be happy you're free?" She asked.

"I don't know what freedom means." Luke's expression floated somewhere between shock and fear. "Am I to live as a human? Am I no longer immortal?"

"You're looking at me for answers?" Sage laughed at the irony.

"*You* did this to me."

"I did nothing," Sage snapped a bit more harshly than she should have. "You and Thalia forced my hand."

"But how? That is not a Terra power." Luke just wouldn't let it go.

"Answers mean death," she warned.

"I get it. Magical gag order, right?" Luke threw the term bitterly at her. "And if my guess is correct, whatever you bargained for to get your newfound ability, you're already paying that price."

Sage shoved her hand deep into her pocket again. "Don't mock me."

"Said with respect." Luke bowed with a flourish. "To be honest, I didn't know how you were going to stop Thalia. ASSET has a reputation for doing whatever is necessary to get the job done."

"You can say that again," Sage whispered under her breath.

Luke turned his eyes skyward and took in a deep breath. "Seems we both have to learn how to exist with our new impediments." How many centuries had he lived with his magic? To be suddenly cut off from it had to have been a huge shock. Confused as he appeared, he seemed to be taking the news in stride. No tears. No pleading. Just quiet acceptance.

"How are you going to deal with mortality?"

He shrugged. "I've never had a problem making friends."

"Don't go around calling people Master. They might get the wrong idea."

"I'll take that under advisement."

He'd failed to laugh at her joke. She couldn't blame him for being humorless. She'd been fighting the doldrums herself.

Luke lowered his gaze to meet her face. "I hope I can still count you as a friend."

"Don't think you're going to couch surf. We're all full up on crazy." She smirked to make sure he understood she was teasing.

"Wouldn't dream of it. You have done me a favor, freeing me from my curse." He put on a good front, though, keeping his expression neutral. "I'm in your debt. If ever you need help, just ask, and I will do what I can." He offered his hand.

She met him halfway and gave him a squeeze as she shook his. "Thanks."

"As someone who has lived many lifetimes cursed by the gods, can I give you a word of advice?" Luke turned her hand over and gave the black mark a closer look.

Sage nodded.

"Curses that can affect a Terra are not to be taken lightly, no matter how nobly they were enacted. You need to find a cure before this one blackens more than your skin."

"Working on it." She pulled her hand back. He knew much more than he was letting on. But even so, she couldn't discuss it openly.

Luke backed away a few steps.

"Thought you were tagging along for dinner."

He bowed out. "I need to figure out how to be human again. Can't do that too well with an ASSET agent ruining my game. You know where to find me when you need me."

Sage waved him off, wondering how much he actually knew. Everyone had secrets. She continued her walk to the pub, running the conversation through her mind.

Luke had said "when you need me," not "if." *Why?*

TEN

The feeling of unseen eyes prickled at the back of her neck as she meandered toward the pub.

For a half second, Sage debated whether or not she should just turn around and go home, but the reality was, this was her life. She could either live it, or hide from it. Affliction or not, she couldn't hide from the world. She needed to be around people, not wallowing in self-pity alone in her home. Much better to eat her feelings in the form of chocolate cake.

Julie's truck sat in the parking lot, a cute little pickup bedazzled with bumper stickers from every concert she'd attended. The thought of a familiar face affirmed her decision to come out, even if she had a stalker watching her from the shadows.

"Luke, I already said you could join me," Sage called out, hoping she was right.

She spun around, looking again for his telltale trail of smoke, but came up empty.

"Zack. Matty, not funny," she tried again. They were on the hunt. It would stand to reason they might use her as training.

"Well, whoever you are, best not to screw with me. I'm in no mood," she warned the breeze.

The pub was all but empty inside. Slow, even for a weeknight. Sage walked to her favorite booth in the back and waited for Julie to come around.

Julie greeted her with a pint in hand. "Bad day, eh?"

"The worst." Sage reached for the glass.

Julie gasped as she saw the bruising on Sage's hand. "You tried cooking again, didn't you?"

She swapped hands, hiding her left one under the table, and reached for the beer with her right. "Never let me do that again." Julie had provided an excellent lie to explain her condition. All Sage had to do was keep it going. "Chocolate. Lots of it. And extra icing if you've got it."

"You have someone look at that hand?" Julie asked.

Sage gulped down her beer, giving her time to come up with a response. "I did. Just a few burns and bruises, nothing really bad. It's healing. You should have seen it a few days ago."

"I was wondering why game night had been cancelled." Julie seemed to have accepted the lie, but she hadn't walked away.

What else could she say?

"Sorry. Yeah. My hand. Matty sick. Josh out of town. Just a bad week in general."

"I'm just a phone call away, hon. Next time, call and let me know what's up. I was worried." Julie nodded and turned to put the order in.

That was the problem with having human friends now that she'd learned about the magical world. Living a double life meant keeping all kinds of secrets, and remembering who knew what. It wasn't fair to Julie to be kept in the dark. She'd always been a good friend. She deserved better.

Sage needed to work harder to keep her as close as she could.

The front door opened, and a couple walked in. A man, tall and slender. Hipster type complete with skinny jeans and a goatee. Next to him, holding his hand was a woman who matched him in height, but had a punk vibe about her. Pink and purple pixie hair, nose ring, and enormous gauges in her ears. Definitely not the normal sort to patronize this neighborhood pub.

The moment Sage laid eyes on them, she picked up on their otherworldliness. As if they were wearing costumes to blend in.

All at once, the ambient noise in the bar silenced. More than just quiet, it was as if her ears had been turned off. She could no longer hear music, conversation, or the hum of the refrigerators behind the bar. Sage glanced around and spotted Julie standing at the bar, only her posture was wrong. She appeared to be hovering.

No, not hovering. Frozen.

Sage turned her attention back to the couple, the only other people in the bar not frozen in place. They were staring intently in her direction.

Ethereals.

The word materialized in her mind.

Before she could get the word from her lips, the male and female blinked out of focus. When they blinked back in, they stood two feet in front of her.

The seed in her palm awoke with a fiery roar, ravenous for the magic within reach.

"Get out of my bar," Sage warned.

"Didn't realize you had ownership of this place. Surprised, given how meagerly you live," the woman responded.

"So it was you two following me. Not very smart, are you?" Pain gave Sage's voice a powerful edge. Her left hand moved on its own, drawn toward the magic in reach. She forced it back, pinning her wrist with her free hand.

"What makes you so special?" The male stood dangerously close, looking down his nose at Sage.

Stupid man. He'd picked the wrong day to mess with her, dark as she'd been feeling. How long had he and his partner been following her? How much had they heard of her conversation with Luke?

If he didn't back away, she wouldn't be responsible for what she did. The seed's pull tempted her hand to move. A slap across the face would do him in. He'd feel more than a sharp sting as his magic was absorbed. Teach him to mouth off.

At least his partner seemed to have some sense about her. She stood behind the jerk, using him as a shield. She might make it out with her powers intact.

"ASSET does not take too kindly to Ethereals disrupting human establishments." Sage spoke with unquestioned authority. "You've done enough here for me to haul you down and hold you indefinitely. Sound special enough for you?"

The woman giggled. "You're all alone tonight. Not very intimidating." She moved in closer and thumped Sage's shoulder.

The momentary connection sent a shock wave through Sage's body, traveling all the way down to the center of her palm. These two had power. More than enough to sate the seed's hunger for at least a few hours.

Sage growled with the effort it took to hide her discomfort. She glared up at the woman. No words were needed. She knew. The punk was slowly backing away, having felt a small part of her power devoured. She pawed at her male companion, pulling him just out of reach.

They weren't intimidating. They got it.

Sage smiled wickedly and slowly rose to her feet. "I'm Terra. If you were smart, you'd know what that means. But seeing as how you've chosen to physically assault me, I think you need a refresher in exactly why my people should be respected." She pointed a finger at the woman. "My magic negates your magic. But it goes a bit further." She poked the woman in the chest. Ready for the zap, she held her breath through the pain. "You see, when provoked, I can use my magic to not only neutralize yours. I can also destroy it." She poked the woman again. This time the pain had morphed into pleasure. She wanted more. Sage turned on the male. "Want to know what that's like? Having your very essence zapped away, one" – she jabbed a finger at him – "little poke at a time." Laughter bubbled up from her chest as pain and pleasure combined with this new feeling of ultimate power. "I can do this all day."

The male backed up.

"Stop it!" The female stood her ground, snarling with rage.

"Why? Isn't this what you came here for?" Sage taunted. "You have some kind of grudge and thought you could take it out on me?"

The woman's hand cocked back. Sage watched eagerly for the swing, and when it happened, caught the woman's hand in the air.

The agony and ecstasy of their connection had Sage moaning with pleasure. The woman crumpled to the ground.

Somewhere in the back of her mind, a voice begged for Sage to hold on tight, but as her gaze traveled toward the bar and she saw her friend standing frozen, she realized what she was doing. This was wrong. The woman wailed in agony, begging for her partner, the man, to save her.

Fear, it seemed had, him trapped where he stood. His eyes like saucers, witnessed every agonizing moment of his partner's torture.

Sage finally found the strength to let go, panting from the sensation. She clutched her hand to her chest. Pain returned with the seed's incessant demand for more power. She'd taken more than she should, possibly blowing her cover. If they realized how she was doing what she was doing… No, they couldn't. She needed to say something. Warn them off. Put the fear of the Goddess into them.

"ASSET has been lenient. The Terras have restrained their magic long enough. Too many have died in recent months. We will stand for it no longer." Sage delivered the decree, hoping it would be believable enough. "You want to test us, you will be the ones to fail. Now get out of my sight before I relieve you of all of your magic."

They turned tail and left. The moment the doors closed behind them, time restarted.

Sage collapsed into the booth, her hand hurting more than it had in the last week. But more disturbing than physical pain was how close she had come to giving in to the seed's demand. It had spoken to her, tempted her with pleasure to consume all the power she could. And she nearly had. She was supposed to serve magic, protect it, not destroy it.

By the time Julie had come round with her extra-large slice of chocolate cake, Sage had lost her appetite.

"What's going on?"

"I'm not myself today," she answered honestly.

Julie slid onto the bench and wrapped Sage in her arms. She hesitated at first, scared of her magical affliction, but eased into the warmth when she remembered Julie was human. Thank the gods for that.

Tears began to fall unchecked down her cheeks. She sniffled and buried her face into Julie's shoulder.

"It's okay, girl. You let it out. Bet you haven't had a good long cry since your mom died. You've been so busy. And Matt's been such a grump. You let it all out."

Julie was so right. She had not let it out. She'd been forced to suck it up and deal. And she had. This sudden permission to cry had her blubbering like a great big baby.

"Thank you," Sage said when she found her voice again.

"Hey. I'm not just an alternate for game night, you know. I'm here whenever you need me. We're friends."

She needed friends more than she wanted to admit, but Julie was also human and she'd failed to protect one human friend already. She'd die if she failed and lost another to the deadly side of magic. But she appreciated the gesture all the same.

"When I get my head on straight, we need a girls' night." Sage wiped away her tears. The smell of chocolate reinvigorated her hunger.

The door opened again. Sage held her breath as she looked to see who'd come in.

A regular barfly strutted up to his usual place and swiped his player's card in the bar-mounted slot machine.

"It's on. You name the time and place!" Julie stood. "Duty calls."

Sage dove into her cake, feeling conflicted about what had happened. She'd have to report it to Ava. Depending on how well she took it, Sage might not live long enough to have that girls' night out.

ELEVEN

Devon called first thing in the morning with exciting news that he'd arranged a meeting for Sage with Quarn. The Elemental had an extensive personal library, and she needed all the information she could get her hands on. After the night she'd had, Sage worried about being so close to another magical being, but at least she'd have Grey at her side. And the longer she stayed away from ASSET, the more time she'd have to figure out how to report what happened at the pub.

Sage pounced on Grey the moment he parked his bike, blurting everything out in a rush of hazy details.

"Just can't let you out of my sight, can I?" Grey groaned wearily. "Did you at least get names?"

He had her there. That would have been the smart thing to do. Her cheeks warmed with embarrassment. "It kind of happened quickly. They attacked me."

"You're an agent, right?" She couldn't see his face, but Grey's tone smacked of annoyance. "You should always be on your guard. Prepared for any eventuality."

So much for expecting him to be on her side. She knew she'd be dressed down by Ava, but Grey was supposed to be on her side. Her partner. "How? What was I supposed to do? I defended myself."

"Sounds like you nearly killed them." Grey pulled his helmet off and raked his fingers through his hair. "And then sent them on their way to go report what just happened to them."

"I warned them not to act like assholes and that the Terras have more magic than they have been told."

He looked around, everywhere but at Sage, as if the sight of her annoyed him. "That was a really stupid move considering no other Terra can do what you can."

"Would you rather I kill them?"

"You could have brought them in," Grey fired back at her.

How could he stand there and pretend she was at fault? She hadn't sought out those Ethereal assholes. She'd been ambushed. She was winging it. Like he could have done better in her position.

"Yeah, I guess I could have done that." She slammed her hands on her hips and glared up at him. "Put them in handcuffs. Drag them down to headquarters. Oh wait… That requires touching, which leads to… Bye bye, magic."

Grey growled in frustration. "You can't be alone at all."

"Yippy, more babysitting." She rolled her eyes. At least then it would absolve her of being at fault for everything. He could take a few lumps.

"I'm trying to protect you," – Grey pointed to her hand – "until we can get rid of that thing."

"Totally appreciate it," she snarked.

"Could have fooled me," he replied in kind. "Remember as you roll those indignant eyes. You chose to use the seed."

"Ava was the one who told me to use it…on Luke." She sneered at him. He knew she'd had no choice. How dare he stand there and act all superior.

"Okay, we're getting nowhere. Bottom line is you need protection while we undo this curse or whatever the seed is doing. Deal with it. Okay?"

"Fine."

"Now get on the bike so we can go." He held a helmet out for her. "And remember, Quarn cannot know the true nature of your affliction. Let me do all the talking."

"So, shut up, Sage?"

"You're learning. I'm so proud." Grey put his helmet on and brought the bike to life before Sage could try to get in another snarky word.

He drove them out to a small community of expensive homes around Lake Las Vegas. Quarn's home was like a Mediterranean palace surrounded with gorgeous fountains and water features.

Her palm ached, sensing the magic radiating off of Quarn even before they made it to the door. Grey rang the bell and Quarn answered.

"You are most welcome to my home. Please come in. Would you care for refreshment?" Quarn asked.

"Thank you," Sage replied pleasantly. "We appreciate you seeing us on such short notice."

Quarn extended a webbed hand to shake. Grey stepped in and took the hand before Sage made the mistake of doing it. She shoved her hands in her pocket to prevent herself from accidentally touching something, and let Grey stand between her and Quarn.

If the webbed hands and rubbery look to his skin hadn't been obvious enough that he was a water-type Elemental, his house practically screamed it. It was one thing to install a fountain. But to have entire walls of cascading water was a bit over the top. Of course he was a merman after all. Living in the desert. That seemed stranger still. She had to wonder what kept him around. Magic most likely. She could feel it throbbing in her palm. Certainly not the puddle of Lake Las Vegas. Questions for another time, if she had it.

"A case we're working on has brought us into contact with magic we have not seen before," Grey began. "Devon speaks very highly of your ancient wisdom, and the vast library he's turned to for resources in the past."

"It warms my heart to hear how highly he speaks of me." Quarn bowed his head and motioned for them to walk into his study. "I am always willing to assist ASSET in any way that I can."

"We're not at liberty to discuss specifics, but we believe the nature of the artifact we have come into contact with is of godly origin." Grey followed behind Quarn as he led them through a large, comfortable living area and into his library.

"Then it is nothing to trifle with," Quarn warned as he moved toward a bookshelf that had been piled all the way up to the ceiling with leather-bound tomes.

"We don't trifle. We protect magic," Grey defended quickly. "And those potentially affected by it."

"Of course. I did not mean to imply anything less. I was merely commenting on the seriousness of your assumption." Quarn fingered a few of the books' spines.

Everything he had on the shelf looked as if it belonged in a museum. Devon had been right to send them here for information. Sage dared allow herself to feel hopeful.

Quarn selected a few books and brought them to his desk. "Has someone been negatively impacted by this artifact?"

"Yes," Sage answered.

"Godly magic behaves differently than the magic you are probably used to facing. Terras, even the most ancient of your race, are not immune to the will of the Mother. Should she wish to strike you down, it would take naught but a thought for her to do it," Quarn preached. He thumbed through one of the books, his eyes lighting up as if finding something he'd been looking for and placed a length of ribbon to mark the page.

"But this isn't a god come down to earth to strike someone down. It is an ancient artifact of unknown origin," Grey said.

"The same applies to artifacts that have had power imbued in them by the gods," Quarn answered as if expecting Grey's question. "They do what they have been created to do, acting upon the will of their creator."

"All items of magic can be neutralized." Grey's brow creased in disbelief as if Quarn's revelation went against everything he knew. "I've never come across one that could not."

"Do not confuse a conduit of divine power with an item cursed by magic," Quarn replied sharply. "The power it contains cannot be banished with simple alchemy or abjuration."

He seemed to know quite a lot about artifacts. Sage felt confident he'd have all the answers she needed. How could he not? "So you've come across items like these before?"

"Never." With one word, Quarn wiped away all the hope she'd been holding on to.

Sage slumped against the wall, her eyes on the Elemental as he continued to browse through the books he'd selected.

Grey glanced over his shoulder at her. She straightened up, hiding her defeat, and waited for Quarn to finish with his book.

"There are accounts of ancient weapons. You were searching for one such weapon the day we met Miss Cynwrig." Quarn looked up from his book, spearing her with a curious gaze. "I understood ASSET located and safely contained that weapon."

Sage cleared her throat, unsure of how to respond. "Yes. If there is one, there have to be others, right?"

"Legends," he answered, slamming shut the book he held in his hand. "You are free to search through the books I have collected." He placed the books in a pile and offered them.

"Thank you. We will." Grey picked up the stack.

"ASSET should have its own accounting of such artifacts," Quarn said suspiciously.

"They do, but this one we have encountered does not come up in our registry. And it is slowly killing the host who came in contact with it," Grey offered that tantalizing bit of information. "As you can imagine, we are eager to solve the mystery quickly."

Quarn's eyebrow arched curiously. "How did the host come across such a powerful artifact?"

"Classified," Grey answered quickly.

"That is a disappointment. Without knowing the facts, I cannot be counted on for accurate council." Quarn's eyes flitted over to Sage. He stared at her as if he were searching for something.

Sage winced as the seed inside her palm throbbed, hungering for power. She made sure her ruined hand was concealed deep within her pocket. But still, she had a feeling he knew. Had he seen it already?

"Our job is the protection of magic." Grey spoke matter-of-factly. His words drew Quarn's attention from Sage. "Secrecy is part of that protection."

"Very well. I cannot promise accuracy in my information without all the details. If you can accept that, I'll tell you what I know."

"Better than nothing." Sage shrugged. "Anything you can tell us will be very helpful."

"If we are to assume that the artifact in question is of godly origin, then it had to have been around since the dawn of the ages. Moving forward with that assumption, if it has been around and kept secret, it would have been housed in something to shield its power."

Sage's hand lifted toward her necklace as if drawn to it. As soon as she realized what she was doing, she lifted her hand farther and scratched her head.

Quarn was staring again. She wondered what was going on behind his eyes?

"The shield would carry its own enchantment in order for it to be effective," he continued.

"Let's say we know what that shield was," Grey offered.

"That would be excellent. You'd need to have someone test its enchantments to be sure that removing the artifact did not break the magical bond between it and its prize," Quarn answered, but his gaze remained curiously on Sage. "I'm sure ASSET has the resources to do this. If not, I will humbly offer myself in service should the need arise."

"And if it is still magically charged?" Grey continued to try and draw attention to himself with the questions. "The shield, I mean?"

Quarn finally turned his gaze to Grey. "Then it should safely house the artifact as it did before it came in contact with its unfortunate host."

"That solves half the problem." Grey sounded hopeful, and that gave Sage a boost too.

"Separating the artifact from its host has, so far, shown itself to be potentially fatal." Grey continued to hold Quarn's attention with leading information.

"Are you implying that the artifact has bonded with its host?" Quarn's tone turned fearful.

"Attempts to separate the artifact from the host have been unsuccessful," Grey answered mechanically.

"In what way, if I may ask?" Quarn turned to Sage, as if he knew.

She sucked in a breath, feeling the pressure of his quizzical gaze, wondering what to say.

"Subject has reported pain," – Grey drew Quarn's attention with his quick reply – "along with dangerously high spikes in vital signs each time an attempt has been made to surgically separate the artifact from the host."

"What about magical extractions?" Quarn asked.

"Ineffective," Grey answered without missing a beat.

But they hadn't tried to magically extract it. Could they? No. Not on a Terra. Wouldn't work.

Sage's palm throbbed in time with the thundering beat of her heart. The seed demanded the powerful magic in the room.

She cleared her throat. "We think it has bonded with the host's body."

Quarn seated himself at the desk. "If what you say is true than it may not be able to separated from the host."

"It is killing the host," Sage blurted out, earning a reproachful glare from Grey.

"That can happen sometimes." Quarn nodded.

"Unacceptable," Grey fired back, surprising Sage with the emotion in his voice.

"Death comes for us all." Quarn, however, seemed less concerned with the lives this artifact could end. Though he did appear to be interested in the details they could offer.

"We need other options," Grey demanded, his voice turning bitter.

"Again, without knowing the details, I cannot accurately give answers." Quarn appeared to be employing the same tactics as Grey, leading the conversation towards divulging details. Both sides clearly knew more than either wanted to let on. "Is there anything you can tell me? What it is doing to kill its host?"

"Let's say it is hypothetically draining the life of the host," Sage offered, hoping her nugget of information would be reciprocated.

"Feeding on energy?" Quarn asked.

"Sure. Go with that." Sage nodded.

"If the artifact is attracted to the magical energy source present within all creatures, it would lead me to think that it would attach itself to the next closest source once the original is used up. Following that thought, it might be persuaded to switch hosts if a more powerful source of magical energy is placed in close proximity."

"You're speaking as if the artifact has a mind of its own," Grey said.

"Godly creations are often sentient on some level," Quarn replied sharply, as if annoyed he had to explain himself. "Who is to say the artifact, especially being hypothetically ancient, does not have some level of awareness?"

"I don't like the implications of that theory." Grey sent another concerned look Sage's way.

"Neither do I," she agreed.

"We must consider it as a possibility," Quarn suggested. "It feeds on something. Energy or essence, whatever you wish to call it, correct?"

Sage nodded.

"If it were created to simply absorb energy, it would have instantly consumed its host," Quarn continued. "But you say it is not only slowly draining them, it has defended itself against removal of its host. It knows what it needs. That tells me it is aware."

"Then why would it kill the host?" Sage asked.

"There is the big question. That, to me, says it is not simply consuming. It is growing. We may not be dealing with an artifact at all. It may very well be a dormant form of a creature the gods created. The host may have given it the spark of life it needed to awaken."

"Hypothetically speaking?" Grey asked nervously.

"Without details, yes. This is all speculation, yes," Quarn replied. "But if we follow the logic, this thing is more than just an artifact. As it grows, so do its needs. Magical creatures, especially immortal ones, are like rechargeable batteries. Even cursed magic the likes of vampires are able to recharge. They renew their life-force from the blood they consume. Elementals draw from the element they are attached to. Ethereals draw from the light, and Shades from the dark. Their energy cannot be totally consumed as they are constantly in a state of replenishment. Only when their inner light, their spirit, for lack of a better term, departs their body, do we consider them dead. Even then, their energy does not disappear. It goes somewhere. To its next life, perhaps, or another reality dimension. If this artifact is not really an artifact, but a sentient being with an appetite greater than the magical host's energy, it must be growing. And when it has consumed the host, what will it go after next? Where will its insatiable appetite end?"

"You're suggesting we offer it better bait in order to lure it out into the open? That's your solution?" Sage asked.

Quarn took a moment, as if debating on what to say before finally answering. "Or wait for it to drain the host and use the shield you have to confine the artifact or creature, whatever it may be, before it attaches to a new host."

"Thank you for your time." Sage balled her aching hand into a fist.

"You are most welcome. I do hope you can find the answers you seek. Death is not for the young." His eyes moved from hers, down to her pocket. He knew. "Perhaps there is something you can uncover in the text I've selected for you. Keep them as long as you need."

Sage was first out the door, her heart thundering, her hand aching. She'd speculated as much, but Quarn had all but confirmed she was going to die.

TWELVE

Devon wasn't in the training room when they made it back to ASSET headquarters, so Grey set the books down in his office. "We're going to be here for a while."

"I will be." Sage stood in the hallway. She crooked a finger, calling Grey to join her. "You are going on a special mission."

A smile broke through his stony expression. "Giving me orders now?"

"You're the only one I can trust to do it." Sage unclasped the necklace her mother had given her. "We need to have this tested."

His brow crinkled as he scrutinized the small locket as if seeing it for the first time. "Why?"

"Because it's the shield Quarn spoke of."

"I can't believe you've been wearing that thing around your neck the whole time. No wonder the damn thing bonded to you."

"You want to keep your voice down?" How weird it was for Sage to have to say that line to Grey. It was if they had momentarily swapped bodies. And she didn't enjoy the way that felt. "Didn't have another choice. I inherited this burden. I was ordered to keep it safe."

The way he glared at her had her feeling about an inch tall. But she had no recourse. Ava had told her right from the beginning that no one, not even her partner, was supposed to know she still carried the stone in her mother's locket. If not for his demand to be by her side when she faced Thalia, he would still be in the dark.

Grey finally broke the silence between them with a loud sigh. He cringed as he reached to take the necklace from her hand, as if expecting it to burn him. He held it up in the air. "Secret maybe, but definitely not s–"

Pain tore through her chest like an invisible dagger. Sage struggled to fill her lungs with air as she clutched at her heart. The seed within her palm had awoken with insatiable hunger, ready to devour her whole. This was it. This was how it would end. Not a quick blink from existence, but she would be treated to a slow death as the seed drank deeply from the well of her magic.

As if her body was being turned off, one by one her limbs gave out. She collapsed under her own weight, meeting the unforgiving ground. The impact pushed all the air she'd struggled to breath out of her lungs. She choked and coughed, unable to breathe or release the scream trying to claw its way up her throat. She prayed for the Goddess to give her mercy.

The necklace found its way back into her open palm, a cold kiss of metal as it touched her skin that sent the world grinding to a halt. Her lungs opened. Had the Goddess listened to her plea? Sage closed her fingers tightly around the locket and gulped in air greedily, filling her parched lungs to capacity. Pain evaporated, leaving only the ghost of its memory.

Grey was on the ground next to her. Had he fallen too? His eyes leveled with hers, wide and glistening with fear that needed no words.

She must have looked really bad to turn him white as a ghost.

The necklace was the only thing keeping her alive. It had nothing to do with her innate magic. She had changed the nature of the seed when she used it. When it bonded with her. A punishment for sure. Sage wished she had never laid eyes on the stupid thing. Tears wet her cheeks before she realized she was crying.

"Speak, Sage. Say something." Grey's voice cracked, betraying the depth of his feelings.

Sage caught her breath, panting through the cresting wave of a full-blown anxiety attack. She had nearly handed over her life. Game over. No extra lives. No redos. She looked down at her injured hand, white knuckles hiding the treasure within her grasp. The rest of her hand had gone black.

"I think we know the shield works." Her voice came out hollow despite the emotions threatening to send her into madness.

"It appears that's the only thing keeping you alive."

"Don't sugarcoat it for me or anything," Sage cackled madly. He was right. The pain she felt. That was no mere shock. Like Westley in the Pit of Despair, she'd just experienced what it felt like to have one year of her life sucked away.

"I've got a very bad feeling about this." Grey held out his hand to help her up. "Can you stand?"

Sage tested her muscles and found them unresponsive. "Nope. No good. Going to have to give me a minute or two." Maybe longer. The Goddess had chosen to screw her over completely. She might be paralyzed for all she knew. Nothing worked except her mind, and her mouth, too, but that wasn't worth bragging about at that point.

"Seriously?"

"I'll be fine," she lied to avoid hearing the worry in his voice. "Just give me time to recuperate."

Grey stood and paced between the doorway to the training room and the hall.

"Not like that. Don't hover. I can't deal with hovering," she snapped at him.

He was much more palatable as a snarky and sarcastic jerk. Mother Hen was not his best look. And it only added to her anxiety. She might not have taken it so seriously before, but now she understood how close she'd tiptoed between life and death. She had to find a way to safely remove the seed quick. As much as she dreaded the Luke Skywalker approach, and prayed it wouldn't come to that, she'd take it if it meant saving her life.

"Put the necklace back on, now!" Grey gave the order as he made his fourth pass between the training room and the hallway.

"Sir, yes, sir!" She tried to lift her hand to mock salute him, but her muscles still refused to budge. "Um…maybe not."

"I have to do something." Grey took off down the hallway without another word. "Don't move. I'll be back."

"Sure thing. I'll just…hang back here…" she mumbled.

Grey had become so hard to read since her affliction. One moment clingy and overprotective – a sickeningly sweet combination – and the next, off he went like he'd given up, running for the hills to avoid seeing her death.

"Pay no mind to the invalid in the hallway." Her snarky comment never made it to Grey's ears. He'd rounded the corner before she'd finished.

Truth was, the joke was on her. She hoped no one would wander by as she sat helpless to move. The pain had gone, but the effects of just a moment of the seed's full power had rendered her helpless. Even with the necklace in her hand, acting as shield, she knew the seed was slowly killing her.

She tested her muscles again, breathing slowly, concentrating on controlling her trembling hands as she brought the necklace around her neck and clasped it. Once on, she worked to stand again, using the wall as her brace. She eased herself up. This must have been what eighty years old felt like. She struggled, but found her footing.

Grey came back into view, sprinting down the hallway, carrying in his hand a clear crystal prism. "Take this." He didn't give her time to argue, slamming the slender rock into her injured hand.

He might as well have stabbed her for the pain that slashed through her already weak muscles. She winced as shock of the seed's hunger caused all the muscles she'd fought to control to spasm. Her legs gave out, and she crashed to the ground once more.

The crystal clattered to the floor as her ass collided with tile.

"Would you warn a girl next time?" she shouted.

"I was trying to help." Grey bent to retrieve the crystal.

Sage didn't rush to her feet. She gave herself time to catch her breath again. Testing her hand, she flexed her fingers and stared into the black mark. Still there. Not that she expected it to have gone. But its necrotic color had not reached her fingertips just yet. Small victories. The pain had subsided, and her muscles seemed to be more responsive.

Feeding the stone magic fed her and rejuvenated her. Like vampirism of a sort. And Sage didn't like the implications of that. How soon would she need more than wands or crystals to sate the seed's hunger before it demanded richer and more powerful sources of magic?

"Thanks." She tried to push herself up again, and failed. "I'm not dying today."

"You're not dying at all. We'll figure this out. At least we have our first clue."

"And that is?"

"Your necklace still serves as a shield. If we can recreate it, we might have step one to getting that thing out of your hand and a safe place to put it when we're done."

"You don't want to put it back in the necklace?" she asked.

"I don't think we can do that without removing the necklace from you. And as we've seen, that thing doesn't like being separated from the necklace. We need a more permanent solution to this problem."

"Then we better get cracking."

"Cracking?" He cocked his head to the side, reminding her of a confused puppy.

"Books. Spines… You know, reading?"

"Oh, I know, I'm just surprised to see you so eager for research. I kind of like this new Sage." The worry lines began to smooth away from Grey's brow. If he could find the strength to smile in the face of so much uncertainty, then maybe she could too.

"It's all in the motivation." She managed a little chuckle despite the soreness of her muscles.

Grey helped lift her off the ground and carried her back into the training room. "If I'd only known threatening your life would motivate you so well."

THIRTEEN

Sage had walled herself in with books. Between Devon's library and the books she'd borrowed from Quarn, there was plenty of reading material. Not the kind of research she was used to, but the subject matter more than made up for how slowly she absorbed it.

"Someone made that necklace." Grey tossed her a book that appeared to be a registry of magical artifacts. "Check this for a record of your necklace or something similar." He picked up another book. "And I'll see if there are any reports of rituals mentioning the *you know what.*"

She cracked open the book and began thumbing through pages. More notebook than encyclopedia, each page had elegant strokes of elaborate calligraphy and illustrations. Gorgeous as it was informative, Sage found herself in awe at the amount of work that had been put into such a large tome. Each page must have taken hours to complete. "The Book of Thoth. Oh, it says it will let you know the mind of the Gods."

"And make you go insane," Grey commented as he claimed his own patch of ground to sit and read. "Keep looking."

Items inside appeared to be in no real order, as if the author had added each listing as they discovered them. That would make her research a little more interesting. "The Hand of Glory, I could use that."

"Only if you want to steal something. Even then, your hand is not a door to be unlocked."

"The one ring!" Sage shouted.

Grey scrunched his face as he looked up from his book. "What?"

"The Ring of Gyges. Says it makes you invisible, and might blacken your soul. It's totally the one ring."

"Don't care," Grey groaned.

"C'mon, even you have to have seen *Lord of the Rings*."

"That the movie where they walk and walk for a million hours?"

"It's also a book."

Grey glared at her, clearly not as excited about Tolkien's possible inspiration as she was.

"I'll keep looking." She smiled sheepishly and turned the page. "Wait. What about a Seer's Stone?"

"That could be helpful. Seer Stones can sometimes allow communication to the gods. Maybe if we can speak with the Mother, she can tell us what needs to be done to remove this curse." He sounded hopeful, and that lifted Sage's spirit.

"So we just get it from the archive? And then what?"

"We need someone who can scry," Grey replied.

"Do what now?"

"Magical Google search for the gods, or their messengers."

"Thanks for putting it in terms I can understand."

He winked. "I'm getting used to dumbing things down for ya'."

"Jerk." She laughed at his little jab. If he was picking on her again, he must be feeling confident about their chance of saving her. Sage held on to that hope, determined to find whatever artifact they needed. "So who do we know that can use this stone?"

"That might be a problem. We need shadow magic for that kind of spell." He closed the book in his hand and set it aside. "Devon is from the Shade branch of magic. But he is so far removed from the baseline. Not sure he can perform active magic like this."

"So, we'll put that on the maybe list and keep looking for something we can actually use." Sage dug out some paper from under a pile of books and wrote down Scrying Seeing Stones, underlining it as important, then returned to her book, flipping through the pages again. "This looks promising. Tears of Isis. Says it can heal magical wounds."

"You mean Vervain," Grey corrected. "Yeah, we keep a healthy growth of it in the greenhouse."

"Really?"

"Not everyone who works here is Terra. Nor are the prisoners we bring in."

"Fair point. Maybe it could help with the extraction," Sage said hopefully.

"Put it on the list, but don't count on it to do too much."

"Unicorn blood." Sage cringed. "Alicorn feathers. Hold on. Feathers. It says here they contain protective properties. Shielding from magic."

"Keep reading. They are only helpful if willingly given by an Alicorn." Grey shook his head and began rummaging through the pile of books for another to read. "Haven't seen one alive in centuries."

"What happened to them?"

"Hunted to extinction. Along with the unicorns. Alchemists use their parts for various potions."

"And our people didn't stop them?" Sage asked, shocked. "Isn't it our job to protect magic?"

"We can only do so much. I don't know if they are truly extinct, but I haven't seen one in a very long time."

"That's sad."

"It will be sadder if we don't find a listing for that necklace and how to recreate it, so keep looking."

Devon came strolling in from the hallway, duffel bag in hand. "I see Quarn was good to you." His gaze settled on the piles of books around the pair of them.

"This feels pointless." Sage let the words slip out before she'd considered their weight. "I mean, we have no idea if anything will work. We're just looking up a bunch of magic items."

"What did Quarn say?" Devon asked.

"He confirmed what you thought and gave us more to read, but we're still sitting on the same problem with no real leads," Sage answered.

"Wait now, we do know one thing." Grey stood and stretched. "That necklace you are wearing is a shield."

"That is something." Devon smiled. "May I see it?"

Sage clutched at her neck. "As long as I continue to wear it."

"Another thing we learned," Grey confirmed. "It is keeping her from the full effects of that thing in her hand."

"That makes things a bit more complicated, but does give us a clue." Devon stroked his chin. "Where did you get it?"

"It was in a box of Mom's things sent down from Phoenix," Sage answered and immediately thought of Mark. She hadn't spoken to him since forcing him to give her the password to the ASSET databases. She owed her surrogate father a call, and a few hundred apologies.

"If we can track down the origin of the necklace, we can learn how it was created. That might tell us how to manufacture one of larger scale that might help us extract the seed without damaging the host."

"You mean me, right?" Sage asked.

"Don't get your hackles up," Devon said. "I was speaking clinically."

"Sure. Let's go with that." She felt as if she had become some kind of medical experiment. No more important than the data they might gain from using her to find a cure rather than curing her.

"Someone is getting hangry," Grey snarked.

He was right. How long had it been since they'd eaten? She couldn't remember the last time. Nor could she remember her last dose of caffeine. It was no wonder her mind was going to the dark side. None could resist the pull when they've been imprisoned without the basic necessities.

"Call it a night, you two. Get some rest. I will see what I can locate on the necklace. And with any luck, tomorrow we might have a mission for you."

"Mission?" That perked her up.

"No magical items are created without ingredients. And once we know them, someone will have to go on a grocery run."

"Sounded so much better when you made it sound mysterious," Sage grumbled louder than her stomach.

"Oh, it will be." Devon winked. "You'll see."

FOURTEEN

Grey dropped Sage at her apartment after a quick bite to eat. "Don't go anywhere. I'll be back in about an hour," he promised.

"Really, you don't have to babysit me. I have Zack and Matt, you know." Sage pulled off her helmet and handed it to Grey.

"All the more reason for me to come back quickly."

"What is that supposed to mean?"

"They're vampires. They'll be heading out for their…nightly activities, I assume."

That was the last thing Sage wanted to think of, especially when it involved Matt. "They won't be gone all night."

"I don't want you alone for any part of the night."

"I knew I shouldn't have told you about the bar."

"Better you did. Now I know how much danger you're in." He still sounded as if he blamed her for how things had turned out. "And I don't want any arguments. Until we fix that," – he pointed to her hand – "you are under my protection."

"I guess I should be flattered," she grumbled.

"Don't go reading into anything. Keeping you safe keeps us all safe."

So much for the connection she'd thought they had. Maybe she'd misunderstood his concern.

"Do whatever." Sage turned and headed in through the night gate.

"I mean it. Don't you leave. I will be back in one hour." Grey revved the bike's engine and sped away.

Home at last. Sage looked forward to kicking up her feet and relaxing, at least until Grey returned. She unlocked her door to find Zack sitting at the kitchen table, waiting for her.

He pounced the moment she came through the front door. "I heard a very interesting rumor about you."

"Not interested." Sage tossed her keys up on the hanger and hefted her bag on the kitchen table.

"You might be," Zack teased.

"Are you going to bother me all night? I have research to do." She hoped he'd get the clue that she needed some alone time. She wasn't that lucky.

"Rumor has it, there's some new magic in town. Caught the eye of some collectors looking to enhance their power base."

"I'm off active duty until I heal."

"Oh, I didn't mean you should investigate it."

"I don't have time for riddles or games," Sage grumbled.

Zack stood and came close enough to whisper, "You are the new prize."

"What the hell?" Sage threw her hand out.

Zack dodged in time to miss the connection. "Watch it there, killer."

"Your fault. You came in too close. You know the danger."

"Noted." Zack rubbed his chin. "But the point remains. Your encounter with the kitsune and the djinn has not remained as quiet as you might have hoped. People are talking."

"If they are talking, then they know I came out the victor. Both enemies neutralized."

"Were they?" Zack asked.

"Yes," Sage replied defiantly.

"You shouldn't be so cocky about that victory." Zack clicked his tongue. "That makes you extremely valuable."

"To who? Who would be stupid enough to come after me? My touch is deadly."

"They likely wouldn't touch you themselves. Consider how many non-magical people there are in the world. You've forgotten about them since learning of the others. Remember your new cursed powers have no effect on humans."

His words struck her like a slap to the face. He was right. She hadn't considered mundane threats. "Who's been asking about me?"

"I rather like being useful to you." His eyes sparkled. "Look at how you hang on my words."

"Every time I think to trust you, you show me just how stupid that is. Stop teasing me."

"You're no fun. Becoming like that partner of yours. Where is he? Grey boy needs to hear this. Your daytime protector needs to be informed as well."

"Out with it, Zack, before I lose my patience."

"And what will you do? I am the only one keeping Matty on a leash."

"I mean it."

"I don't have names right now. Some shadowrunners visited the bar my people run. They were talking about ASSET destroying the lost amulet of Emuri. That provoked a debate with some of my kind. Seems the only way to destroy something that powerful is with a weapon of godly magic. The very same that recently came through here and decimated the vampire clan a short while ago."

"Is there a point?"

"Your name, or rather the Cynwrig name, came up. Momma was made dark, remember. She was known to have been in contact with the weapon. And since you were also on the case with the amulet, they put the pieces together."

"So they think ASSET still has the weapon and let me use it?" Sage asked.

"Something along those lines." Zack shrugged.

"Where did they get their information from, I wonder?" Sage gritted her teeth. Sylvia, one of the more prominent shadowrunners and well connected in the magical world, had been there when she destroyed the amulet. Could she have started the rumor? Sylvia wasn't a huge fan of ASSET.

"Shadowrunners have a habit of seeing things they shouldn't. It's their nature," Zack said.

"Great." Sage groaned, wondering how much worse things were going to get. "Thanks for the warning. I'll watch my back." At least Grey would be back soon. Seems she really did need to have twenty-four-seven backup until she found a way to remove the seed.

"That's all I get? A cold-shouldered thanks?" Zack pouted.

"What exactly did you expect? For me to jump into your arms and plant a big old sloppy kiss on you for bringing me this news?"

"It would be a start."

"I'd kill you."

"Crimes of passion." He blew her a kiss and quickly moved away, likely in case she swatted at him again.

Sage rolled her eyes. "Insufferable flirt."

"At your service." He bowed. "But you know you like it."

"Don't go there."

"I try so hard, and all I get is ridicule."

"Speaking of. Where's Matt? How did your field test go?" she asked.

"You don't need to know the details."

"You didn't? He didn't?" Sage couldn't bear it if Zack had let Matt drain some poor soul dry. Matt wasn't a killer. Even if he was a vampire now, that would destroy him.

"As much as you have learned about our world, you are still so clueless."

"Then enlighten me."

"How much blood do you think is in a human's body?" Zack asked.

"I didn't come here for a science lesson."

"Well, you're going to get one. Because if I have to field questions like this every time I take your friend out for a meal, we're going to find a way to make you our next."

"Back to threats again." Sage pointed a finger at him.

He licked his fangs in response. "On your best day at the bar, how much would you say you've drunk?"

"We're comparing blood to booze now. That's a new one." Sage chuckled with outraged amusement.

"Play along. You might learn a thing or two."

"Fine, three or four pints, maybe." She tried her hardest to avoid the image of Matt drinking cupfuls of blood.

"All at once?"

"Of course not," Sage scoffed.

"Right, because chugging down your drink is neither satisfying nor is it easy. Same applies to me. I like to savor my meals. Which, by the way, come about one pint at a time."

"And you just willingly get people to donate?"

"Oh, I have had plenty of willing participants. But those that are less than willing are very forgetful." He waggled his eyebrows.

"You told me most don't survive the bite." A shiver ran down her spine as she remembered the way his beast had risen to the surface when he'd pinned her to the apartment door, threatening to make a meal of her.

"A stretch of the truth. Some don't, sure. That's generally done on purpose." He snapped his jaw, and Sage jumped despite knowing he couldn't touch her. Zack chuckled, likely seeing how easily he could still get a rise out of her.

"I think I just threw up in my mouth a little." Sage feigned puking.

"I'm teaching Matty the art of snacking. Sate the beast so he can avoid accidentally killing his meal."

"Good to know. Where is he?" Sage said.

"Taking a walk around the complex. Getting a little fresh air and working up an appetite."

"Alone? What the hell are you thinking? Go get him!"

"It's you who should not be alone."

"I can take care of myself."

His eyes narrowed as if he had something devilishly snarky to reply, but Zack allowed a breath to pass before opening his mouth. "As much as I would love to test that theory, since I can't be here to watch you and take Junior out for dinner, I feel it would be safer if you'd call your partner. You two can have a nice little girls' night in while us boys go do vampire things."

The jealousy was certainly strong between those two, but for Zack to actually push for her to bring Grey in, he had to be seriously concerned.

"He'll be here in a minute or so," she replied.

The two of them here in her apartment. It was a recipe for disaster. But seeing as both Grey and Zack were concerned for her well-being, who was she to argue with their efforts to keep her safe?

"Go and take care of Matt before we have an accident to clean up in our backyard." Sage jabbed a finger toward the door.

"As you wish." Zack smiled toothily, his fangs on full display. "Just remember that the moment you take care of your affliction, I'm owed a big sloppy kiss, planted right here." He pointed to his cheek as he walked out of the apartment.

FIFTEEN

Grey arrived, carrying a large overnight bag, ready for a sleepover. Somehow her apartment had turned into a halfway home for wayward magical creatures. And she wasn't too sure how she felt about that.

"So we might have a little problem." Sage met him at the door, all but bursting with the new information Zack had unloaded.

"I was gone for less than an hour. How did you manage to get in trouble in that short a time?"

"I didn't do anything." She huffed. His accusation had her second-guessing the decision to let him stay at her place. Not that she had much of a choice. He'd demanded it in the name of *keeping her safe*. "Zack warned me about potential trouble."

"I'm not going to like this, am I?" Grey gritted his teeth. "Go on. What did Zack warn you about?"

Sage took a breath, mentally preparing for his response. "Okay. According to him, there is a rumor going around about my special ability. And some are already linking it to the stone."

"Shit." The duffel bag slipped from Grey's hand and landed on the ground with a loud *thump*. "That's why those Ethereals tested you."

"You think they're connected?" She knew the answer the moment she asked the question, but prayed he'd have some other explanation.

"There are no coincidences. This is not good. We can't stay here. We're going to have to bring you in."

"And risk another attack on ASSET? Remember what happened last time?" Sage cringed, remembering her mother, those haunting eyes, and the pool of blood after Grey removed her head. "And what about what Ava said? My life is not as important as the secret. She might just as well cut off my hand and put the seed back in the necklace. If it kills me, oh well."

"Calm down."

"I will not. I know I made a vow to ASSET, but dammit, I am not ready to die. Especially when using the seed was not my idea."

"You still did it. And left the safety of ASSET," Grey replied.

The audacity! He'd been there. He knew she'd had no other choice. How dare he throw it in her face like that? As if he would have done better.

"Who's side are you on?" Sage shot back at him.

"This isn't about sides. We need to do what's right. That is the vow we made. We protect magic." His words came cold and unfeeling.

"So that's it? We go back to ASSET?" she asked. "Well. It's been a fun life. Here's hoping the next one will be better."

Grey growled and turned away as if the sight of her angered him beyond reason. He balled his fist, cocking back, as if to strike. Sage thought he might punch a hole through her apartment wall, but he stalked to the couch and threw his anger into a cushion, venting his frustration in loud grunts as he punched the furniture, before finally collapsing down on the couch.

"What are you doing?" Sage asked, confused.

"Thinking."

"Looks more like throwing a temper tantrum."

"No, Sage, that's what you're doing. I'm trying to think of our best course of action." His voice was so full of anger.

She didn't understand why. It was her life that was to be forfeited. She was the one supposed to be angry and hurt. And she was, but his rage seemed to eclipse her own.

"I'm sorry. Okay. But try to understand where I'm coming from. If I'm a little freaked out, do you blame me?"

"Just stop talking, please." Grey covered his eyes, pinching the bridge of his nose as if trying to ward off a migraine.

She didn't want to be shushed. Not now. Not when he was making potentially life-ending decisions about her, without her input. But at that same moment, Sage couldn't make an argument better than not wanting to die. As serious as that statement was, in context it sounded petulant rather than a grounded defense.

His argument, much as she hated to admit it, was more in line with reality. Protection of magic is what she'd signed up for. It was what her mother had done. She'd sacrificed herself in the hopes that the seed would not fall into the wrong hands.

She'd already been tested. How many more would come sniffing around, slowly devising a way to get around her defenses? If a weapon of that caliber fell into the wrong hands, it could cause untold devastation. How many lives would be lost if that happened? At least at ASSET, the seed could be placed back into the locket and hidden away again, somewhere even safer. It was her duty. Sage had made the vow. She had offered her life in service of magical protection. She had risked the secret getting out when she'd used the seed. It didn't matter who's idea it had been originally. She had to own up to the facts. Time to put on her big girl panties and face the music.

"C'mon, Grey. Let's go." Sage grabbed her keys from the hook by the door.

"I told you to shut up."

"And I'm not listening. Haven't you gotten used to that yet?"

Grey lifted his head slightly to glare at her. His hand shielded his eyes, fingers still tightly pinching the bridge of his nose and made him look as if he were saluting. "I'm trying to think."

She stifled her laughter at his odd posture – that might have enraged him further – but couldn't stop the sarcasm from tripping from her tongue. "It was either that, or you'd set the couch on fire, all the smoke coming from your ears."

Grey gave a wry laugh. "Very funny."

"Look. I'm trying to be a big girl here. Let's get on our way to ASSET before I lose my nerve."

"We're not going back there."

"Say what?" Sage nearly choked on her words.

"Not here at least. We have to get ahead of the news before it reaches Ava."

Apparently she'd missed that stop on the train of thoughts. Either that or Grey had taken an entirely different train. She'd only just resigned herself to his decree that they go back to headquarters. "You're going to have to start making some sense before I lose it completely."

"Devon had mentioned wanting to find the origins of the necklace."

They had definitely taken two different trains of thought. Now he was bringing Devon into this. "Okay, um, sure."

"Where did it come from again?" Grey shot up from the couch.

"Can you just spit it out? This cryptic shit is giving me a killer headache."

"The stone is killing you." Grey closed the gap between them and tapped her on the top of her head. "I'm trying to get you to think. C'mon now, use that brain of yours. Where did the stone come from?"

Mark had packed the boxes he mailed to her after Miranda's disappearance. "Phoenix, I guess."

"Which is about five hours away. If we leave now, we can be there before sunrise." Grey opened the front door and nodded for her to follow. "Road trip?"

SIXTEEN

Riding crosstown was bad, but nothing could have prepared her for the ass-numbing experience that was the trip through the barren wasteland between Las Vegas and Phoenix in the middle of the night.

They pulled into the parking lot as the sun had begun to warm their backs. Sage was never more thankful to be off the bike.

"I'd forgotten just how pretentious the Phoenix crew was." Grey stood and stretched hard before removing his helmet. "Compensating for something, maybe?"

A white ten-story building stood before them, the crimson letters *A.S.S.E.T.* mounted across the front entry. She'd never thought the people working in this office were all that showy, but compared to the Vegas office hiding any indication of its building's intention, she had to agree with Grey's remark. Though she wouldn't admit it out loud.

"Jealous?" She pulled her helmet off and worked at untangling the tattered mess of her ponytail.

"At least Vegas tries to blend in."

"Phoenix has a great cover. They don't need to."

"You really think by changing one word, they can get away with pretending they are anything but a supernatural agency?"

Sage shrugged. "I never questioned it. Mom worked for a specialty security and weapons manufacturer."

"And how did she explain the bruises after some of her missions?"

"She was a weapons demonstrator." Sage realized how flimsy the lie was now that she knew the truth, but before it had been revealed, it seemed plausible.

"And all the time away?"

"Conventions," Sage snarled at him as her finger caught in a nasty tangle of hair. "Is there a point to your line of questioning, other than to annoy me?"

"Just feels a bit odd that this branch is so out in the open." Grey pulled his fedora out of the saddle bag and glanced in the mirror as he ran his fingers through his hair and fit the hat on his head.

"Not nearly as odd as your obsession with hats," Sage mumbled. She worked her fingers through a messy tangle, combing out the remaining hair as best she could with her fingers. Best to make a good impression when you're a fugitive. She wrapped her hair into a tight bun at the top of her head and turned to face the building.

The last time she passed through those doors had been like falling down the rabbit hole. This had always been her mother's place. Even after she had gone, it was here that she'd visited, in a prophetic dream, but now it felt foreign and imposing. She would have to face Mark Sorenson again. A surprise. Uninvited. Technically AWOL.

"Are we going in?" Grey nudged her.

Sage wasn't sure she had the strength to walk inside.

Mark had always been a surrogate father. Would he protect her? Or would he lock her up once he knew the truth? Facing him brought up emotions she wasn't ready to feel.

Ava might rail at her and threaten her life. She was getting used to the abrasiveness of her boss. She expected it and in a way appreciated the way Ava ran things with an iron fist. Being responsible for so many lives as well as keeping the peace was no easy task. A job that left little room for familiarity and warmth. How many had she grown close to who had died in the line of duty? Just one would be enough to harden anyone's heart.

Mark, on the other hand, had always operated on a compassionate level. Knowing what she knew now, she couldn't imagine the kind of compartmentalizing he needed to do to maintain his demeanor.

But it was that closeness and compassion she feared most. If he rejected her being here, it would crush her spirit. She needed her surrogate-dad to help her through this. He was the only link she had left to the past.

"Sage?" Grey nudged her again. "Let's move."

With a sobering sigh, Sage resigned herself to facing Mark's anger.

Automatic doors parted, revealing a brightly lit reception area. Another stark contrast to the Vegas office she now called home. ASSET Phoenix was brightly lit and open to natural light. Architecture aimed at making the place feel welcoming. Hiding magic in plain sight.

Behind the reception desk, brightly lit LED screens played the false ads for security and weaponry that ASSET claimed was its business. Sage smiled, knowing the truth as she approached a twenty-something male with purple hair sitting at the reception desk.

"Mark in yet today?" Sage asked.

"Do you have an appointment?" Purple Hair looked up from his paperwork. His weary eyes had enough baggage to travel the world.

Sage could empathize. After the night she had she was in serious need of coffee. She held up her wrist as she had seen Grey do many times in the past. "I need to speak with Mark."

Tired, turquoise eyes moved slowly toward her wrist landing on her identifying birthmark. "I wasn't aware of any new recruits coming in."

"We're from the Vegas office," Grey chimed in. "Level 7 assignment. If you point us to his office, we'll wait for him."

"Hold on. I need to verify." Purple Hair turned to his computer screen. Despite his tired appearance, he typed like a madman on the keyboard.

"I know where his office is." Sage grabbed Grey's sleeve and started walking away.

"Wait. Sage Cynwrig, right?" Purple Hair shouted loud enough to echo against the empty waiting area. "I need to issue you visitor badges."

"How did you know her name?" Grey asked sharply.

"Email from Director Masters. Vegas." Purple Hair cowered, as if afraid Grey might strike him. "She said if you showed up, we were to allow access to whatever facilities needed for your assignment."

Sage and Grey exchanged glances.

How the hell did she know Grey would bring her here?

Sage returned to the reception desk. "When did she send it?"

"A-about five minutes ago," Purple Hair replied, looking just as confused as Sage felt.

"Does Mark...er... Director Sorenson know we're here yet?" Sage asked.

"He does now." Mark rounded the corner, coming from behind the false wall of the reception desk. "I assume you are going to explain yourselves?" He pulled Sage into a bear hug, squeezing the air from her lungs as if trying to make up for all the hugs he'd missed since her mother's passing.

When he released her, he turned to face Grey. "Don't think I've had you in my office before."

Grey stood stiffly and extended his hand. "Agent Maddox. No, I've never been assigned to Phoenix."

"If you're around long enough, you will." Mark shook his hand with a smile. His demeanor so sharply contrasted Ava's it was hard to believe they were in the same position. "How about we step into my office and I can debrief you."

His tone did not betray any underlying anger. Neither did his eyes. But his words had a terrifying effect on Sage.

They followed as Mark turned away from the reception desk.

"What about visitor badges?" Purple Hair called after them.

Mark left no time for an answer. He was already power walking past the glass offices, conference rooms, and elevator bank, heading straight toward the only office with privacy shielding. Still encased in the same plexiglass as the others, Mark's office had soundproofing shutters controlled with a remote that turned his office into a chamber of secrecy. He flipped a switch once they were safely inside. The room went on lockdown.

"Sit." Mark delivered the order sharply.

SEVENTEEN

She felt good getting it all off her chest. Sage revealed every last thing Mark had missed since she'd left Phoenix. He sat patiently and listened to her tale of the kitsune and the djinn, and how she'd been forced to use the seed.

Only when she had finally stopped talking did he break his silence. "Not exactly the outcome I had hoped for."

Where she expected to hear anger, he replied with sadness. Mark sighed and stood from his desk chair. He walked around to a file cabinet, opened it, and began thumbing through.

"You're surprisingly calm," Sage noted.

"One should be calm when problem solving," he replied.

Grey turned to her, his expression all but saying 'I told you so.' Thankfully he didn't utter the words. She might have smacked him if he had. Sage waited patiently for Mark to face them again. His calm demeanor filled her with hope. He moved from one file to the next, searching for something she assumed would help their situation.

"Ah, here it is." Mark retrieved a file and brought it back to his desk. "What you are experiencing appears to be curse-like in nature." He sat down and thumbed through the small stack of yellowing pages in the file. "Similar to the vampire's stolen magic. You are familiar with that, right?"

Sage nodded. "To maintain their immortality, they must feed on the life essence of another."

"Same concept. Yes. Starve the stone and it will eventually eat your magic, leaving you nothing but a dried-up husk," Mark spoke clinically.

"Right." Hope faded from Sage's voice. "But we already knew that. How do we fix it?"

"Always so impulsive. Let me finish."

"Sorry."

"Miranda did extensive research during her time as the stone keeper. She came to me with a theory. I'd dismissed it as rubbish, but after hearing what you've been through, I now think it might just be what we need."

Sage wondered if she'd ever be able to hear her mother's name without feeling the pang of grief in her heart.

"There is a… We'll call it a purification ritual," Mark continued. "Miranda had a theory that doing such might reverse curse-based magical transformations like vampirism. If her theory holds water, perhaps a similar approach might be used to separate you from the stone so it can be safely returned to its containment vessel."

Sage's mind jumped straight to Matt, bypassing her own affliction. "There's a cure for vampirism?"

"Now, hold on." Mark held his hands up to stop her. "Don't jump to conclusions. We're talking in theories. And what's happening to you is not exactly vampirism."

"But my best friend. Maybe it could help him too." Sage sat up taller, on the edge of her seat. With one spell, everyone could live happily ever after. Well, maybe not to the fairytale extent, but at least they would be back to normal.

"The roommate?" Mark asked.

"Yes."

"Not sure if it's worth the hassle. This is a pretty complicated ritual. And it requires some special items." Mark picked up the paper and handed it to Sage.

The tight, fading script was hard for her to read, and some of the words looked more like gibberish. "Does that say burn in wax? Translation, please."

Grey snatched the page from her. "A wax figure. Like a voodoo doll?"

"Anointed candle wax," Mark answered them both.

"That's a relief." Sage chuckled nervously. "I don't exactly fancy the idea of becoming barbeque to purify my blood."

"No. You won't burn. But if I'm reading this correctly, you're going to be boiled in a soup," Grey teased.

"Stop joking like that." Sage punched him in the arm.

"This doesn't look too complicated. But where are we going to find a cauldron that big?" Grey continued to study the list. "Am I reading this correctly? We need to access a spiritual vortex under the light of a full moon?"

Mark cracked a confident smile. "That'll be the easy part. Sedona is just north of here. But to perform the magic, you're going to need people capable of channeling that magic."

That was a potential setback. Sage slumped against the back of her chair. "But we're sworn to secrecy. Ava's probably already ordered my death, an accident of course, for coming here and speaking to you."

"I was the one to inform Ava of what you were carrying." Mark threw her a stern, fatherly look. "You're safe talking with me, though I wish you'd told me you were on the way."

"Snap decision. We had to move quick. Too many people were snooping around her." Grey offered the explanation quickly before Sage had the chance to stick her foot farther into her mouth.

"Understood." Mark's fatherly disappointment extended to Grey. "But you do have a phone, don't you?"

Sage hung her head sheepishly. She had owed him a phone call well before this snafu. "Sorry."

"That's your catchphrase these days." Grey chuckled and dodged the punch Sage threw at his arm. "Careful now. If you're not nice, I won't help you." He squinted his eyes and read from the page in his hand. "Anoint your body in the Oil of the Ages." He mimed throwing up. "Nope. Not doing that."

"I'm going to seriously regret this, aren't I?" Sage groaned. "That is if we can even manage it. What kind of people are we going to need to employ to channel this magic?"

"Ideally we would use branches of each magic. Shade, Elemental, and Ethereal," Mark replied. "Copy down the ingredients and you two start collecting them while I coordinate with the Las Vegas office for practitioners."

How the hell were they going to do that? And even if they did, would the spell work? This was a ritual aimed at removing vampirism, not godly curses.

Grey pulled a notepad from his pocket and snatched a pen from Mark's desk. He quickly scribbled down items and set the pen and Mark's paper back on the desk. "Shouldn't be too hard to locate the items. C'mon newbie." Grey stood, notebook in hand, and turned to face the door.

"Sage," Mark said. "A word alone, please."

She nodded to Grey and waited until he left the room before rushing over to Mark and giving him a long overdue hug.

"You had us all worried, Sage." Mark held her tightly, as if he feared to let her go. "You have to stop being so secretive."

"I was scared. I didn't even know what we were doing. One minute Grey said he was taking me back to the office to turn myself in, and the next we're on the bike heading here."

"But before that. Why did you wait to tell me about the stone?"

Sage pulled away and shrugged. "Ava basically said I'd be killed to protect the secret."

"From those who don't already know. Kiddo, I was the one who sent the thing to you."

"But can you blame me?" Her cheeks burned with embarrassment. "My whole life has been kept in secret, and then suddenly, bam." She punched her palm for effect. "Now I'm part of this crazy, insane world of magic. And rather than allow me to finally speak freely, I'm told to keep everything secret. I'm struggling with who to trust and how to handle everyone I meet."

"I wish you could have worked here with us. It would have made the transition so much easier for you, but I'm sure you realize now why we had to move you around like a pawn," Mark admitted sorrowfully.

"I know why. And I understand that. I'm here now."

"You can't stay."

"Why not? Ava hates me."

"Not true. And you know that."

"Do I?"

Mark's fatherly glare fell on her once more. "Don't do that. You're not a baby. Don't act like it."

He must have been practicing that look. Sage hung her head in shame. "Yes, Dad."

"Speaking as your father, you need the kind of tough love Director Masters offers. Here, I'm afraid you'd be singled out for favoritism. Your achievements would be overshadowed by rumor, and you'd never know the accomplishment of hard-earned respect."

She shuffled her feet, keeping her gaze on the ground. "You're a terrible salesman."

"Director Masters cares more than you know. She alerted me the moment you hit town. She and I have been in direct communication since your arrival. And though you might not like him, she assigned you to Grey because he's the kind of agent who'd willingly sacrifice his life for his partner."

"What is his record with partners?" Sage asked. Grey was also the type to be completely silent about his past. Every time she had asked him about the rumored girlfriend or other agents he'd worked with, Grey found a way to change the subject.

"Classified."

"C'mon." She batted her eyes at Mark, giving him that innocent daughter look that had worked well for her in the past.

"You're an agent now, Sage. If he chooses to tell you his past, that is one thing. Otherwise, his record is classified to all but his immediate director."

"See. Look how well you tough loved me there. You could totally be my boss." Sage smirked. She'd eventually learn Grey's secrets.

"You're assigned to Las Vegas. You will return to Vegas."

"After we've done our little ritual?" Sage asked for clarification.

"Possibly before that. We've got a week or so to the full moon. You need to concentrate on obtaining the items for the ritual."

"Do you think this would work to save Matt?"

"I wish I could say. I'm not sure this will work on you. One at a time. And you may find that he does not want to be saved. Have you asked him?"

"I know him. He doesn't want to be a vampire," Sage said.

"First you. Okay?" Mark walked her to the door and opened it. "Off you go."

EIGHTEEN

The day had far too many ups and downs to be dealt with on such a little supply of caffeine. Grey brought them to a diner to refuel before they started on the shopping list Mark had given them.

Sage slid into a booth, grabbing the menu, eager to devour everything listed in the breakfast column.

Grey flagged a waitress down and ordered the coffee. He must have read her mind. After all the driving they'd done, she could probably polish off a pot all on her own.

"Did you know Ava would track us?" Sage asked, keeping her face behind the plastic menu.

"Are you really that surprised?" Grey chuckled.

"So all that back in my apartment, about turning me in, was for show?" Sage hated the way she just couldn't read that man's intentions.

"Someday you will have to trust that I'm on your side."

She glared at him over the top of her menu. "You didn't answer the question."

"Yes and no. How's that for an answer?"

"I hate you," Sage grumbled.

"You're so cute when you're angry."

The waitress set two mugs down and filled them to the brim with liquid energy. Sage ordered herself a lumberjack's breakfast. Grey ordered the endless stack of pancakes.

"I'm serious, you know," Sage whispered as the waitress walked back to place their order.

Grey's brow scrunched with confusion. "No. I don't know. What?"

"I can't read you."

He shifted uncomfortably in his seat. "We're back to that again, are we?"

"Truth time. I want to know what's going on in that head of yours."

"I could ask the same of you." He fidgeted with his coffee, adding sugar and staring down at it as he stirred it well past the point of mixing his drink.

"When we first met, you were a royal ass who made no secret of your unhappiness in being tethered to me as a partner."

"Newbies are insufferable." He leaned back and put his arms over the edge of the booth.

"I'm still a newbie. But you've changed." She stared into his eyes. "What's with the mother hen act?"

"Is it a crime to care about the welfare of my partner? Let me ask you this. If it were me cursed and possibly facing down death, how would you act?"

"Not fair. I'm—"

"A girl?"

"I was going to say I wear my emotions on my sleeve. I'm not the one acting out of character here."

"So now I care too much?" He chuckled, clearly amused with his ability to get under her skin.

"No. Stop twisting my words around. I just mean that you're acting different than expected, and I want to know if there is something else going on."

"I told you we're not talking about my past or partners."

Exactly what she thought he'd say. She sipped her coffee, black, hoping the hot infusion of caffeine would spur her brain into action. She needed all the help she could get, playing the mental game with him. "Probably an insufferable girl, right?"

"You don't give up, do you?" He moved in closer, hovering over his coffee as if looking deep into its murky depths for an answer.

"We agreed to honesty and laying it all out there so that we can better understand each other and work together," she whispered softly so the waitress wouldn't hear as she passed the booth on her way to another table.

"You don't need recounted war stories and death tallies to understand me."

His evasiveness, more than anything else, made her want to dig deeper. He could have given her any small detail and she might have dropped the subject, but the fact he continued his blockade had her curiosity up to an eleven.

"But I do need to understand you." She gulped down the rest of her coffee, giving time for her words to sink in. "I have nothing to go on. I don't even know where you live."

Grey was as thick as a brick wall. He shrugged her off. "Why would you?"

"You know where I live."

"Because you need a damn chauffeur."

The transportation issue was going to become a serious problem if she didn't get a car eventually. "I'll ride the bus," she snapped.

"You don't have to get so defensive. Not everything is an insult."

"Sounds like it coming from you." Her coffee gone, Sage glanced around for the waitress, and motioned with her cup when she got her attention.

"That's just you being sensitive."

"Hey." Her mouth hung open with no snappy reply finding its way to the surface.

"You said it." Grey smirked, clearly satisfied he'd silenced her. "You wear your emotions out there for all to see."

Her instincts would normally have her fighting back, but that would only egg him on. She needed a better way to wipe that self-important grin from his face. Kill him with kindness. That had thrown him off his game in the past. He expected her snark.

"You got me there." She conceded his victory sweetly.

The waitress came by, hot pot of coffee in hand, and refilled their mugs. Sage took a long pull from hers. Black coffee wasn't exactly her favorite flavor, but slugging it down the way she did worked wonders in jumpstarting her mind.

Grey, on the other hand, looked as if he'd lost something. Her plan was working. He just couldn't compete against her when she played nice.

"You're right. I'm sensitive to those I care for. And you're my partner. I want to know more about you." Sage gave him her most innocent smile. "So tell me about Grey, the guy, not the agent. Where do you live?"

He glared at her suspiciously, his brow forming deep creases, crow's feet creeping out from the corners of his eyes, aging his eternally youthful face. "I've got an apartment down by Boulder Highway and Trop."

"Any roommates?" She fired off her next question eagerly, a few more ready should he take the bait.

"We are really doing this? The whole first date line of questioning?"

"This is not a date."

"I don't know. We're at a restaurant, about to share a meal, talking about our feelings."

Damn him, he was onto her.

"Whatever." She pretended to shrug him off. "Poke fun all you like. I've learned more from you in five minutes here than I have the entire time we've been partners."

"That's just because you don't pay attention." He took a swig of his coffee. "No roommates."

"Pets?"

"Nope," he responded with mild amusement.

"Hobbies?"

"Please stop."

"Girlfriends?"

Grey looked up from his coffee, meeting her in a dead stare. "Enough!"

She'd hit a nerve there. "See? You're a closed book. I can't read you. And anytime I get you to open up slightly, you slam shut."

"You're not trying to get to know me. You're fishing."

"Semantics."

"You want some truth? I appreciate genuine people. And I can smell bullshit a mile away."

"*I* smell bullshit," she mocked him.

Grey's phone went off. He picked it up, and his already angry expression darkened.

Sage's phone went off next. She reached to answer it, but Grey snatched it from her and dunked it into his cup of coffee.

"What the hell!"

"Time to go." He grabbed her by the arm, threw two twenty-dollar bills on the table, and pulled her toward the door.

Sage didn't fight his grip on her arm. As mad as she was, he'd just destroyed her phone. The fact he'd done it meant some major kind of shit was hitting the fan. "Are you going to tell me what's going on?"

They came to an abrupt stop at his bike. Grey glanced around cautiously before showing her his phone.

Text from Ava.

Agent Cynwrig: location unknown. In possession of artifact id: SPONGE. Apprehend and return to Las Vegas HQ.

"What the hell?" She gasped and immediately slapped her hand over her mouth. Things had truly taken a turn for the worse.

"That text just went out to all active ASSET agents." Grey didn't need to explain it. She'd already guessed as much. "You've been marked. We're not safe here any longer."

"But why?" That was the bit she didn't understand. Ava had always been two steps ahead of them. She had even known they were in Phoenix. Why send this? Why was she a marked woman *now?* Why not contact them personally instead of sending in all of ASSET?

"My guess," Grey spoke calmly. If he was worried, she'd never be able to tell. "Word of your little escapade with the Ethereals just got to her."

"Didn't take long."

"I was hoping we'd have more time before that piece of information crossed her desk." Grey sighed.

"So you're taking me in, then?" She held her hands out, ready for cuffs, really wishing she'd have gotten a last meal. She'd been so looking forward to bacon and eggs. No luck of that while locked up in ASSET's prison.

He slapped her hands away. "What do you think?"

"Ava gave you an order."

"You're not good at reading between the lines, are you?"

"Apparently not." She huffed.

"Ava told you if your secret got out, your life was forfeit."

"Yeah."

"So taking you in to headquarters right now is a death sentence."

If she hadn't been stressing out, she might have called him Captain Obvious. At best she might lose her hand and be locked away in ASSET for the rest of what remained of her life. At worst, she might get a quick death. Either way, she'd run out of time.

"You're a company man," she said. "You do what you're told, right?"

"You wound me."

"Just tell me what the hell you plan to do. I can't read you. So stop the cryptic crap because I'm about two seconds from a heart attack."

"You'd survive a heart attack." Disappointment soured his tone, but it was the look of outrage that struck her as hard as a slap to the face. Had she really misread him that badly? "I'm not about to march you in to die when we have a shot at fixing you." He turned away from her and grabbed his helmet. "And I can't believe after all we have been through together, you'd think so lowly of me."

She hadn't realized how much her offhand comment would affect him. With his helmet on, Sage could no longer see the pained look in his eyes, but somehow felt the weight of her words more strongly. She hadn't intended to insult him. Calling someone a company man would normally be a compliment. More evidence to her argument of not knowing him, but this wasn't the time to bring that back up.

"I-I'm sorry." She stumbled for the right words. "I just thought… Not following a direct order from Ava will get you in trouble."

"I'm always in trouble." The helmet hid his face but couldn't disguise the disappointment in his voice. "That's why Ava assigned me to you."

"Should I be worried or impressed?"

"Yes," he answered quickly.

She'd meant her question as a joke, but he'd responded as if she'd lobbed yet another accusation at him. Best she keep her mouth shut. At least until things blew over. Despite all her confusion, one thing was clear: As long as she was with Grey, she was safe from ASSET.

Grey threw his phone down in the dirt and stomped on the screen a few times before mounting his bike. "We better go before they track our phones here."

NINETEEN

They rode aimlessly around the city. It felt that way as far as Sage was concerned. She'd lived in Phoenix all her life and recognized various landmarks as they passed. Grey drove silently, never once asking her for directions or telling her where they were headed. Only when he stopped for gas, near a strip mall with eclectic shops, did he finally speak.

"Time to go shopping." He pointed to a sign across the parking lot as he filled the tank on his bike.

Sage had almost forgotten about their grocery list. She'd had so much else running through her mind that even the constant throbbing in her palm had taken a back seat. If the spell Mark had told them about worked, she could fix all of her problems, and maybe reinstate her good name at ASSET too.

"That place looks fun," Sage noted as they walked through the parking lot. A wafting scent of patchouli hit them as they closed in on the new age shop.

Grey opened the door and held it for her to enter. "Best place to get the practical supplies from this list."

"I know I shouldn't laugh, but the way you said that without any hint of irony feels so very wrong."

Herbal perfumes choked out the air. Incense burned in all four corners of the tiny shop.

"How are you still so surprised by everything?"

"Not that. Just how it's so in your face. But hidden."

"Some humans share distant links to magical blood-lines. And they, too, enjoy tapping into it."

"While others just like to play pretend."

"Not everyone can wield magic. Some do love to play though."

How many times had she tried to explain that to him when he teased her for enjoying game night with her friends? "I'm going to let that one slide."

"Like the tokens on a game board?"

"Did Grey try to make a joke?" She gasped and clutched her chest.

"Apparently it was a good one."

She faux punched his arm. "Don't let it go to your head. It wasn't that good."

"We going to stand here all day?"

"And the fun-slayer returns."

"We're being watched." Grey angled his eyes toward the shopkeeper behind the counter.

Sage looked around nervously, suddenly feeling as if she had extra limbs and didn't know how to use them. She shoved her hands into her pockets, and stumbled toward a display of rocks. "So what's on the list?"

Grey pulled the notebook from his pocket and ran a finger down the list. "Selenite."

"That's a word."

"Look for a milky white crystal rod. We want the wand-shaped ones, not the polished pebbles."

"Gotcha. Superman's Cave of Solitude décor." Sage headed toward a stocked shelf of rocks and wands.

"Your world is one hundred percent pop culture, isn't it?" he asked.

"Pretty much."

"There is a real world out there, you know."

"Don't."

"What?"

"Don't pretend to lecture me on being super serious and all that. It's okay to enjoy a little fantasy."

"But you live it. Why cling to what you know is false?"

"Because it's still fun. It was fake then. It's still fake now, but knowing that doesn't kill the fun of it. Something you need to learn to embrace. The world is a shitty place. Even with magic. Let yourself enjoy whatever brings you joy."

"Surprisingly wise." He smiled. "Fine, then, go find Superman's home décor."

She fingered through piles of multi-colored rocks and wands before locating a small basket of cloudy white crystal wands. "Got 'em. What's next?"

"Fluorite pillars," he called out. "We need four of them. Purple and green."

"I've got purple here." Sage picked up a pillar of amethyst.

"No, both purple and green."

The shopkeeper wandered over, smelling so strongly of lemongrass it overpowered the patchouli that had been making Sage's eyes water.

"Anything I can help you with?" he asked.

Grey eyed him suspiciously before answering. "We're needing supplies for a purification ritual." He put his left arm behind his back as he showed the shopkeeper his handwritten list.

"No problem. We got a kit for that. C'mon over to the register." The shopkeeper led the way and pulled up a basket from under the cabinet. "Got your Negative absorbers here. That's the Selenite. You're going to need one for each of the corners if you're banishing. Same as with your Fluorite. We got a few varieties of quarts. Can't ever have enough of those. We charge ours here every moon cycle...."

The door behind them chimed. Sage glanced over her shoulder, spotting a man entering the store. Definitely not the type to be buying any kind of magical ingredients. He had tool written all over him.

"We've got a bundle of sage for cleansing your altar." The shopkeeper continued talking as if he hadn't taken notice of the new customer.

Seeing her reaction, Grey turned his attention to the newcomer. He likely saw the same thing she had. Definitely not the kind of guy who'd be in a shop like this.

Sage pretended to be interested in a pack of white candles bundled on a small table next to the register, using the new angle to get a better view of the stranger.

Baseball cap, hoodie unzipped over a tight-fitting shirt. As he moved, she saw the shadow of something else there between his layers. She blinked and looked again. The man busied himself thumbing through some pamphlets by the door. As his arms came down, she saw it again. The butt of a gun. He was packing. She tried to get a look at his wrist, but the angle was wrong. She couldn't see if he had the mark.

"Now, I see you have alchemy oils on your list. Oil of the Ages is kind of a broad term. What specifically are you banishing? I might have something special in the back." The shopkeeper continued to prattle on.

Sage's spidey senses were tingling, and it had nothing to do with the seed in her palm. That, thankfully, had been silent. They might've been in a magic shop, but nothing here was charged enough to set her off.

"We'll take whatever you have," Grey responded mechanically. He, too, had his eyes elsewhere. Was he thinking the same as her?

Grey tapped the basket. "Just toss in whatever you think will work. I'm not working the spell. Just the errand boy." He turned away from the shopkeeper and took a step toward the stranger.

"Are you working the spell, then?" the shopkeeper asked Sage.

"Just a lackey here as well." She faked an innocent smile. "Whatever you think we'll need."

"Let me see what I have in the back." The shopkeeper ducked behind a beaded curtain.

Grey moved toward the door, eyeing the man standing there, practically blocking the exit. "What about you? Know anything about these banishing spells?"

The stranger smiled. "I don't need spells." He moved his open jacket just enough to confirm what Sage had suspected.

She never liked guns.

Grey smirked. "Me either." He brushed aside his leather jacket, and Sage spotted the twin machete handles at his belt. "I prefer to do my own banishing."

"A bit old-fashioned, don't you think?" The stranger laughed.

"Well, I normally prefer my bolo, but we're traveling. Thought I'd pack lighter, so the kukris will have to do."

"Assuming you have the chance to use them." The stranger took a step back from Grey.

"Am I going to need to?"

"Well, that depends on if you're going to get in my way."

"What are you here for?" Grey asked.

"The girl."

"You ASSET?" Grey asked.

"Don't worry who I'm with."

"See, that's where we have a problem. She's not going anywhere unless it's with me."

"Then I guess you're in my way." The stranger moved to pull his gun.

Grey snapped into action. He took the strangers hand with the gun and twisted hard, using his momentum to push the gun away from his body. A shot fired, destroying a potted fern across the room.

She'd seen Grey take on vampires before. Guys with super strength, too, and win. But the stranger was no vampire. Couldn't be. It was broad daylight outside, and the shop was flooded with it. She hadn't seen the mark on his wrist but doubted he was ASSET. They couldn't have found her that quickly.

The gun clattered to the ground. Grey kicked it toward Sage as he grappled with the stranger.

She threw herself toward it, picked it up, and aimed at the two men. "Stop," she shouted.

The stranger hesitated, and Grey locked him into a sleeper hold.

"Who are you and why did you come after me?" Sage yelled.

"You think I'm afraid of you?" The stranger laughed despite the blood dribbling down the side of his face. He had a nasty gash on his eyebrow.

"Between the two of us, she's the one you should be scared of," Grey said. "Do you know how many people she's killed?"

"Shut up. That's not nice." Her arms trembled as she tried to maintain her posture, aiming the gun at the stranger's stomach.

"I'm telling you. Don't piss her off. She's deadly, that one," Grey continued to taunt.

"I'd believe it more if she weren't shaking like a damn leaf." The stranger stared at Sage, all but daring her to do it.

"I don't want to do it, but I will," she threatened.

"Just make sure you get him and not me," Grey added.

"You trust my aim that much?" Sage replied. How could she not hit him? Clean shot at close range, the bullet would likely pass straight through the stranger and get Grey with nothing else to stop it.

"I've got him nice and still. Aim low. Angle down," Grey spoke calmly.

"So, shoot him in the balls?" Sage wondered if he truly wanted her to fire.

"Do I get a say in this?" The stranger sounded worried for the first time.

"You came here, threatening me, attacked my friend, and you think you get a say in where I shoot you?" Sage found her courage and stilled her shaking arms. "You're lucky to still be alive right now. And the only reason I haven't shot you yet is I want to know who hired you to come after me."

"They'll kill me if I say."

"And we'll kill you if you don't. The difference is, giving us the information we want gives you a chance to run."

A glimmer of understanding lit in his eyes. "They call themselves Mystics. That's all I know. Weirdest group I've ever contracted with. Serious ren fair types, but they pay well."

"When did they contract with you?" Grey asked.

"I've been doing surveillance for the last week. When you left Vegas, they ordered me to bring you in."

"What did they tell you about her?" Grey asked.

"Just that she's valuable and I shouldn't hurt her."

"Damn right you shouldn't," Sage agreed.

"You got your intel. You going to let me go now?"

"Sage, you know how to unload a gun?"

"Only by shooting it," she replied.

"Not in here," Grey said. "As for you, I catch wind of you sniffing around her again, I will kill you." He shoved the stranger toward the door. "Start walking."

The shopkeeper came out from behind the beaded curtain looking visibly shaken. "I'm going to have to ask you guys to leave now."

"Soon as we pay for the supplies." Sage turned, still holding the gun in her hand.

"Take them," the shopkeeper said.

"We'll pay for the broken vase too." Grey tossed a pile of cash at the register. He took hold of the gun from Sage, pulled the clip, and removed the round from the chamber.

Sage picked up the basket from the counter and waited patiently for a receipt. "We're very sorry. You see now why we need some serious banishing supplies."

"You're going to need more than banishing if the Mystics are after you," the shopkeeper warned.

"You've heard of them?" Grey asked.

"I don't want to say." The shopkeepers eyes darted all around the room, everywhere except where Sage and Grey stood, as if he feared he was being watched, and didn't want to be seen associating with them. "Can't get involved. Don't want trouble."

"Please. If you know anything, tell us. My life is in danger. You heard that guy," Sage pleaded, hoping to appeal to the shopkeepers' good nature.

"You have to leave now. I won't call the cops. Just please, take your stuff and go." The shopkeeper backed away, disappearing through the beaded curtain.

TWENTY

Grey drove them deep into the heart of downtown where the streets narrowed and the buildings grew tall enough to block out the sun, before finding a parking garage to pull into.

"Want to clue me in to your plan here?" Sage looked around, searching for signs of familiarity. She'd grown up in this city, but downtown was only a place she'd visited for comic conventions. Beyond that, it had been no man's land.

Grey swapped out the helmet for his fedora. "We're off grid. No resources." He reached into the saddlebags, feeling around as if looking for something special. "This is a long shot, but I used to have a connection that worked downtown." He pulled a small metal case from the depths and opened it briefly.

Sage closed in for a peek. Badges, ATM cards, and a few official-looking identification cards.

Grey picked through them, choosing a small leather billfold, and stashed the box back in his saddle bags. "We just need a little leverage."

Their usual leverage came from showing the very con-spicuous tree-shaped marking on their left wrist. Magic types of all kinds knew exactly what that meant.

Her curiosity was more than piqued. "Corporate type?"

"Hardly." He pulled out a pair of aviator sunglasses, completing his flimsy disguise. "Computers guy. Techie. Gremlin." Grey opened the billfold, revealing an official-looking inspector's badge before placing it in his inside jacket pocket.

"Wait, like Gizmo?" Her mind immediately went down the rabbit hole of movie references. She was just about to ask what would happen if he was fed after midnight, when Grey's laughter stopped her.

"Be sure to ask that when we see him."

"Thanks, partner." File that one under 'never say out loud.' She glared at him, more angry that he'd finally found a better response to her newbieness than simply calling her that. "Way to have my back there."

"Don't be like that. I can only enjoy your ignorance for so long. Let me savor it a little, please?"

"Of all the people I could be on the run with…." Sage sighed. "Where's my douchebag sunglasses?"

"I'm going to pretend I didn't hear that." Grey led them out of the parking garage toward the street. "And re-member, when we get there…"

"If you tell me to shut my mouth, I will smack you."

"You're learning. I'm so proud of you."

Sage smacked him in the arm.

"Did a fly just land on me?" Grey dusted the spot where she'd hit him.

Sage wouldn't admit it out loud, but she enjoyed these moments. The playful banter they shared made for a much needed distraction from their current situation. She couldn't dwell on it. She might go insane. How could a life change so much so quickly? Her thoughts began to go down the dark path as they walked on in silence. She wanted to speak but had nothing of value to add.

Grey at least seemed to know where he was heading. He walked swiftly, his head up, eyes to the skyline as he moved them from the street to the alleyways in between the towering buildings. "If he's still around, Tito is a bit twitchy. He doesn't like surprises."

"I'm sure I'll be ridiculed for eternity for asking, but what exactly does he do?"

Grey turned as he came out of the alley, merging into a swarm of people heading toward a crosswalk. "Hotel security."

She'd never been on the run before. Public places were probably best, lots of people, less chance of incident. But as they filtered in with the pedestrians crossing the street, Sage felt as if she had stepped into the crosshairs. Her neck prickled, and so did the seed in her hand. Tingles like that of a waking limb ran outward from her palm, joining her pulse to send the sparks throughout her body. Magic was close. But that wasn't the only thing.

Someone was watching. Whether it was the street musician looking for someone to stop and listen to their work, and maybe drop a buck or two in their hat, or something more sinister, Sage couldn't shake the unnerving sensation.

If Grey felt it, he didn't show it. Swiftly moving through the crowd, he'd reached the other side of the street, and stood waiting for her by the glass front doors of the hotel.

Sage stopped short, waiting for him to open the door. "You might want to let me sit this one out at the bar."

"Funny. I'm not letting you out of my sight." He looked down, spotting her twitchy fingers. "You sense something?"

"Yes and no. I don't like this. I don't feel right. Someone is watching."

Grey glanced up toward a domed security camera. "With any luck, it's Tito."

"When was the last time you talked to him?"

Grey shrugged. "His type like the cave life. And usually don't stray far from home."

"And you think he can help us how?"

"I'd have thought by now you'd have learned not to underestimate anyone."

"Just saying. If he never leaves…"

"He doesn't have to. Hotels are international hubs. He can access anything and everything he wants. And let's not forget the lost and found. We need a phone, computer, IDs, etc.…"

"I'd have never thought of that." *Learn something new every day.* Sage smiled to herself.

"Just keep your hands in your pockets, and we'll be fine." Grey started walking again, away from the hotel door.

She hadn't expected that, and rushed to catch up. Grey walked like a man on a mission, every few minutes looking up and around as if hunting for something. She followed along, mimicking what he did, noticing all the domed security cameras placed around the building, and it began to make sense. If that Tito guy was watching the cameras, he'd spot Grey and know exactly where they were heading. She'd have much rather used the front door and found some back of the house entrance that way, but Grey would have a reason for keeping them on the outside. He hadn't led her astray yet.

He stopped at the back corner of the building and nodded toward another security camera. "This way."

Sage played follow the leader down a narrow driveway behind the hotel that smelled like a dumpster marinated in tar. The aroma burned her nose, searing the smell into her nostrils. She pulled up the collar of her T-shirt and covered her nose. It was all she could do to hold back the chunks.

Grey came to a stop at an unmarked door. He knocked in a strange pattern, then reached for his machetes.

"Why do I get the feeling you might not be as good of friends with Tito as you let on?" Sage worried aloud. She'd accept frenemies as long as it meant an invite inside so she could escape that horrid smell. How could the hotel get away with such a stench? Trash burning wasn't still a thing, was it?

Grey didn't appear to be as bothered by the smell as she was. He had his hands on the handles of his blades still sheathed in his belt and kept watch on the security camera. "Always be prepared."

"Boy Scout." She snickered. "Should I be armed too?"

He jerked his head so fast his sunglasses looked like they might fall off his face. "You mean to tell me you aren't?"

"We left in such a hurry." She feigned an innocent smile. The arsenal of bladed weapons she'd inherited from her mother was an impressive collection. She hadn't picked a favorite yet, but wished she'd at least brought a dagger or two with her.

"Never leave home without protection." He hadn't growled at her like that in a while. But she deserved it and hung her head appropriately in shame.

"Lesson learned."

Grey knocked again, a bit more urgently than before.

"You sure he's here?"

"No. It was a longshot." Grey tapped his fingers on the handle of his machetes and let out an impatient sigh. "We'll give him one more minute."

"I don't like this." The eyes-on-the-back-of-her-neck feeling prickled again with renewed intensity. Sage stared into the lens of the camera as if trying to see through to the other side. Unfriendly or not, that Tito guy watching would be understandable, but the feeling wasn't coming from that camera. Sage looked for another. "We need to go."

"Your hand?" Grey asked.

"No." She turned around, still trying to pinpoint the direction her weird feeling was coming from. "Something else. We're being watched."

Grey's jaw tightened as he scanned their surroundings. Without a word he turned, putting her at his back, and waving her to follow.

She didn't need to be told twice. They walked double speed back down the small drive and came out along the side of the hotel. Out in the open, Sage felt the pull of eyes stronger than before. Someone was definitely following, but who? Another human looking to pick up a bounty? More Mystics coming to test her powers? Or was it the worst of all the options? Had Ava caught up to them? She scrambled behind Grey as he carved a path through the busy streets, heading toward the parking lot with his motorcycle.

Sage looked over her shoulder, her intuition confirming the unknown watchers were close. Two shadows were following, moving as rapidly as she was. "We've got company."

Grey took hold of her hand and jerked her on a new direction. "Not that way." He led her down a service road between two huge buildings. On either side of them, warehouse bays sat in various stages of use. Dockworkers took their breaks a few feet from the wide roller doors smoking cigarettes. Sage took comfort in the potential of witnesses to keep the ones following them from doing anything rash.

"Do you know where we're going?" Sage panted as she pushed her tired legs to keep up with Grey.

"Just keep moving."

She looked over her shoulder again. The shadows had gone, but the feeling remained

The service road connected with another, like a secret passage, that brought them straight to the parking lot they'd been looking for.

Just across one more street and they'd be able to put miles between themselves and their shadows.

Grey watched the traffic pattern, looking for the best time to run.

A gun cocked behind them. The unmistakable sound stole the breath from Sage's already burning lungs.

"Sage Cynwrig, you are to come with us." A man gave the order with all the authority of a police officer.

She turned to face the voice and found an ASSET Agent, uniformed all in black. Option number three. The worst possible shadow that could have been following them. She gave Grey a hard time for looking like a tool, but this Phoenix agent, complete with faux hawk, sunglasses, Bluetooth earbud, and SWAT-style vest with A.S.S.E.T. embroidered in bright gold on it, clearly had the market cornered on douchebaggery.

Her hands went up instinctively as the barrel of the gun leveled with her body. Not again. Nerves fired all at once, quickening her breath, as her heart raced to keep up. She fought against the urge to run, forcing herself to stand perfectly still.

"She's not going anywhere with you." Grey reached for his machetes, ready to pull them. He stood two steps closer to the gunman. Not quite in the crosshairs but an easy target. Not that he appeared worried. Even from where she stood, Grey gave off a fearless vibe. "We're on assignment. You're going to blow our cover. Drop your weapon and walk away."

Every breath became a conscious effort. In. Out. In. Out. Focus. That was the key. She scanned around, hoping Faux Hawk was the only one in the area, but she knew better. She'd seen two shadows in her peripheral a moment before. If they were armed, too, things were going to get messy.

Gun versus machete. Not the best matchup. And she wasn't ready to test her pseudo immortality against bullet wounds.

"I'm afraid your assignment has been cancelled. Our orders are to bring her in." Faux Hawk motioned with his gun. Sage was definitely in the crosshairs. "Peacefully would be best."

If she made a break for it, could she get to the other side of the street? What did Devon always say? Run in a zigzag pattern to avoid getting shot. But what about Grey? He stood menacingly, staring down Agent Faux Hawk.

No secret signals or nods. What was she supposed to do?

"The last person who pulled a gun on us regretted that pretty quickly." Grey spoke with confidence that gave Sage hope. "Lower your weapon before this gets ugly."

"Stand down, Agent Maddox." He spoke the command louder, as if that would make a difference. "My orders come from the director himself."

"We're not under your director's jurisdiction." Grey matched him in volume. "You're interfering in our investigation, and threatening a senior officer."

"You didn't see us. Simple as that," Sage said, trying to plead to the agent's good nature. "The director doesn't need to know."

Agent Faux Hawk narrowed his eyes, possibly considering her words, but kept his weapon trained on her.

Moving forward wasn't an injury-free option. Behind them, the alley opened to a street. The only way out. Another option that wasn't exactly injury-free either. Grey was the combat guy. Why hadn't he made a move yet?

She held her breath waiting for the gunman's reply. All the while her skin crawled with the sensation of being watched again.

Agent Faux Hawk was stalling. Because of course he would be. She picked up on shuffling noises behind her. Footsteps. Someone, hopefully only one, was creeping up, closing the back door option.

Sage angled her head slowly, enough to look from the corner of her eyes. The shadows were closing in. They were surrounded.

"Two behind us, one in front," Grey whispered. "Time to put your training to use. Get behind me."

"Last chance, Ms. Cynwrig. We have been authorized to use lethal force, but do not wish to do so with a fellow agent." Faux Hawk's tone smacked of apathy despite his choice of words.

Sage had never seen his face before. If he was a Phoenix agent, he had to be new. As much time as she'd spent there, growing up, she'd learned of many of the regulars.

Sage lowered her hands, balling her fist as she sidestepped into Grey's shadow.

"When I give the word, drop low. The gunman is mine. You take the shadows." Grey's voice betrayed no emotion. Cool and collected. If he was as good as he was cocky, he might be able to deflect the bullet. Otherwise, he'd just offered to take one for her. She'd owe him big-time if they made it out of this alive. *If.*

Sage set herself ready to fight. She still had two shadows creeping up behind her.

Grey unsheathed his twin blades.

An arm came around her neck. She gasped for air as the warmth of a body pressed up against her backside. Python-like pressure squeezed her throat. Grey hadn't given the word yet, but if she didn't act, she'd run out of air. While she still had the leverage, Sage put everything she had into a hard elbow aimed at her attacker's abdomen.

A painful shout worked like a shot of adrenaline, kicking Sage into a new level of focus. The pressure at her neck released enough for Sage to fill her lungs. She chopped again blindly, and connected with soft tissue. Her attacker doubled over with a strangled grunt. Muscle memory took over. Sage sent a foot out to trip him. She pushed her hips back and twisted, grabbing for any bit of skin or clothing to yank. Using his momentum, she sent her attacker to the pavement.

A gun went off. Sage flinched, waiting for pain or confirmation of someone else taking the bullet.

Oh gods! What if it's Grey?

A meaty hand took hold of her wrist. Shock tore a cry from her throat before she could prevent it. Shadow number two, the other agent. His grip was tight. She should have been ready for him, but she hadn't finished immobilizing the first guy yet.

Where is Grey?

Quick and dirty, Sage stepped out and twisted her arm, rotating her wrist in his hand. Using the strength of his hold, she aimed a forearm strike right above his elbow, putting everything she had into it. The crack of his joint vibrated through their connection before Sage heard the sound.

Agent number two screamed but didn't let go.

Damn. Some people just don't know when to quit.

She planted her feet and yanked his freshly injured arm forward. He began to topple, releasing her hand as he windmilled his arms to regain balance.

"Oh no you don't." Sage elbowed him between the shoulder blades hard to finish the job.

Agent two went down harder than Han Solo in carbonite. He should have been down for the count, but still the creep tried to get back up. Using his good hand to push against the ground, he flopped like a freshly caught fish.

"Leave us alone!" Sage stomped his back.

His head smacked the concrete and his body went limp against the pavement. Killing another agent hadn't been her intention. All her aggression turned to fear when she realized he wasn't just staying down—he wasn't moving at all.

She knelt next to him and felt for his pulse. It was there. Weak, but there. He'd heal with the right medical attention. She sighed, relieved for the moment, then stood to look for Grey.

Shadow number one, the first guy to attack her, had made it to his feet, because of course he had. He faced her, fists balled, ready to strike. "Let's finish this."

"Really? You want more?" Sage all but rolled her eyes. "You did just see what happened to your partner here, right?"

He lunged at her, wrapped his arms around her waist, and tackled her to the ground.

Her ass hit first, then her shoulders, scraping concrete. Her head came down next. The impact sent a flash of brilliant light blotting out her vision. She fought to blink away the blindness. Pain kept her riveted to the moment. Whether she could see or not, she still needed to get away, or at the very least fight the good fight until Grey could come to her aid.

She tried to roll away but met with a foot instead. Pain bloomed across her chest. Something cracked. It had to be her rib. She howled, unable to hold back the cry. Her vision blinked back just in time to see her attacker drop down on top of her. The weight of his body crush the air from her lungs while the pain focused down to a single point.

"You were warned. We wanted to do this peacefully." He took control of her hands, pinning them as if to cuff her. "We have our orders."

Devon had run this drill with her so many times it should have been easy, but pain short-circuited her memories. She struggled, biting back tears, as she searched for the leverage needed to break free.

He gripped her wrists tight and brought them center. "If you stop fighting, this won't have to hurt."

She lifted one leg and set it down just outside of his. "You've already hurt me." She tucked her hands against her chest, forcing him to hold tight, and threw her hips sideways. "You're going to have to come up with a better lie."

He went down hard. His grip loosened as he rolled to the ground. Sage roared with the pain of her damaged ribs as she came back up and threw all her fury into a hard punch to his jaw.

Another hand grabbed her shoulder. She pivoted with another pain-filled shout, and threw a wild punch.

Grey caught her fist before it connected with his face. He brushed her aside, and knocked out the guy she'd been fighting.

"You okay?"

"Better now." She hugged her ribs tight and forced herself to stand. Her pain level had already dropped from a ten to a manageable seven. As long as the fighting was over, she'd be okay. Sage glanced down to the fallen gunman. Grey had him hogtied and gagged lying like an offering on the pavement.

"Hold this." He handed her the gun. For the second time in as many hours, he had disarmed someone and passed the weapon to her. "If he so much as coughs, pull the trigger."

Grey pulled zip ties from his jacket pocket to tie the two unconscious men the same way he'd left Agent Faux Hawk.

"Remind me never to come at you from behind." He chuckled as he bent down and checked for a pulse.

"He's not…"

"Just knocked out. But when he wakes up, he might wish he were dead. What the hell did you do to his face?"

"That was the concrete, not me." She groaned. Talking hurt. Laughing was worse.

"He's not going anywhere for a while." Grey finished zipping the men up and took the gun back.

Agent Faux Hawk glared at Grey as he pulled the magazine and threw the empty gun to the ground.

Grey crouched down low. "Here's what's going to happen. When you are picked up, let your boss know not to send anyone else after us. We're all on the same team here. Got it?"

The agent squeaked out a "yes," nodding his head emphatically.

"And while you're at it, your team needs to go back for some serious retraining. Newbie here took down two of your guys, unarmed." He clicked his tongue. "She's barely been active a month. I'll be adding that evaluation to my report when I get back home."

Sage wasn't sure whether she wanted to punch Grey or hug him for that little jab. He was clearly riling them up, but at her expense. Sage held her tongue for the sake of the moment, but he'd hear about it later on.

"C'mon, newbie. Better clear out before the cavalry comes." Grey waved her on, and took off down the street toward the parking lot and his bike.

TWENTY-ONE

"We'll stay here tonight." Grey opened the door marked B22.

The motel room smelled of stale cigarettes, but it had beds and a shower. Things Sage desperately needed after the day she'd had. "Dibs on the shower."

The only thing missing was a good meal. That would have to come later.

"Have a look at your wounds." Grey closed the door and immediately turned to the window. He peered sideways through the edge of the blackout curtains. "We need to be ready for the next fight when it comes."

Sage made a beeline to the sink and mirror to inspect her wounds. The pain in her chest had dropped from a seven to a five during the ride to the motel.

"Is this how it's going to be from now on?" With any luck, she would heal before the next fight broke out. Though she really hoped she'd met her quota for fighting, at least for the night.

A little cool water and soap washed some of the evidence of her day from her face. Her clothes were not as lucky. Ripped jeans were in fashion, at least. But that was all she could get away with. The collar of her shirt was stretched over her shoulder, the seam bloody and fraying. She pulled it off, leaving her with only a tank top for cover.

"Going to need to go shopping." The back looked even worse. Completely shredded.

She twisted to look at the wounds on her back. Her damaged rib made itself known. Sage struggled to contain her yelp.

Grey left the window and threw his bag on the bed closest to the door. "We'll pick something up when we have time."

"So we have ASSET after us and the Mystics, whoever they are. What's our play?"

"Not sure. I need to think." He pulled off his jacket and unbuckled his weapons belt, then laid his twin machetes down along with the bag.

"That's what I'm trying to get you to do." She paced the thin strip of carpet between the beds and the TV cabinet. The shower was calling her name, but with the twitchy way Grey was acting, she couldn't relax enough to listen. "Think. Out loud, with me. It's called brainstorming. Something that teams do." She threw her hands on her hips as she rounded the bed to face him. "Partner."

"I'm not trying to shut you out. I'm just gathering my thoughts." He laid two more daggers on the bed next to his weapons belt, taking far more time than was necessary to disarm himself.

"Same difference."

"Stop it." He slammed his fist into the bed and glared up at her as if ready to unleash his anger.

She hadn't intended to be a pest, but not knowing what to do had her jumping at everything. She was the reactionary type. Wearing her emotions out there for all to see. That was her job. Seeing Grey on the edge… Nope. He didn't crack under pressure. He had no emotions. He was the Spock to her McCoy. Not the other way around. Things were worse than she had imagined. And she'd already imagined so many doomsday scenarios. Just another reason for her to panic. She couldn't panic. Someone had to be the calm one.

"Okay. I came on too strong." Sage sighed in frustration. "Ever been in a situation like this before? Not knowing who to trust or what to do?"

He closed his eyes tight as if trying to shut out the world and took a deep breath. Her first instinct was to push him for the answer, but Sage fought that urge and waited for him to collect his thoughts.

Minutes passed in silence before Grey relaxed and opened his eyes. "Part of the job actually."

"Not like this," Sage said the first words that came to mind. But even as she spoke them she knew they'd be misconstrued. "I mean, you...we... work for the good guys. Right?"

Grey snorted. Not exactly a laugh, but far better than the yelling or screaming he could have done. "ASSET's mission is good. But even those who claim to be good screw up sometime and do bad things."

"But they do them for the greater good, right?"

"That's the company line we use to make ourselves feel good." Grey sat, perching himself on the end of the bed. "But you said it yourself, Sage. It was Ava who asked you to use the seed."

He had her there. Not that she wanted to admit it. Sage looked down at her palm, and the hideous blackness that had nearly taken over her hand. Where would she be if she'd never come in contact with the stupid seed?

"Ava felt there was no other choice."

"You see?" Grey smirked. "Greater good and all, she still asked you to do something very bad. I saw it in your eyes then. I still see it now. You were scared. You didn't want to do it."

She tried to hide her shame by folding her arms tight against her chest. "But I did."

"Not the way she wanted. You were forced to use it, for personal gain, I might add."

"What?"

"Easy now." He jerked backwards, catching himself before falling off the bed. "You were spurred into action by your friend Matt being kidnapped."

"He's more than just a friend."

"I know. He's family." Grey held his hands up passively. "You ultimately did good, with a lot of bad in the mix." His gaze softened. "And paid a heavy price for it."

"I feel we're talking in circles."

"Exactly the point. We don't always know who to trust. Because even when we have the best of intentions, we are all capable of doing very bad things."

Grey might have calmed down, but the conversation had done nothing to ease her anxiety. She resumed her pacing again, feeling as if the walls would close in on her if she didn't push against them.

"So ASSET is Chaotic Good in the grand scheme of things?" she asked.

"Is that gamer talk again?" he scoffed.

"Yes."

"If it helps, let's go with that. You want brainstorming? Okay. We have to think the same way to keep ourselves from being swallowed up by the chaos."

Thinking. Working. Yes. That was exactly what they needed to do. Of all the people she knew, how many could she trust? Grey, abrasive as he was, always had her back. That was one. Who else? Devon? He'd been her confidant, but even he had secrets. He knew more than he ever revealed, and Ava had given him private information before revealing it to her. But Ava wanted her brought in. Technically, that made her the enemy. Even if she was, as Grey had put it, doing things for the greater good. Who else could she trust? Who in this new life had given her a reason?

"Mark," she blurted out as she came round her third lap.

"What about him?"

"He's like family. We can trust him."

Grey's mouth hardened into a scowl. "Are you sure?"

"Yes," she said without hesitation. "And he has the spell we need still."

"No. Absolutely not. We can't go back to headquarters, Phoenix or Vegas."

She caught herself before the word 'duh,' left her lips. She might be Captain Obvious, but even that was too stupid for her to suggest. "We don't have to. I know where he lives."

"If you're wrong about him, we'll be walking straight into a trap."

"I'm not wrong." She rushed toward Grey. "And if I am, it's me who will pay the price. I'll go alone."

"I can't let that happen. You're my partner."

"But I'm a fugitive. Wanted by the Agency and whoever else these Mystics are."

"Which is why I can't let you do this. I have to protect you."

"I appreciate that. I know you have my back. I know I can trust you." She reached out and allowed her fingers to graze his shoulder. A tender nudge of solidarity. "Mark has had my back for a long time. I know we can trust him too."

Grey's muscles tensed. He turned away from her.

"You okay?" she asked, reaching out again, but he recoiled as if her touch might sting.

He stood and walked across the room. "Trust is important. But are you prepared for the pain of betrayal if it comes?"

"How can I be? I can't even think that way right now. It's taking everything I have to keep up some hope that I'm not going to die the minute I leave this room."

"You're not going to die. I won't let that happen."

"Which is why I trust you."

"But are you putting your trust in someone who will? I don't like us going to Mark. He's top level. The director of this area. You called me a company man, but he *is* the company. His priorities trump whatever loyalty you think he might have to you."

She couldn't believe that. Mark had been like a father to her as far back as she could remember. "He loves me like a daughter. That's a bit different."

Grey gritted his teeth and hissed as if her words had hurt him. "I really didn't want to…" He stood across the room, as from Sage as he could be, his body rigid as a statue. Grey clenched his fists as if ready for battle.

Sage wasn't sure what to expect, but if it was a fight he wanted, he'd get it.

"Let me tell you about love." His voice turned to gravel. All the light seemed to drain from his eyes, leaving them cold and unfeeling.

Sage had seen the look before. But not from Grey. It was as if he'd shut out all the parts of his humanity, leaving only an empty shell.

"A few years back, I was involved with someone who I thought I could trust. Someone I loved."

Sage gasped. Not an empty shell. He'd buried his emotions down deep to avoid feeling the pain.

"Yasmine." Grey winced as he spoke her name. "She was smart, beautiful, and a vampire. Despite our obvious differences, we were good together. She stayed out of the way of my job, and I stayed out of the way of her…business. Occasionally, we'd trade secrets to keep each other safe. For the most part, she was cool with the way ASSET controlled things in the city. Fast forward a year and new leadership moved in, shaking up the vampire covens." He took a breath and unclenched his fists.

Sage relaxed, slowly letting herself sink down onto the bed as she listened.

"My partner, Carrie, warned me that I shouldn't put so much faith in Yasmine." Muscles still tense, he walked stiffly to the other bed and took a seat. "Carrie had always been the practical one. By the book. Damn good agent. She believed that vampires were not inherently bad, but at the end of the day, they answered to a higher power than their hearts. They only truly loved one thing. Blood. I didn't want to hear it. Just figured Carrie… Well, you know how girls are."

Sage smirked. "I'll let that one go for now."

"Yasmine and I had a bond. We loved each other. We were a team just as much as Carrie and I were." He took a stuttering, deep breath, slowly pulling the air into his lungs.

She stared into his eyes, as if truly seeing him for the first time. The windows to his soul. She explored deeper, past the wall he'd put up to hide the pain. He was so much stronger than she had given him credit for.

"ASSET ordered a raid at the night club where Yasmine worked. Too many dead bodies. Police had been investigating too closely. Too much noise is the enemy of secrecy. So, we were told to shut it down and round up the coven for trial. Standard operation." His voice warbled. "I sent word to Yasmine, warning her not to be at work that night. There was no way she was part of the problem. She was one of the good ones." He tensed again, clenching his fists, and sat straighter on the bed.

As much as she wanted to open her mouth and offer sympathy, Sage knew better than to interrupt. If he had been closer, she'd have hugged him.

"We walked straight into a trap. The coven knew we were coming. It got dirty. Young vampires. Stupid. Unschooled. They hadn't been taught to feed by the rules. They hadn't been taught to fight. So many of them. It was like they were being created en masse. Like a small army of pawns."

An army? The words stuck in her throat. Sounded like someone had been planning to start a war long before she'd been introduced into the fray. Vampires. And now her roommate was one of them too. Something she'd have to deal with later. If there was a later.

The pain in Grey's eyes turned to anger as he continued his story. "I did what I could to restrain them so I could bring them in, like I was ordered to. A lot of vampires died that day."

"And your partner?" Sage asked timidly.

"Found her in the middle of a scuffle with Yasmine."

Better than being dead, or worse, but Sage didn't utter the word "darkling" out loud. "That had to be difficult."

"Carrie could hold her own when it came to vampires." Grey stood and walked toward Sage like a man on a mission. "I didn't intervene. Our orders were to subdue and bring in. Not kill. Yasmine might still be able to prove her innocence."

She expected Grey to come and sit next to her, but as fast as he came up to her, he walked past, rounding the corner of the bed to retrieve his jacket.

"But something wasn't right. Yasmine wasn't herself. I called out to her. The fighting had stopped, but it wasn't my love looking at me. I'd never seen such feral hunger. Her eyes had eclipsed, totally black. Blood smeared all across her beautiful face. It was like looking at a complete stranger."

Sage knew the look he was describing. Zack had revealed his demon side. Matt, too, had shown the signs of the beast within.

"Carrie turned to see me in that same moment. It wasn't like her to do that. She was by the book. She should have taken Yasmine out. Or at least restrained her." He reached into his jacket pocket. "It happened so fast. Yasmine had Carrie, teeth bared, and told me to choose."

Sage understood why he always cautioned her against getting too close to Zack. "What did you do?"

He pulled a throwing dagger from his jacket pocket and flipped it around in his hand. "I chose."

"You killed Yasmine?" The woman he loved. He'd chosen the job. His partner. Over love.

"Put this straight into her left eye. Should have dropped her. Should have bought Carrie some time. But it didn't. Yasmine opened her throat. Severed the carotid. You know what that means?"

Death. In minutes maybe, but death all the same.

"I'm so sorry." Tears streamed down her cheeks. So much pain. She felt it as if it were her own.

"Yasmine said the same, the minute she came out of her frenzy. But it was too late. Carrie was lifeless in her arms." He set the small blade down and pulled one of his machetes free of its sheath.

"What did you do?"

In one smooth stroke, he swung the blade like a golf club with a hard, upward arc. "I did what I had to do."

Sage felt the break of air tickle her face. "Was Carrie…dead?"

"She didn't make it." He focused on the metal of his weapon, bringing it back down slowly, and used his sleeve to wipe it, as if removing the stain before returning it to its home.

"Did you love her?"

"What kind of question is that?" Grey snarled.

Sage jumped to her feet again, holding her hands in surrender, not wanting to rile him further. "Just trying to understand how hard that was on you. Choosing between job and heart."

"It wasn't just the job. Carrie was my partner."

"Yes. I'm sorry." The more she tried to explain her question, the more Sage shoved her foot in her mouth, but she just couldn't stop talking. "I didn't mean it that way. I just wanted to understand."

"We were a team. It was hard. That's all you need to know."

Sage held her hand out as a peace offering. "Thank you for sharing."

Grey stared at her. He slowed his breathing. Sage waited, keeping her hand out. He had shown his strength in more than just ability. The pain he'd endured. The choices he'd made. He deserved her patience.

Her arm began to ache, trembling as she maintained her physical offering of peace.

"Be careful who you put your trust in." He closed the gap between them and took her hand in his, but rather than shake it as she'd expected, Grey brought her palm up to his heart. When he met her eyes, the anger had evaporated. "Especially when your life is at stake."

"You have my trust. Do I have yours?" she asked.

"You should know by now…you have so much more than that."

Her heart swelled with emotions Sage couldn't allow herself to process. If they survived, maybe, but with their lives on the line, they both needed to focus on the mission.

"We have to survive." Her voice cracked as she struggled to keep the words coming. The tears still fell, but no longer for the pain of his loss. "To do that, we need the spell. Without it, I will eventually die." What was the use of pursuing her feelings if she wouldn't be around long enough to enjoy them?

"You can absorb magic to stop the effects." His heart beat hard beneath her palm. Strong and steady. He had the answer right there as he gazed deeply into her eyes. Confidence ran straight through to his core.

It would be so easy to give in to the temptation. Fall completely off the grid. Explore the possibilities, the excitement of these new feelings. She dropped her gaze. Her free hand, the one bearing the mark of the Terra, had also been blackened by the seed. Head or heart? Sage had to choose.

"How long until I run out of magical artifacts to tap? What if I need something stronger?"

"There's never been a shortage of people abusing their magic." His words stunned her. So quick to accommodate her condition to keep her alive. Proof that these new feelings could undo them both.

"That's a slippery slope. One even I can't wrap my head around. I've already got too much blood on my hands. I don't want it to become a necessity to continue my life."

"If you go to ASSET now, you will be put down. Ava has already told you that."

"I don't blame Ava."

"Well, you should."

"Grey, stop. We can't go down this path. You're supposed to be the voice of reason."

"Sage, I have been in this business for a very long time. I know how the agency operates. I can't let you do this. You don't deserve this. You're…"

"You think I'm turning myself in. But I'm not. I have no desire to die or become some prisoner. And I sure as hell am not going to become some kind of killing machine for the Mystics or whoever else wants to use my abilities. I'm going to fight like hell to make things right."

"That's more like it." Grey's eyes lit with renewed excitement.

"We can trust Mark to give us the spell. I know that much. He gave me the seed. He doesn't want me die because of it. He might be a company man, but he doesn't want the company to lose its best asset."

"You leave me no choice." He squeezed her hand before letting go. "But we do this together. Shower and get some rest. Tonight, we'll go see if you're right."

TWENTY-TWO

Under cover of darkness, they rolled into the master-planned community where Mark lived. Sage kept her eyes open, searching for signs of surveillance watching the di-rector's home as they rounded the block.

She'd been so certain when she convinced Grey to go on this little side mission with her, but being out in the open, exposed, so close to a major member of the ASSET organization, she couldn't help but wonder if she'd made the wrong choice.

Even if he was on her side, who was to say Ava wouldn't have pulled strings of her own? She'd entered a whole new level of secret agenting, unprepared for the consequences that were sure to follow.

If Grey was as bothered as she was, he sure wasn't showing it. Sage took courage from that. His head was in the game. Hers should be too. Focus on the mission, leave no room for nerves to screw things up.

They rounded a corner, and Mark's modest ranch-style home came into view—a single-story, stucco house with desert landscaping and a two-car garage.

His green beast of a Jeep sat in the center of the drive-way. Mark always stripped it down during the summer. No top. No doors. Nothing separating him from the ride. He claimed it gave him the feeling of freedom, like flying through the air.

She never truly understood it before, but the Jeep was his touchstone to the regular non-magical, normal, and mundane. Amid the insanity of the world Sage found herself in, any connection to a solid baseline was worth its weight in gold.

"Looks clear," Grey announced. "We can't be too careful though." He drove the bike around the corner and found a spot just outside the halo of a streetlight.

From their vantage point, Sage had a clear line of sight, looking directly at Mark's Jeep, while at the same time, the bike appeared to vanish into the shadows.

Grey cut the engine. "Let me be clear. I don't like this plan."

"I know, you've only said it a hundred times," Sage snarked. As against this mission as he'd been, she didn't want to reveal her own apprehension. She hopped off the bike and removed her helmet.

"I'm serious. If we do this, we do it my way." Grey took hold of her arm. His grip was gentle despite the rough way he'd grabbed her. "You listen to what I say. If I tell you to run, no questions asked. You run."

"Sir, yes, sir!" Sage jerked free.

"Be serious or I'll cancel this insane plan of yours. We're walking straight into the jaws of death. You do understand that, right?"

"Sorry, I…" His concern was more than valid. She shouldn't have let slip such an ill-timed quip. This mission wasn't just risking her life. If things went south, Grey was going down with her. Not a price she wanted to pay. "I was just trying to lighten the mood."

"Don't! I need you one hundred percent focused."

"I am." She straightened up and nodded. "Let's do this."

"If something goes bad, this is the rendezvous point."

"No one knows where we are." She threw a quick glance over her shoulder, making sure the coast was clear. "And as you pointed out earlier, we'd be stupid to walk right through the front door, so who would ever expect us to do it?"

He whispered a curse under his breath. "Just because it is an extremely stupid move, doesn't mean it is an unexpected one. Mark knows you, remember? The queen of bad ideas." Grey dismounted the bike and pulled off his helmet.

"Really? We're going there? Right now?"

"Yes, because unlike you, I have a very bad feeling about this." He set down his helmet, and for the first time since she'd met him, didn't immediately reach for his hat. Grey pulled his machetes, one by one, sliding them free from their sheath and replacing them, as if making sure they were still there. Next came the blades in his pockets. Each one pulled and replaced as if inventorying his weapons. "You might trust him. You might even think of him like family. But what is he really?"

Before she could open her mouth to answer, he cut her off.

"Director of ASSET, Phoenix," he said. "Don't you forget that. He has a duty to uphold the magical laws in this jurisdiction. It's not a position that allows for playing favorites." Finally, Grey pulled one his throwing daggers and held it up for her to see. The same one he'd used with Yasmine. A silent but poignant reminder to her of what was at stake.

"Head over heart." Sage understood the message, but still held out hope. "I hear you loud and clear."

"For both our sakes, I hope so." Grey slid the knife back into his pocket. "We all eventually have to make that choice. It's tough as hell, but it has to be made."

She appreciated his concern, but deep down, this felt like the right play. "Mark's the reason I'm in this mess. He's going to do what he can to fix it." He'd given her the seed. He'd given her info to help her figure out what it was. He would not want her to die because of his actions.

"Can you at least compromise and let me take precautions to keep you safe?" Grey pulled his hat from the saddlebag and put it on.

"Okay, fine. What do you want to do? And don't say leave. We need that spell."

"The front is too accessible. Too easy for us to be spotted if he has someone patrolling. If we're going to face the beast, let's do it on our terms. Stick to the shadows and go around back."

"Not a bad idea." She wondered why he hadn't mentioned it before. Maybe he had seen something during their round of the neighborhood she hadn't. "Oh. But he's got a dog in the backyard. Fox."

Grey's nose crinkled with surprise. "Dog or fox?"

"Dog."

"Great, an ankle biter."

"Not exactly." She snickered. Seeing his reaction would be priceless, and if they weren't trying to be covert, she'd have let the surprise play out. But for the sake of the mission, she had to warn him. "She's got the colors of a fox. But she's a giant. German shepherd, malamute mix. About one hundred pounds."

Grey's surprised expression hardened. "Friendly?"

"Super. Maybe a little too friendly. Her size throws most people off, and the fact that when she meets someone, she tackles them to the ground. But don't worry, she just wants to play."

"Should have said something earlier. I'd have picked up some treats."

"You didn't mention the backyard until now."

"Honestly, I was hoping to find a way to talk you out of this nonsense. I didn't really think you'd go through with it."

"Have you met me?"

"Unfortunately. You'll be the death of me. Or maybe it will be the dog."

Between his cold expression and the deadpan delivery, Sage couldn't tell if Grey was trying to be funny or serious.

"Fox is a great big baby," she assured him. "Give her some love and she'll move on."

"Does he have a dog door?"

"Funny you should ask." Sage couldn't help the smile spreading across her face. How many times had she stayed at Mark's house? How many nights had she snuck out through that dog door? "Yeah, you want me to slip in through there and let you in?"

"Not at all." Grey shook his head. "The house is a potential trap. We need to keep all of our escape options open. Bring him out to us if possible."

She hadn't thought of that. But it made sense. The front door was too public. But leveling the playing field by bringing him outside and around back might work.

"How do we get him to come to us?" Sage glanced around the darkened street. The neighborhood appeared to be asleep. Most of the houses had gone dark. Only a few left their porch lights on.

"Fox," Grey announced. "Follow me." He took the lead, cautiously heading toward Mark's house.

Suspicious of every shadow, bush, and parked car, Sage gave each a second glance as they passed. Sleepy as the neighborhood seemed, she wasn't about to let her guard down. In the previous twenty-four hours, she'd found herself facing the barrel of two loaded guns. Third time was not about to be the charm. What would Devon say if he were there? *Head up, eyes open.*

They ducked into the gap between houses, becoming one with the shadows as they came upon Mark's home. A brick wall standing at least eight feet tall divided his front and backyard. The only way through was a wrought-iron gate fitted with a metallic mesh screen.

Grey drew his hands around the gate to the padlock securing it. "Got any hairpins?"

Lucky for him, Sage pulled two from her bun and handed them over.

"The dog knows you well, right?" Grey bent one of the pins into an L shape. "When I get this gate open, I want you to call the dog."

"She'll probably hear you picking the lock, if she hasn't already. She *is* a dog."

"We don't want her barking." He started working on the padlock. "Do what you can to keep her quiet. As soon as I get this gate open, get her to follow you to the bike."

Not what she had expected him to say. "Okay."

"Can you do it?"

"Hold a hyperactive one-hundred-pound dog without a leash, sure." She didn't bother to hide her sarcasm.

"You're going to have to." Grey struggled with the pins, working in the dark. "My plan revolves around you having the dog."

"As a hostage?"

"I didn't mean it like that. I'd never hurt an animal."

"You say that now." Sage heard the flap on the dog door seconds before Fox barreled toward the gate snarling and growling. Too late for their covert operation.

Grey fell backwards as Fox threw the full weight of her body into the gate.

"Foxy, sweetie, it's me." Sage approached the gate and bent down. Despite the dog's aggressive behavior, Sage placed her hand against the metal mesh for Fox to sniff.

Her snarling quieted. She sniffed cautiously at first. Then her tail lifted and began to sway.

"There's a good girl. You do remember me," Sage spoke sweetly.

Fox's tail dropped, her ears went up like little radar dishes, then she turned and ran back to the house.

Grey redoubled his efforts to unlock the gate. "What was that?"

"I don't know. I've never seen her act that way."

"She trained?"

"Mark never had the time. I taught her to sit, but she was just a pup."

"That was a while ago, I take it." He unclicked the lock and stood aside.

"I've visited since. She's always been happy to see me. Dogs don't forget. They're not like people."

Grey's scowl said he wasn't convinced. "We stick to the plan. Call her back."

Sage opened the gate enough to fit inside and crouched down. "Fox," she whispered. "C'mon, girl."

She listened for the flap on the dog door to open again. Nothing.

"Foxy. C'mon, baby. It's me."

A shadow played against the corner of the house. Shapeless, it grew like a monstrous blob stretching out beyond the borders of the porch light.

"Definitely not Fox," Sage whispered under her breath and rose to her feet, ready to meet the owner of that ominous darkness.

Mark stepped out from the corner of the house, Fox at his side. "More than you bargained for, I'd imagine?"

His tone matched the shadow, dark and foreboding. For maybe the first time in all her life, Mark didn't seem happy to see her. Had she made a huge mistake?

"I thought you'd have more sense than to come here." Deep lines had etched into Mark's brow and the creases of his eyes as if he'd aged thirty years since their last meeting. "You had to know that once the order was given, I could no longer protect you. You're smarter than that. Why didn't you run?"

Grey's words, but echoed in another voice. Everyone was telling her to run and hide, but that wouldn't save her in the long run. Her palm ached with constant hunger as it slowly devoured her from within.

"You know why." Her voice cracked as she struggled to control the sinking feeling in the pit of her stomach. "You sent us on a mission."

"A fool's errand, I'm afraid." Mark blinked slowly, as if trying to shut her out as he admitted his failing. "I'm so sorry for what's been done to you."

"Are you? Because it's all your fault." She hated throwing that in his face, but if he planned to betray her, she'd at least make sure he felt every inch of the knife he'd buried in her back.

"You're not entirely wrong," Mark agreed. He refused to look at her. Instead, he seemed to take more interest in Fox, standing dutifully at his side.

When had she become so important to him? No doubt his overwhelming guilt was manifesting as this sudden inability to look her in the eye. *Good. He should feel shame.* He'd raised her like a daughter. *You don't betray family.*

"Do the right thing now. Help me." Sage hoped if there was some shred of decency left in him, Mark would help her.

"I am doing what I must to fix this unfortunate situation," Mark replied. "ASSET can't let word get out about the WMD. Its power cannot be unleashed. That is the reason it must be carried by a Terra. It must constantly be on the move so those who would seek to abuse its power can never find its true location."

"And they won't," Sage blurted.

Mark lifted his gaze, revealing tear-filled eyes, already mourning her loss. "The moment you used the seed, you revealed its location. The shadow clans, Mystics, and every other power-hungry mob in our realm will have heard of your power. They'll hunt you to the ends of the earth and claim you or the power you wield."

"Sage." Grey's distant call barely registered past the thundering of her heart. "We need to go. He's stalling."

"Not yet." Sage clamped down on her fear with rage at the implications of what Mark had just revealed. Not simply a betrayal. He'd groomed her to stand before the firing squad. No. That couldn't be. She had to have heard him incorrectly. "What exactly are you saying," – she couldn't speak his name; the word caught in her throat, – "Director?"

Mark looked away again. *Coward.* "The seed must be protected at all costs."

Rage, fear, disappointment. Everything came crashing down on her like the weight of the world. "But what about the spell?" she pleaded. "You said the spell would separate me from the seed safely."

"A hunch." He sighed, shaking his head as he looked down at Fox. He didn't deserve her. Unconditionally loyal, she stood waiting, tail wagging, happy to comply with his every wish. No ulterior motives. No betrayal. "The ritual is not a guarantee."

"And that's not enough to try?" Her voice broke as she fought back tears. He didn't deserve to see them. She struggled to hide her trembling arms, desperate to unleash all the pain. She'd punch the wall if only it would give her some relief.

"My hands are tied, Sage. You've topped the magical most wanted list. We're past the point of quiet containment. It's time to hit the reset button."

"This is my life you're talking about. There is no reset button."

"Be reasonable, Sage."

"You were like a father to me once. I can't believe you would be so willing to sacrifice me. I see now what matters most to you."

"You're upset. You're not seeing this clearly." He took a step forward, his hands held out as if he were closing in for a hug.

Sage balled hers into tight fists, bringing them up, ready to strike if he so much as came within reach.

Fox remained at Mark's side, but her tail no longer wagged freely. Sage prayed he would not use the dog against her.

The sound of Grey unsheathing his blades from his belt, soft as it was, stopped Mark in his tracks.

"I am not sacrificing you." Mark's calm tone did nothing to soothe Sage's nerves. "But I do need to bring you in where you will be safely contained so we can remove the seed."

"Ava already tried that and failed," Grey answered gruffly.

"You will be dealt with as well, Mr. Maddox."

"Keep threatening. I'm fast losing any respect or loyalty I might have once felt for you." Sage held her ground, though every muscle in her body trembled with unspent energy.

"Don't be so dramatic." Mark employed his fatherly voice.

"He's shown his hand. He's stalling for reinforcements." Grey spoke with more urgency. "Why aren't we leaving now?"

"Because I'm afraid if I move, it will be to do something I will regret," Sage replied.

"Anger will not stop the inevitable. Nor will guilt. But your accomplice is right. The longer you stay, the faster you march towards fate." Mark dropped his fatherly tone, letting all emotion fade from his words until all that remained was the mechanical ramblings of a tired, hollow old man. "Our purpose is to balance magic. To prevent wars and the death that follows. You saw, during your awakening. You witnessed the horror. We all get a glimpse of destruction that led to our creation. We all swore an oath when we joined ASSET. We all must do our duty. No matter how hard it is. No matter the sacrifice."

"Purpose, balance, bullshit. Go preach to someone who gives a damn. This is my life, and I will fix it myself! Give me the spell."

Grey came to stand in front of her. "We will fix this together. But now we really need to leave."

"You know I can't just let you leave." Mark crossed his arms as if the act alone amplified his authority.

"I don't see a team here to stop us," Grey replied, his machetes at the ready.

"Don't need one." He whistled and Fox snapped to attention. Mark pointed a finger toward Sage. "Fetch."

Fox took off in a sprint toward Sage. She turned and made a break for the street. The dog was fast. Before she reached the curb, Fox tackled her to the ground. She rolled away, bringing her arms up to cover her face. Fox stood over her, snarling, teeth bared and ready to strike, but she did not make the killer blow even when she had the opportunity. Sage wasn't taking any chances. Trained or not, it didn't take much for a dog to do some serious damage. And she didn't want to injure Fox. She pushed against the animal's chest in a vain attempt to move her. One hundred pounds of stubborn, snarling dog was a lot harder to budge than she had anticipated. Her fingers slipped through Fox's soft coat as she tried to find a grip that wouldn't cause pain. Her pinky finger caught on the dog's collar. Perfect. She threw both hands up and took hold of the collar, intending to use it to force Fox aside, but the collar broke off in her hand.

"Call your dog off!" Grey shouted.

Mark whistled and Fox stopped snarling. The dog and Sage both turned to look at Mark. Grey had him up against the side of the house, machete at his throat.

"Call her back now," Grey ordered.

"Come," Mark gave the order.

"Sage, get to the rendezvous point." Grey's tone was not to be argued with.

She took off just like Fox had, running in the opposite direction. Her lungs burned as she pushed herself to move fast toward the bike.

When she got there, she jumped on and started it. "C'mon, Grey, get here." She glanced over her shoulder, around the corner. Every shadow could be an agent hidden, waiting to follow her. Waiting to strike.

Grey appeared, sheathing his machete, looking as if he'd lost all faith in the world. "Sage, I'm so sorry."

"You didn't…" She couldn't finish the sentence. As angry as she was, she might have done it herself. But even as betrayed as she felt, knowing his fate wasn't something she wanted.

"No. I didn't. He is the director of ASSET after all."

She blew out a breath and brought her hand up to wipe the sweat from her brow, realizing she still had Fox's collar. It had snapped off. Strange for it to do that. And now that she had a better look at it, it wasn't a typical collar at all.

"…we'd definitely be on the most wanted list." Grey continued speaking even though Sage wasn't looking at him. "We need to get the hell out of here. All that stalling, he's sure to have alerted his team. This place will be crawling with them any moment."

"Yeah. Sure." She stared down at the collar in her hand. Why was it so thick? She turned it over and found a zipper hiding under a flap of nylon cloth.

"What are you doing?" Grey asked.

"Fox's collar." She held it up.

"Could have a tracker in it." Grey grabbed it and turned it over in his hands. "Here." He fished out the zipper's pull and opened a hidden pocket. "Wait. It's paper."

"Let me see." She opened it up.

Notes scrawled in Mark's handwriting described the spell and its components. Sage sat numb, the note shaking in her trembling hands. Tears she had fought so hard to hide came bursting to the surface, flooding her vision. Despite all he'd said, and the horrible way she had just treated him, Mark had come through for her.

"Thank you," she sobbed.

Grey took the note and pocketed it.

"Save the tears for later. We're not out of the woods yet." He mounted the bike and put Mark's home in the rearview mirrors.

TWENTY-THREE

Their ride back had been a disturbingly quiet one. Sage spent most of it trying to understand Mark's true intentions. At face value, he'd been a company man, but placing the spell in Fox's collar had been a conscious effort, meaning he must have known she'd come for him. But if he'd known it, chances were others might have made the connection too. It was no secret how close he had been with her all through the years. And still, no one was there waiting to take her in. It was hard enough being a magical secret agent, but to be a double agent... How could anyone keep their allegiances straight?

Grey rushed into the motel room like a man on a mission. "Pack up. We can't stay here tonight."

"But I thought you said we'd be okay." All Sage wanted to do was fall face forward into the mattress and sleep. Things might make more sense in the morning. And if they didn't, at least she would be well rested and less achy. Fox had really knocked her hard. "Mark let us go."

"He may have let us go, but ASSET wants us, and you've had a tail since we left Vegas."

Sage looked behind her, almost expecting to see one wagging at her backside.

"Followers," Grey groaned. He pulled the hat off his head and flung it on the bed. "You're being hunted. The Mystics won't have given up so easy, and both they and ASSET know we are in Phoenix. There's no reason for us to stay any longer."

Sage moved to the bedside table and pulled on the drawer. The crystals, candles, and smudge sticks they'd bought earlier were the only things worth packing. She hadn't brought much to begin with.

"Is this how it's going to be?" She didn't mean to sound so angry, but the day had taken its toll on her, and looking down the barrel of another sleepless night – on the run – didn't help her temper.

"We can't stay in the same place for too long. Not when we're so close to fixing you."

Her hand ached less than her bruised hip or sore ribs, but Grey's choice of words coaxed out the pain she'd been trying to ignore. The seed hadn't been fed since…she couldn't remember when. Her fingertips were beginning to blacken. Darkness crept down the heel of her hand like weedy vines searching for new skin to cling too. How long before they reached her mark – the Tree of Life –and erased it?

"Don't do that." Grey's order stopped her from sinking down into the pit her mind had created. When she looked up, there he was, taking her blackened hand in his, as if he could shield her from the darkness. "You can't lose focus." His eyes lingered on hers even as he gently massaged away the pain of her ruined hand. "We're only a couple nights to the full moon, and we still have a lot of ground to cover."

His confidence was infectious. Their plan was a long shot at best, but Grey talked as if it were a guarantee, and all she needed to do was believe and it would be so. She wanted to believe it, but short of true faith, having tasks to accomplish – goals, a purpose, at the very least a distraction – was exactly the thing she needed.

"Right, where do we go?"

He released her hand and pulled the folded page Mark had given them from his pocket. "We need allies." Grey flopped down on the mattress and stared into the crumpled paper for a few moments. His eyes moved swiftly from side to side as he went over the lines. The corners of his lips twitched, not quite lifting into a smile or hardening to a frown.

Sage watched the war going on over his features, all the while wondering if he might not have an answer at all and was simply stalling for time.

"The spell calls for the essence of the three families. And we need a practitioner to perform the ritual."

"You have someone in mind?"

He set the page face down on the mattress. "Devon is normally the one to go to for this kind of thing."

"No!"

Grey stared at her as if she'd just slapped him. "What?"

She hadn't meant to blurt it out so loudly. Devon was exactly the person she would have chosen. Her go-to guy for information and a good ass kicking. But for exactly those reasons, he was the worst choice. "I had a feeling deep down that Mark was on our side."

"But you don't get that feeling for Devon?"

"Let me finish," she cut him off impatiently. "I'm not saying I don't trust him. I do. In any other circumstance, I would go straight to him. But..."

"Oh, I can't wait to hear this." Grey chuckled in disbelief.

"He's in Ava's inner circle of trust. Think about it. Of all the people she could have had me work with during my" – she air quoted – "administrative leave… Who did Ava send me to talk to with her blessing to be honest?"

"He's been around for a very long time." Grey looked as if he were about to call her Captain Obvious again, but she beat him to the punch.

"Exactly. We can't compromise that by bringing him in. To maintain his good reputation, we have to keep him out of the loop."

"You've got a point," Grey agreed. "He was our best resource, though."

"But not our only one." She winced at the thought of having to resort to such a risky prospect, but desperate times… "We have another." It meant going out on a serious limb, totally thinking outside of the box, but her instincts had been pretty good lately, and if her plan panned out, it could be a huge victory.

"You don't mean…" Grey looked like he was going to be sick. "We can't trust… No. Have you learned nothing about their kind? That's suicide! Might as well turn yourself in before you're hand delivered to the Mystics."

She hadn't even gotten the name out, and Grey was already throwing in the towel. Understandable after what he'd told her about Yasmine. Even when you think you know who to trust, someone can always stab you in the back, or rip out your throat. But the fact remained they had no good options, and rather than fearing every shadow, they'd have to learn to move with them.

"I get what you're saying. But the fact is, we can't do this ourselves. We do not have magic."

"No. The answer is no."

"My life is on the line. No ritual, no more me." Sage held up her hand again, her blackened palm a few inches from his stubborn face. "We have to do what we can to fix this."

"Haven't you learned anything? You cannot trust those creatures. I'd rather risk Devon's reputation than the alternative."

"I'm not destroying someone else's life to save mine."

"I didn't mean it like that."

"Yes, you did." She moved to sit next to him and rested her head on his shoulder. "I appreciate how much you want to save me, but we can't bring others down to do it." Great big jerk that he was, his heart was in the right place. The longer they spent together, the more she saw the depths of his caring. He tried to hide it, pretending to be the tough guy, but she'd seen what lay behind his emotional armor. "We don't have any other options. We're going back to Vegas, and you're going to help me sneak into the Sortilage Staffing Solutions building."

"Wait. What?" Grey sprung from the bed so fast he nearly knocked her over.

"Sylvia's office." Sage could have sworn she had said it earlier. Maybe she hadn't. That would certainly explain Grey's crazy eyes.

"Is that who you were talking about?"

"Yeah, who did you think I meant?"

"Zack," Grey announced as if it were obvious.

He was the last person she'd have thought to go to. Zack already had his plate full with Matt's training. "Why? What could he do to help us?"

"I just thought… You two… No. Never mind. You want to talk to Sylvia?"

"Yeah. She saw me take out the amulet. She saw me drop Luke, but she hasn't made any threats against me. And if you remember when Devon called his secret meeting when the seed was thought to be missing the first time? If we all trust Devon, then by extension, I believe the people he trusted are just as worthy."

"That's a big *if.*" Grey sat on the opposite bed, facing Sage. Shock had not faded from his eyes. If anything, he appeared even more apprehensive about Sylvia than he'd been under the assumption of going to the vampires. "How do we know she's not in league with the Mystics?"

"We don't. But short of anything concrete, we have to go on faith." Even as she was trying to convince Grey, deep down, Sage still needed convincing herself. Their backs were to the wall. Do or die, and in her case, the division wasn't exactly fifty-fifty.

"You have a death wish." Grey scrubbed his face with his hands, growling like a wild animal before flopping backwards on the mattress. "I get it now. You want to die."

"I want to live. More than anything. And that's not going to happen if we go back to ASSET. And good as you are with those blades, you can't protect me twenty-four-seven, for eternity, or however long I have before the seed kills me. We don't have good options. Not a single one. What we have are a fist full of really shady options, and if even one pans out, it's better than the alternative."

"Is this from some nerdy war movie?"

"What?"

"The whole inspirational speech thingy you just tried to do there."

"Really? Why do I bother talking to you? It just passes through that dead space between your ears, doesn't it?"

"Struck a nerve, didn't I?"

"Do you want me to talk about the hat?" she teased.

"It's a great hat." He picked it up off the bed and spun it on his finger.

Sage whispered a curse under her breath. How does a man like Grey, with all his weapons and combat training, get all bent out of shape over a stupid hat? "We need to talk to Sylvia and see what she knows and if she might be able to help us."

"I'm going to regret this."

"Think positively. If we die, you won't regret it for long." Sage picked up her bag, threw it over her shoulder, and headed for the door.

TWENTY-FOUR

"For the record, this is the worst idea you've ever had," Grey said as he sprayed a can of paint over the dome of a security camera. The backside of the Staffing Solutions building appeared more warehouse than office space. He went to work on the locked door, while Sage stood guard. They'd made it back to Vegas before sunrise, and headed straight for Sylvia's office. She seemed the type of boss who'd be there before her minions had their first cup of coffee so they couldn't afford to waste time.

Grey struggled to get the lock to release, grunting and growling as he slid a length of bended metal between the sliver of a gap on the back doors. "Just a little more."

"Is this going to work?" Sage asked.

"These doors should have a panic bar to exit. One of those safety mechanisms so that employees can't get locked inside. I just have to get the metal in the right spot and be touching the door to trigger the magnetic release."

"When do I get to take the class on lock breaking?" She laughed.

The door clicked, and Grey pulled against the handle. It opened. "It's called life experience." He ushered her inside and pulled the door closed behind him.

They found their way through the dark easily enough. Sylvia's office was at the back of the building, and there were only so many executive offices. Her light was on as they approached. Sage's palm began to burn with hunger at the prospect of such powerful magic within her reach. She clenched her fist tight.

Sage had hoped to have the element of surprise on her side, but nothing had worked as they'd expected so far, so why should this be any different? She took a breath to ready herself for Sylvia's abrasive personality, reminding herself that she needed help. She had to play nice.

Now or never. Sage rounded the corner and stepped into Sylvia's office, head held high. "Good morning!"

"Of all the people I would expect to break into my office, you were the last on my list." Sylvia smiled with an eerie, satisfied look. "I do hope you will clean the mess you made on my security camera before you go."

"That will depend on how well this meeting goes." Grey followed Sage through the door.

"Should I be afraid, Agent Maddox?" Sylvia's tone was anything but fearful. Her body began to shift into inky smoke.

Sage had noted Sylvia's tell. Her emotions were tied to the way she appeared. Keeping the shadowrunner corporeal was the goal.

"We're not here in any official capacity." Sage took the lead, slowly approaching Sylvia's desk. She kept her damaged hand behind her back, out of sight. Better to save that reveal for when she absolutely needed it. "I know you don't like ASSET as it is—"

"From what I hear," Sylvia interrupted, "ASSET doesn't like you these days."

"Where are you getting your information?" Grey snarled.

"You're here because you need something from me, Mr. Maddox, so I suggest you drop the machismo aggressiveness before I decide to turn you in to your bosses myself."

"Mercenaries, agents, and a crazed wolfhound have all tried to take us out in the last twenty-four hours," he fired back. "You think you can top them? Please, be my guest."

"Fox is not a wolfhound," Sage added.

"Might as well have been." Grey shrugged casually, but gave Sage the side eye all the same. "She was bigger than any dog I've seen."

"A dog?" Sylvia returned to her fully corporeal self, laughing madly. "Agent Maddox was scared off by a dog? Oh, I do need to hear this story."

"Maybe, if you drop the hate and help us." Sage slipped onto the chair in front of Sylvia's desk.

"I do have a serious distrust for an agency with so much control and so little oversight." Sylvia folded her hands on the desk. "Do not mistake that with my annoyance at your lack of respect in breaking and entering, Miss Cynwrig."

"We can discuss our fundamental differences later. If there is a later." Grey came up behind Sage and placed a hand on her shoulder. "At this moment, however, we need to know if you will be willing to help us."

"Why come to me? Out of curiosity." Sylvia leaned forward, her coal black eyes scanning Sage's face then moving up toward Grey as if hunting for some clue.

"You're smart, Sylvia," Sage began sincerely. "You and I both know that the amulet you were trapped in couldn't have been shattered by a simple Terra's touch."

"A curiosity for sure." Sylvia brought her hands closer to her mouth, fingertips touching her lips gently.

"And with your distaste for the agency I work for, a curiosity like that could be valuable," Sage continued.

Sylvia's eyebrow arched. "You are not wrong."

"And if Devon had not vouched for you on our first meeting, I would be stupid to come to you." Sage stared straight at Sylvia defiantly.

"And yet you came to me and not him." Sylvia smirked.

"He's got a reputation to maintain here, and as you have put it, we're at odds with our employer at the moment. Not going to tarnish his reputation with my plan."

"She has a plan now." Sylvia's gaze flitted upwards to Grey again. "Enlighten me."

Sage tapped Grey's hand, still resting on her shoulder. "Show her. Please."

He pulled the spell from his pocket and moved between Sage and Sylvia to lay it out on the desk.

Eager excitement brightened Sylvia's eyes. Her form shifted again, disappearing into a puff of black smoke and returning just as quickly. They definitely had her interest piqued.

"May I?" Sylvia asked as she became solid again.

Grey nodded and let his hands fall to his side.

Sylvia took the spell in hand. Confusion furrowed her brow as she studied the crinkled paper. "What exactly are you trying to remove with this spell? Terras are impervious to magic."

Sage took a deep breath, hoping she'd read Sylvia's body language right. Praying that she wasn't making the hugest mistake of her life. She held up her blackened hand, aching to absorb all the magic from the room, and opened her palm to face Sylvia.

The shadowrunners' eyes lit up like a child at Christmas. It took all of Sage's strength to hold her hand still. The seed's pull was magnetic, wanting to connect with the powerful magic only a few feet away.

Sylvia reached out as if planning to take Sage's hand, or perhaps she, too, was feeling the pull of the seed's hunger.

"Don't touch!" Sage used all her strength to pull her hand back and clutched it tightly to her chest. She clamped her free hand over the damaged one, shielding it from view as the seed burned with raw hunger, punishing her for daring to deny it the prize. Sage panted through the pain. No doubt Sylvia saw the effect it was having, but Sage wouldn't give her the pleasure of seeing her cry.

"Is that what I think it is?" The question came with a much softer tone than Sage had ever heard Sylvia utter.

"I can't confirm exactly what it is, because I myself have no name for it, and ASSET couldn't classify it either." She stretched the truth as far as she could, not wanting to be caught in a lie. "What it does, however, is remove magic from anyone I touch, and when it's not feeding on magic, it's killing me."

"The rumors are true." Sylvia spoke with hushed surprise. "I suspected as much when I saw you with the amulet."

"Did you speak of your suspicions with anyone?" Grey asked.

"What kind of a fool do you take me for, Mr. Maddox?" Annoyance turned Sylvia's voice up sharply.

Sage wanted to reply in defense of Grey but found it hard to speak with the seed burning its way through her hand.

"I know better than to speculate wildly about such powerful magic." Sylva's form began to shift again, fading into vapors. "But I do keep my ears open when that magic is revealed. You, dear," – she solidified again, spearing Sage with her dark stare – "are the subject of a great deal of gossip these days. The Mystics are offering a bounty for anyone who can bring you in alive."

"We know," Grey mumbled.

"The dog?" Sylvia snickered.

"No." Sage's voice broke. "That was ASSET."

"You will have to tell me that story sometime." Sylvia chuckled lightly.

Grey folded his arms across his chest, clearly not amused. "Sage is being hunted right now, and we believe that spell is the key to saving her, and removing her from the magical most wanted list."

"If it works. I seriously doubt that was what this spell was intended for." Sylvia waved the handwritten page in the air. "If I've read this correctly, you're trying to invoke the Gods' own power here."

"It's the best lead we have right now," Grey said. "Just look at what that thing is doing to her."

Sage struggled to regain her composure. The proximity to Sylvia had more than just her hand on fire. The pain was spreading across her entire body. She stood and began pacing the office, hoping the motion would help lessen the pain.

"What exactly do you want me to do?" Sylvia's tone softened again.

"Hide us, for one," Sage replied, pain sharpening her voice.

"In the center of one of the busiest Supernatural Staffing Agencies on the West Coast?" Sylvia scoffed.

"Don't pretend you lack the resources," Grey replied.

"What you lack is a sense of diplomacy, Mr. Maddox."

"We're all tired and grumpy. No one has slept much in the last forty-eight hours." Sage completed another circuit around the office, trying as hard as she could to maintain her cool. "You're going to have to forgive the attitude. Please."

"From you, I can," Sylvia replied. "He, however, has never once shown an ounce of respect for me or my operation here."

"He's doing his best to keep me safe." Sage reached across the expanse as she closed in and took his hand. A show of solidarity.

Her pain reflected in Grey's eyes. Sage knew he couldn't feel the burn, but it was there in his expression, empathy for what she was enduring. And somehow, holding on to him helped to distract her from the constant ache.

"If I hide you, what then?" Sylvia asked.

"You have access to an impressive amount of resources," Grey replied. He squeezed Sage's hand before letting it drop. "We need participants for the spell. People who are trustworthy enough to respect the sensitive nature of the curse affecting Sage."

"Well now, you don't ask for much, do you?" Sylvia let out a full belly laugh. The paper fell to the desk as she shifted again between smoke and skin.

"At least give us a place to lie low," Sage pleaded. Whatever the answer, they needed to end this meeting soon. The sun had risen, brightening the office window, and as employees began arriving for work, she could feel the seed's intensity amplifying. "If you don't want to help further, I understand. We can figure out the rest."

Sylvia took out a small notebook and scrawled a few lines before folding it and passing it to Grey. "Go here. Ask for Jemma to set you up in a room. My account." She looked at the spell one more time and then to her desk calendar. "You only have a few days to pull this off. You have a location?"

"Sedona," Grey replied.

"Spiritual vortex. Smart." Sylvia nodded approvingly and added a note on her calendar. "Which location?"

"We haven't scouted yet, but we'll need a place away from prying eyes." Thankfully, Grey had the answers and was giving them civilly so Sage could focus on keeping herself calm.

"Let me see if I understand. You need a team to assemble, in Sedona, by the full moon? Again. Don't ask much, do you?"

"We may not need a full team," Grey replied.

Sylvia's eyebrow arched. "Explain?"

"It calls for essence from the magical families." Grey pointed to a line on the paper. "But farther down, blood must be offered. I'm willing to bet that's what is needed more than a physical body."

"The practitioner should be easy." Sylvia pointed to herself with a sly grin. "It doesn't appear to specify a family lineage for that, but blood of the houses is going to be tricky to obtain."

"I might have the Elemental covered," Sage spoke up.

Grey's jaw tightened. He didn't like it when she surprised him. They hadn't discussed anything further than asking for Sylvia's help.

She'd apologize for that later, maybe after she put her hand on ice. "Our first priority is a safe place to operate from."

"And what is my compensation for helping?" Sylvia tapped her pen on the desk calendar.

"What exactly are you after?" Grey crossed his arms again and stared down his nose at Sylvia.

"Quid pro quo. Of course," she replied sharply. "You are asking me to go behind ASSET's back. In the future, I may need to do so again, and I need assurances that my friends will keep the agency off my back."

"You know we can't give you a blank check," Grey scoffed.

"If you trust me as you say… Because Devon vouches for me." Sylvia smiled sweetly. "Then you would know my desire for a little autonomy is not for nefarious reasons."

"In my experience, those who feel the need to clarify the good of their intentions rarely ever are," Grey replied without missing a beat.

"I've given my terms." Sylvia turned to smoke again, but her voice maintained its resonance. "You want my help or not?"

Grey and Sage exchanged nervous glances. Sylvia was one of the best connected people in the magical community. She had the access they needed, but the favor she'd asked in return had dangerous implications for the future.

"You're asking for something we have no power to give," Grey replied earnestly. "Even if we do succeed, we're wanted by our own people. You think they're just going to let us go with a slap on the wrist? If we're lucky, we'll be re-stationed in some remote location in Siberia serving our time where they can assure we won't cause trouble again."

"And if we're not lucky…" Sage found the strength to control her voice. "After this curse is removed, I'll be sent to the firing squad for abuse of magic."

"Ava will have her brought before the Magical Confederacy for sentencing," Grey added. "It will not matter to ASSET if we break this curse or not."

"But it will matter to me." Sage's voice broke like a teenager going through puberty.

Sylvia's smoky silhouette solidified again, her expression surprisingly empathetic as her gaze returned to Sage.

"You are in trouble, aren't you?" Sylvia asked.

"All magic comes at a price." Sage attempted to look casual as she shrugged.

"Doubly so for those who were never meant to have any," Sylvia added.

"So if a night in a safe house is all you can offer us, we will gladly take it and be out of your hair." Grey reached across the desk and retrieved the spell.

"I've always liked you," Sylvia said, her attention locked on Sage standing as far across the office as she could. "You are genuine."

"Thank you," Sage replied.

"Unlike Agent Maddox here who goes in with strength and superiority, you try reason, and dare I say, a bit too much truth. Loose lips sink ships and all. Your partner really needs to teach you a thing or two about what you reveal when dealing with potential threats."

Sage held her breath. She ran through the last few minutes of conversation, wondering if she had revealed more than she should.

"We were hoping you were not a threat." Sage's arms trembled. She balled up her fists and held them behind her back.

"First rule of espionage, dear—never trust anyone. You know the cliché. Keep your enemies close." Sylvia's haughty attitude returned as if someone had flipped on a light switch.

"Okay, I get it," Sage replied, not really sure how to take that comment. She turned to Grey for help, but he, too, appeared confused by Sylvia's sudden change of attitude.

"No. You don't." Sylvia smirked. "Not yet at least. But I do look forward to seeing how your career pans out. Each time we meet, I'm reminded of your potential. If you were my assistant, I could mold you into something great."

"I'm not really sure where all this is going," Sage said.

"Trust is a two-way street," Sylvia replied. "I'm offering you a safe house. Cloaking you within my shadow as it were. Knowing that the secret you're failing to keep is one ASSET would gladly kill over."

"We have no intention of naming our helpers," Grey assured her.

"I should hope not." Sylvia turned her attention to Grey. "Your partner doesn't have a reliable history of keeping secrets. And I would very much hate to see my name dragged through the mud."

"You'd be surprised with how wrong that statement is," Grey replied. "If you choose to help us, I'll make sure your name does not come up."

"Go, then. I'll be in touch if I can be of further assistance." Sylvia waved them off. "And I'll be billing you for the security camera."

TWENTY-FIVE

Sylvia had been as good as her word. The address she gave them belonged to a weekly rental motel. Three star at best, but being blessedly free of magic made it feel like a resort.

Grey moved swiftly around the room, inspecting the door and windows. "Three potential points of exit. The window is large enough but too close to the door for a smooth escape if more than one person comes at us." He wandered into the bathroom. "There is a window in here. It's small. Above the shower. Might want to practice getting up to it."

Sage tried to listen to his assessment, but her throbbing hand demanded attention. She squeezed it into a fist and opened it again, testing the weak muscles.

Grey came out of the bathroom, his gaze fixed on the point of her pain. "How long has it been? Do we need to find you something?"

Sage fought to keep a straight face, but even absent of magic, the seed's insatiable hunger was becoming too much. "I don't know. Maybe."

The alternative wasn't appealing either. The destroyer of magic. All her life, she had wanted to be part of something supernatural. She and her roommate did more than just play at it with their weekly game night. They became clerics, druids, paladins, and wizards, if only for a short time. Magic was beautiful. It could do amazing things. After learning it was real, Sage felt a new level of reverence for it. To become its end was the ultimate betrayal.

Grey was at her side. His hand found her chin, gently lifting he urged her to look up at him. Somehow he knew exactly what she needed, as if he had a direct line into her thoughts. His hand slid from her chin, cupping her face. She was losing it, her strength fading with every passing second.

"Breathe. It's okay." His fingers tangled in the soft strands of her hair. His eyes held her captive. How did he always have such confidence in those gorgeous eyes? He stared at her, *through* her, as if willing some of his own strength to become hers. "I can't pretend to understand how this feels. I'm sorry. Try to hold it together for a little longer."

He was right. Big jerk that he was. Only, he hadn't been a jerk to her since this whole ordeal started. She almost missed it. Playful banter was so much easier to deal with. A distraction she desperately needed. Matt was always good at snapping her from the doldrums. He'd find some way to pick a fight with her over which Doctor Who was the best.

Matt! She hadn't even considered how he might be feeling. Nor had she made any attempt to contact him or let him know where she was. Even at a distance, her roommate still proved to be the distraction she needed to get over her own drama.

"Dammit, I'm the worst!" She pulled free from Grey's grasp.

"Don't do this to yourself." He stood frozen, his hand hanging in the air, looking utterly confused by her reaction.

"No. I mean… You're right." She struggled to get the words out. Grey's sudden tenderness mixed with her own inadequacy had short-circuited her brain. So many thoughts and feelings she wasn't capable of handling attacked her all at once, reducing her to a neurotic mess. "Matt… I'm terrible… He's…worried" – she scrambled to put words in the right order – "or stressed…or something."

Grey let his hand drop like a dead weight. "Take a breath and try that again."

"I did it to him again. When you came to me the first time, I left Matt wondering if I was dead or alive. And here I did it again."

"Extenuating circumstance."

"I have to get word to him. At least tell him I'm okay. So he doesn't worry."

"But you're not okay yet. Can't this wait until we've fixed…" He pointed rather than finish the sentence.

"What if it doesn't fix this?" Sage brought her throbbing hand up to eye level. "I can't leave him worrying forever. Especially since he's a…you know."

Grey's expression darkened. "Are you afraid to say the word vampire around me now? I shouldn't have told you about Yasmine."

"You were right. I'm glad you did. I'm just…" Her mind ran slower than her mouth. The words weren't coming as quickly as she needed them. How could she make Grey understand the swarm of fear and uncertainty that had suddenly enveloped her? Concern for her friend had given her the strength she needed to hold up against her own pain, but knowing she was the cause of someone's pain brought on another level of stress that at any moment could snap her in two. "Part of his control, according to Zack, was me being around. What if my leaving has back-fired? Made him go feral or something?"

"You really do go from zero to apocalypse at the drop of a hat, don't you?" Grey's lip quirked up as if he were ready to laugh at the joke he'd just made.

She hadn't found it all that funny.

"Zack will keep him plenty busy while we're working to solve your issues."

"How can you be sure?" She clearly hadn't articulated herself well enough for Grey to understand. "Zack only turned him for me, and if I am out of the picture, what's to stop him from giving up and returning to business as usual?"

"It's not the vampire way." Grey flopped down on the bed closest to the door and pulled his hat over his face. "They get in trouble for siring someone and not training them to function in society."

"I'd feel a whole lot better if I made sure his motivations were genuine," Sage said. "And let Matt know I haven't died yet. Maybe I could just call."

"You really do have a death wish." Grey lifted his hat just enough to make eye contact. "But seeing as you won't take no for an answer, can you at least try and think like a secret agent?"

"Meaning?"

"Don't call him directly. Phone lines could be tapped. Whatever message you want to get to him, do it through another channel." He dropped his head and let the hat cover his face again.

Sage thought for a moment then walked to the bedside table and picked up the phone. "I know what to do."

"Think like a spy." Grey's muffled voice filtered through his hat.

"Secret Agent Sage here." She saluted, dialed, and waited as the phone rang.

It continued to ring. Longer than normal. Her hope of hearing a human voice began to wane, and then the voice mail prompted her to leave a message.

"Hey, Josh, I dropped my phone in the toilet. Can you get a message to Matt and let him know I won't be able to make it to Taco Tuesday. Stuck on a business trip in Phoenix. Be back as soon as I can." She disconnected the call.

"Nicely done." Grey's chuckle coaxed her into a smile.

She noticed her hand wasn't hurting quite as much either. Perhaps stress had something to do with the pain. Maybe the seed fed on more than just magic.

Grey rolled over on his side, letting the hat fall to the mattress as he faced her. "Now, are you going to tell me about this second contact you alluded to back there with Sylvia?"

She'd forgotten about him. Really, it had only been a flicker of inspiration, but as she recalled their first meeting, Devon had brought together three of the magical families. Sylvia, a Shade. Nyx, an Ethereal. And Aquaman. "Another one of Devon's guys."

"The Elemental? Quarn?" Grey nailed it on his first guess.

"What's your read on him?"

"I don't trust him," Grey replied without hesitation.

"Do you trust anyone?"

"He seemed a little too eager to find out what the artifact was when we questioned him before."

She might have been too naïve, but Grey swung hard in the opposite direction. Together, they equaled the right amount of hope and skepticism, but that didn't make agreeing on anything easy. "You don't think he was trying to help?"

"I think if given the choice, he would keep the weapon for himself."

She hadn't gotten the power-hungry vibe from Quarn. Collector maybe. Religious type for sure. Probably would do anything to hold a relic of the Great Mother in his wet hands. "To use or keep as a trophy?" She wondered aloud.

"Are we really having this conversation? Either way, the answer is no."

"Of course we can't let anyone keep it. But motive makes the difference in how far you can trust someone."

"You really are trying to think like a secret agent, aren't you?" Grey laughed.

"I'll pretend I didn't hear you actually complimenting me."

"Good, because I'd deny it, even under torture," he replied with unexpected playfulness that coaxed out her smile.

"I don't know if you're that strong," she teased.

"Haven't broken yet." He dared her to try with a cocky waggle of his eyebrows.

"See, that's the thing. You're assuming torture is the rack. What if…" – she crawled onto the mattress next to him and reached out slowly – "someone were to employ more devious methods of information extraction?"

He sucked in a breath, his chest expanding as if his muscles were reaching for her open palms. His pupils dilated. "What nefarious methods are you planning?" His voice came on a low rumble, like the purr of a predatory cat.

This was a side of him she hadn't seen before, but could definitely get used to. Desire vibrated in the pit of her stomach as she closed in on the heat his body radiated. His heartbeat pulsed into her palm, and Sage froze.

She'd planned to start a childish tickle war with him, but now that the moment had come, it suddenly felt…forbidden. Dangerously uncharted territory that had the potential to destroy them both.

She let her eyes linger on Grey's face. For all its hard lines, his eyes held such softness. No doubt his lips would be equally soft. Tempting. Delicious. What price would she pay for a kiss?

Nothing. She wouldn't be the one paying that price. His would be the bill that came due.

He'd shown her his vulnerability, revealing the truth of his past. She'd seen for herself the hard armor he wore to hide the scars left by the death of someone he loved. Sage's life teetered on the edge of that same abyss. Even if they attempted the ritual and invoked the Goddess, her survival wasn't guaranteed. If she died, Grey would yet again be the one left to endure all the pain.

Still, knowing what she should do didn't stop her heart from kicking into overdrive as she gazed deeply into the turquoise depths of Grey's eyes.

Say something! Anything!

"You're right. There's no breaking through your defenses. You're like a rock." She retreated awkwardly.

Grey caught her by the wrist, preventing her escape. "Not with you."

She fought to keep upright, but her legs were turning to jelly. "You forget your training, agent."

"It's agent now? Not jerk, tool, or whatever colorful nickname you want to call me?" He let her go, but the delicious warmth of his grip clung to her skin.

Temptation threatened to do her in. It would be so easy to give in. She clenched her thighs tight against the tingle of arousal beginning to warm within her. As enticing as the fantasy was, for both their sakes, she needed to keep things professional. Sage refused to be the cause of any more pain.

"For now. Yes, Agent Maddox. We're on the run. We have to keep our head in the game. Think like secret agents," she repeated his earlier suggestion. "But maybe, if this mission is a success, we can come up with another moniker for you."

All the softness she'd seen in his face vanished. Grey rolled to the other side of the bed and stood. "Right. We still have much to do. You need something for your hand before we go visit Quarn."

If only she could have held on to that tender moment they'd shared a bit longer. Scary as it was, she wanted to see where it might lead. Reality was the clock counting down. They had a job to do. If it worked, they might have a chance of clearing their names. And then she'd be free to let herself feel something other than fear. If not, she'd have to learn to live on the lam. At least until the seed finally killed her.

Reality left a bad taste in her mouth. Almost as bitter as the side-eye Grey was giving her.

"Thank you," she spoke tenderly. "I wish I could make you understand how much you mean to me. There's just so much fear. I'm drowning in it. I can't pull you down with me."

"So dramatic." Grey scoffed. "I'll be back later. While I'm gone, don't answer the door, phone, or get any wild hairs to go off on your own."

She couldn't blame him for putting the wall back up. Emotional self-preservation and all. If only she had that kind of control. Compartmentalizing. Shoving the emotions down deep. Might make focusing on the end game a lot easier.

"I mean it," Sage said again. "I am so thankful to have you protecting me."

"Then make sure you follow my orders. Stay put until I return." Grey sheathed his machetes into his weapons belt and left the motel room without so much as a look back.

TWENTY-SIX

Grey returned with a silver coin that contained enough magic to quell the seed's hunger. She didn't dare ask how he'd obtained it. Details like that were best left unsaid. Once the pain had subsided, Sage found herself finally able to relax into a deep and dreamless sleep.

Morning came as quick as blinking, but Sage awoke feeling as if she had slept a week.

"You look like you're ready to take on the world." Grey startled her with his chipper greeting.

How long had she slept? Sage turned to the clock on the bedside table. Not quite seven yet, but Grey appeared fully dressed and armed.

"Yeah. Just give me a few minutes to splash some water on my face." Her hand looked as if it might shrivel up and fall off. Still a bit on the stiff side, but Sage moved with less pain than in days past. "Aquaman today, right?"

"Are you going to be able to handle being around that much magic?"

"I've got no choice, do I?" Sage tested her bad hand again, squeezing and flexing. "We should make it a quick trip just to be safe."

"What exactly are you after with him?" Grey asked. "You didn't really explain your plan to me."

"You..." *Nope*. She wasn't going to go there. He hadn't let her reveal her plan. The evening ended quickly with him practically storming from the motel room. She was just as guilty as Grey for daring to cross the line between partners and something more. No use blaming. "I mean, I didn't really have a plan. Just an idea. Something you said."

"I said plenty last night."

"Blood."

His eyebrow lifted.

"You said we would need blood of the families. So, if we can get a donation...maybe." She wasn't really sure of what she needed, and hoped he would be able to fill in those banks.

Grey unfolded his arms and reached for his machetes. "Blood is easy."

Was he trying to be funny? Sage wasn't sure how to read him. "Maybe less hack and slash though."

"Sure, we try diplomacy first. But if that doesn't work..."

"Please tell me you're joking."

"You're too easy. Newbie." Grey chuckled and dropped his hands from his weapon belt. "But we do need to be aware of our surroundings. Also, it might be best if you let me do the talking."

"Are we back to smile and nod status again?" Sage grumbled.

"Sylvia did warn me to keep an eye on what you say, remember." Grey waggled a finger at her, clicking his tongue disapprovingly.

"When did you become all chummy with her?"

"How do you think I was able to get that little trinket for you?"

"I don't like the idea of being in her pocket." Sage let out a defeated sigh. The day had started with such promise, but not even ten minutes in, she was already feeling the grip tighten around her neck.

"We do what we have to do. Focus on the goal." Grey closed the gap between them. He reached out his hand as if to take hers, but stopped before making the connection. "We should get going." He retreated, making his escape toward the door.

TWENTY-SEVEN

Grey had conveniently forgotten to mention that Sylvia had also traded him the use of a car in exchange for his bike. It made sense as his motorcycle could be easily tracked, but without the roar of the engine or the cover of their helmets, the quiet drive to Quarn's estate only served to amplify the unease between them. They'd have to address these feelings. She'd seen the flicker in Grey's eyes. She'd felt it in his touch, and missed it when he'd shied away. But for all her courage in the face of magic, opening herself up to such a powerful connection felt like facing down a dragon armed with nothing but her birthday suit.

By the time they pulled up to the security gate and punched in the code, Sage was ready to jump out and walk the rest of the way to the house herself.

Grey pulled the car up the driveway and cut the engine. "See anything?"

They sat in silence for a moment.

"You thinking Mystics would be here?" Sage hoped not. Surely he would have spoken up if that had been a concern earlier.

"Just keep your eyes open for anything suspicious. Be on our guard. You might trust him, but I don't."

She held back the snarky reply she would have normally employed against his attitude. He was right. Time to put on the game face. Sage gave him a quick nod, and exited the car. The pull of magic had already awoken the ache in her palm. She squeezed her hand tight.

Grey came around to meet her. "You sure you can do this?"

"Yes." She shoved her hand in her pocket and followed behind Grey up to the front door.

Quarn greeted them at the door before they had the chance to ring the bell. They hadn't called ahead, but that didn't seem to matter to the Elemental. He looked as if he'd been waiting.

Grey and Sage exchanged knowing glances. Her intuition had been good thus far, but the fact Quarn didn't register surprise at their sudden visit definitely sent up some red flags.

"Have you made progress with the unknown artifact?" Quarn held open the door, standing just inside the frame, as if waiting for the right phrase to allow them access.

"We have," Grey replied. "Thanks in no small part to the information you provided us."

"It was my pleasure." He held his webbed hand to his chest, and bowed his head ever so slightly. "Please, won't you come, sit, and tell me what you have learned." He stepped aside and waved them into his home.

Sage clenched her fist tight against the pain and followed quietly along behind Grey.

Quarn led them into his living room. Before they had the chance to take a seat, he began, "I must know. Was my theory of a godly artifact correct?"

"We're still under orders to operate with extreme secrecy." Grey took the lead, answering as if they were still operating under ASSET's guidance.

"Of course. ASSET would have a gag order on something of that nature." Quarn smiled as if he'd gotten the answer he wanted. He either did not know or care that they'd been cut off from their employer since the last meeting.

"The artifact is still causing problems," Grey continued without missing a beat. "But we believe we have located a way to neutralize it."

"I had hoped you would be more forthcoming. I have spent my life in study of the gods and their machinations." Quarn took a seat facing them and folded his arms neatly in his lap. "The Great Tree, for example, which bore the fruit that changed three classes into four."

"How many other godly creations have you studied?" Grey leaned forward, his elbows resting against his legs, propping his head in his hands.

Quarn sat in quiet contemplation. The gentle trickle of fountains kept the room from going completely silent as they patiently waited for his reply. "There are so many powerful items that come to mind. Sadly, none have lived up to the rumored power of the tree of life, or the seeds it left behind."

"Seeds?" Sage blurted out.

"Merely a speculation. I do not mean to alarm you." Quarn's calm voice did not betray any emotion, despite the frightening implications of his words. "There was rumored to be one seed. But does not fruit bear more than just a single seed?"

"Let's hope this one is more plum than apple," Grey replied.

"It is a frightening prospect, is it not?" Quarn's tone bordered on excitement rather than apprehension. "Seeds of destruction lying in wait for an unknowing someone to pick them up and use."

"Frightening is certainly an apt word for it." Her aching hand throbbed as if being repeatedly stabbed. And with each passing moment became more unbearable. She breathed through the torment, fighting back the tears watering her eyes.

Grey glanced over, his lips tightening with the strain to keep his tone light. They hadn't yet gotten what they'd come for. "Thinking along those lines, we have discovered a ritual of sorts that might help in neutralizing this kind of god-level magic."

Quarn leaned forward, his calculating gaze darting between them both. "Where did you come across such intriguing data?"

"We pieced it together from all the resources you gave us, and the databases within ASSET," Grey replied.

"I would love to see such a ritual. Perhaps I can document it so that future generations will know." He smiled, all teeth, and for the first time, Sage really noticed how shark-like they were. "So they can be…neutralized…should a wayward seed of destruction be unearthed."

"I'm afraid that's above our paygrade," Grey replied. "ASSET calls the shots when and where people are brought in, especially when we're dealing with such potentially powerful artifacts."

Sage shifted nervously in her seat, trying to find a comfortable position while keeping her hand hidden. Grey reached down, placing his hand in the gap between them.

His touch helped to dampen the pain. She let his arm rest against her, shielding her hand from view.

"Just speculating here. Combating god-level magic would require some kind of invocation. Calling down the god's own power to wield. Never heard of someone actually accomplishing it." Quarn leaned forward so far Sage wondered how he hadn't fallen over. If only she could read his thoughts. "I'm sure ASSET would be aware that improper invoking of magic can have extremely destructive consequences."

For someone simply speculating, he seemed to have hit the nail directly on the head with his assessment. Sage wondered if he'd already known that, why hadn't he offered up the information the last time they'd met?

"Of course." Grey nodded casually. He played his part well, giving an answer without even the slightest hesitation. "And we'd all like to avoid unnecessary casualties. I'm sure you understand."

"Only too well." Quarn's eyes narrowed to slits, but as unhappy as he appeared, his voice remained congenial. "You'd need to perform such magic far away from prying eyes. But if I may, there is a flaw in the plan you have proposed."

"And that is?" Grey asked.

"Pardon my stating the obvious, but you are Terra." Quarn waved a webbed hand between them. "Neither of you can actually channel the magic needed to power the ritual. Without that connection to active magic, you would simply be playacting."

"We have arranged for a practitioner under oath with ASSET," Sage blurted out.

Her partner gave her an annoyed glare, but the longer they sat, the more uncomfortable and twitchy she became.

Coming here was a bad idea. She should have sent Grey alone.

"It saddens me that you did not ask me to take an oath." Quarn straightened up in his seat. "I would have happily offered my services to have the chance to witness a historical event such as that."

"ASSET felt you were too valuable a resource to risk on such a dangerous ritual," Grey offered, so convincingly Sage almost believed it. "As you say, no one has ever accomplished a ritual of this magnitude."

"If I may, why come here to tell me all of this if you did not want me to participate?" Quarn asked.

"We came to ask for a favor of a different sort," Sage said. "The ritual requires some items we do not have at the moment. And some are a bit… How do I put this…unusual."

"You have my attention."

"Mystical Oil of the Ages," she said.

"That's hardly unusual. I can provide you with a book that outlines its recipe and ingredients."

"That would be very helpful, thank you." One step closer. She hoped the next would be just as easy, but she was losing the ability to control her voice. Her hand felt as if it were on fire. She needed to get out of the house fast.

"But that is not all, is it?" Quarn's dark eyes were narrow as slits, but he wasn't staring at her face.

"No." Sage struggled to still her twitching hand. She cleared her throat. "We also need direct links to the original three classes. Blood offerings."

Quarn grew quiet again, leaving Sage to wonder if she shouldn't have let him in on the ritual. Grey had said he seemed too opportunistic and that brought up red flags, but excluding him and then requesting he donate to the cause felt like a slap in the face.

"I may have Elemental blood running through my veins, but I cannot attest to its level of purity," Quarn finally replied.

Was that a polite no?

Sage glanced over at Grey. He'd threatened taking what was needed by force earlier. She hoped that had just been a joke.

"We understand if you are uncomfortable with what we are requesting. It is a lot to ask." Sage stood, the pain in her hand too much to handle. She needed to leave the house now. "We thank you for your help thus far. If ASSET agrees, we will provide you with the results of the ritual once we've had the opportunity to test it." She reached her blackened hand out as if to shake his and immediately pulled back. Her palm pulsed with hungry energy. "Door is this way, right?"

Those shark-like eyes of his shifted quickly. He'd seen the full extent of the damage to her hand.

Stupid, stupid Sage! She shoved it back into her pocket and turned away, hoping to hide her embarrassment.

Quarn cleared his throat. "Please, Agent Cynwrig. You misunderstand me. I was not rejecting your request I was only offering knowledge. My blood might not be pure enough, but you are welcome to use it if it is necessary for this powerful ritual."

"Grey will handle that part. You'll have to excuse me if I don't watch. I need some air." Praying she had not just revealed more than she should have, Sage made a break for the car, leaving Grey and Quarn alone to their donation.

TWENTY-EIGHT

A red light flashed on the motel room phone as they came inside.

"Message from Sylvia maybe?" Sage suggested hopefully, and walked to the bedside table.

"We're not that lucky." Grey closed the door behind them and moved to peek out of the window. "Don't get too comfortable."

Sage hesitated, wondering if she really wanted to tempt fate and pick up the receiver. Bad news on an empty stomach—never a good idea. But what if Grey's pessimism proved wrong? Good news would be reason to celebrate with a burger from that greasy spoon joint they'd seen on the way in. *Yes. Positivity will out.*

She followed the instructions on the phone, and Josh's recorded voice played back her worst fear. Score one for pessimism.

Grey remained at the window, his head tilted, observing the parking lot, leaving his left ear like a little radar dish to hear the whispered curse she uttered. To his credit, he didn't reply with 'I told you so,' or anything snarky at all.

She wished he had. If only to give her a flimsy excuse to lash out. But even then, it wouldn't be fair to loose her rage on him just because the universe failed to provide a punching bag to go along with all the bullshit it kept throwing at her. There was no enemy she could look forward to destroying. She had become the villain of her own story, the root cause of everything going wrong in her life.

The path of self-pity was a wicked little demon whispering in her ear. Mark might have been right. She did belong under lock and key at ASSET where her destructive force could be contained.

Where was Devon when she needed him? He'd never let her entertain such a victim's mentality. He'd kick her ass into gear or knock her out cold so she couldn't wallow.

Her eyes burned with tears, but she refused to let them fall. She didn't need to bother Devon. Sage knew exactly what he'd say. She could either lie down and accept defeat or get up and do something about it.

Josh's message was just another hurdle to get over.

"One problem down, one more to go." Sage hung the phone back on the receiver.

"One more?" Grey spun around to face her.

"Josh hasn't seen or heard from Matt in days."

"How did he get this number?" Disbelief crinkled the space between his eyebrows.

"I don't know, probably just redialed the number from his call log." She shrugged off his question with a huff. Grey wasn't focusing on the important part of what she'd just said. "I need to check up on Matt. Just to be sure he's safe."

"Zack's far from a rookie. I'm sure he is just keeping Josh and Matt apart for safety reasons."

Grey had no loyalty to either of them. No reason to care about their well-being. Zack was nothing more than a means to an end. He knew nothing of Matt except that she thought of him like family. How could he possibly understand the fear turning her blood to ice?

"I hate leaving things to question, especially when someone I love could be in trouble." She kept her voice calm and level. "I just need assurances that they're all right. I'll rest a lot easier once I know."

"We can't risk it," he protested, moving slowly toward her, hands held up passively. "One thing at a time. It will do us no good to lose you on a fool's errand when we are so close."

"What's the point of fixing me? If my whole world is just going to fall apart anyway," she argued. "Let the damn seed kill me and give ASSET my body to do with as they need."

"Don't talk like that." He closed the gap between them, reaching out to embrace her. "Where the hell is this coming from?"

She swatted at his arms, refusing the pity hug he'd offered. "Matt is family."

"He is safe with Zack."

"You willing to bet your life on it?"

Grey's shoulders slumped. "Clearly you are."

Her first instinct was to sneak off and meet them under cover of dark, but she knew better than to listen to that troublesome devil on her shoulder. Time spent with Grey was beginning to have an effect on her. She'd likely get herself killed going out alone, or worse, and that would do little to help Matt if he was in some kind of trouble. She needed to calculate her moves, convince Grey to help her. Together they could manage a quick field trip. All she needed was confirmation that they were okay.

"What about a quick recon mission to find Zack? You know where he can usually be found."

"Where Zack goes, Matt will go too." Grey crossed his arms. "But you already knew that."

"Confirmation that they are okay, that's all I ask."

"Wouldn't Josh make a better ferret than us?"

"Where do you think I want to send him?"

"Round your apartment?"

"Josh is human, the most vulnerable of us all. I don't want to send him into potential danger. Matt's probably not in full control yet. If he barges in on the vampires…"

"And if no one is there? What's the harm?"

"If no one's there, then we're still left wondering if they are okay. You know the other places where Zack likes to frequent. Not exactly somewhere you want to send a human."

"I can't let you go to those places either. Newbie like you, and topping the magical most-wanted list," he scoffed. "You'd walk straight into a trap."

"I'm not that stupid."

"Stupid is not the word I used, but yes, when it comes to your roommate—"

"Fine. I'll give you that," she conceded before he said anything more damning.

"You must be desperate if you let me win that easily."

She was beyond desperate. She stared straight into his eyes, silently pleading, her lips quivering as she awaited his answer.

"Fine." He looked to the sky and released a loud growl. "If I do this, you promise to leave them alone until after we have fixed your hand?"

"Scout's honor." She crossed herself and held up three fingers.

He pointed to the bed. "Sit. Stay. Don't open this door for anyone. Do not leave. You hear?"

"Sir, yes, sir!" She saluted.
He left with another loud growl of frustration.

TWENTY-NINE

She hadn't had a moment's peace in the last week. Being under constant watch had been uncomfortable. Being on the run, even more so. But as much as she'd wished for time to collect her thoughts, she found the silence she'd longed for suddenly unnerving.

Gusting wind sent tree branches clawing at her window. Her imagination conjured thoughts of mystic mercenaries closing in for the kill. She jumped to secure the locks, and mentally ran through the exits Grey had outlined when they arrived. Small window above the shower in the bathroom. That was her best way out.

Putting her trust in Sylvia had felt right when she'd accepted the safe house key. But what if the well-connected Shade had simply provided a pretty package for delivery. Sitting there, alone, unarmed, Sage had all but put a bow on her head.

Maybe not mercenaries or Mystics. Sylvia might have sold her out to ASSET. With all their resources, it was a wonder they hadn't found her already. Maybe there was something to it. Mark, for all his covert help, had told her where the line in the sand lay. She had crossed it. But ASSET wasn't the type to make a move until the board had been set. What if she were still being played? Who was truly the game master here?

Television didn't help. Nor did reading. She thought time spent researching the Oil of the Ages would occupy her mind, but Quarn's book had outlined everything like a recipe. A few minutes of notes and she was back to overthinking and anxiety. She tried it all, showers, pacing, yoga, meditation. Every trick in the book. Nothing helped shut her mind off.

Her imagination ran amok as the time passed. Grey had been gone for a while. Was he safe? She shouldn't have let him go alone. She should have demanded to go with him.

The air conditioner kicked on, and she envisioned a special ops team loading their weapons, waiting for the signal to strike. Then came the *crack* and drop of ice cascading into the ice machine outside.

Where was a weapon when she needed it? Grey had left with his machetes. Sage had only *Faith* and *Courage*. She held up her hands and made fists, remembering Devon's speech about fighting with what she had. They might be the worst fist names ever, but she held them at the ready.

A rapid knock against the door sent Sage climbing the walls.

"It's okay, it's me." Grey's voice did little to calm her nerves.

Sage snuck up to the door and tried to spy him through the peep hole. As dark as it was outside, she couldn't make out more than just his silhouette. "What's the password?"

"We didn't make one," he grumbled. "I don't know, coffee?"

He remembered

She breathed a sigh of relief and opened the door. "That was last week's password."

"Which is why I knew you'd accept it." Grey lumbered into the room and tossed his weapons on the bed. "Zack hasn't been seen for two days."

"Because he's busy babysitting Matt?" Sage asked hopefully.

"If Zack were smart, he'd have gone to ground immediately after learning you were on the hit list."

"But we can't count on that without evidence."

"No one admitted to seeing Zack. If he'd been taken in, someone would have said. These Mystics, they have a lot more power than I originally assumed. I heard a lot of buzz about ending the reign of the Terra. Game-changing magic. And rewards for those who play their part in obtaining the magic they're after."

"I'm so glad you made it out of there alive. I should have never sent you." Sage hugged him.

She hadn't realized the extent of the danger. From what it sounded like, the whole Terra family was about to come under fire. All the more reason they needed to get the seed out of her hand, and if that didn't work, she'd have to surrender her hand. Anything to prevent the Mystics from gaining control of it.

"Okay." Grey pulled out of her grasp, staring at her as if she'd lost all reason. "Let's take the positive approach. Let's say the Mystics don't have Zack. He's gone to ground, lying low with Matt." He backed away slowly and collapsed onto his bed.

She hated being in the dark, but short of any real information, or a way to get it, Sage resigned herself to hoping for the best. She followed Grey's lead and retook the spot on her bed, picking up the television remote for a little mind-numbing entertainment. The motel offered only the very basic of local channels. She scrolled through the limited offerings, stopping on the nightly news. The weatherman stood in front of a map of Las Vegas where all the temperature readings remained in the triple digits.

"I need a distraction." Sage sighed.

"You're barking up the wrong tree watching that nonsense." Grey pulled his weapons one by one and laid them out on the bed. "Why don't you locate the ingredients we need for the oil of the ages?"

Sage tossed him the notebook they'd been sharing. "Here's our shopping list."

Grey perused the list, smirking occasionally as he silently mouthed some of the words. "We'll need a hot plate, small pot, lavender buds, sweet almond oil, myrrh. I'm assuming that's an essential oil."

"I know a store where we can pick up most of that." Sage flipped through the limited channels on the television, coming round to the news after a few clicks. "Whatever we buy needs to be pure. We aren't going to cut corners with this ritual."

"Thank you, Captain Obvious." Grey chuckled. "What the hell is ashwagandha root?"

"I'm telling you I know a place. North Town. Herbal something or other. They have whole bins with plants and dried herbs. I'll bet they have oils too."

"There you go. You wanted a win. You got one."

"Excuse me if I don't celebrate just yet." She rolled her eyes.

"Why not? Especially when you've been through hell. Every win, even the tiniest, is worth celebrating."

How could that man still remain so positive? He'd been through the same crap she had. It had to be an act.

"I'm waiting for the other shoe to drop," she admitted.

"If you concentrate on the negative, you will get negative. Law of attraction."

Sage grumbled as she rounded the short list of channels again. Nothing to watch. Even the news seemed to be having a slow day. Though she had to admit the segment currently on screen was worth a few moments' pause—an animal shelter offering free adoptions for the weekend. On screen was an adorable Husky mix dressed up with a bandana. She watched in silence as they had the dog show off its tricks, sitting on command and giving high fives to the reporter.

"Fine," she said. "Woo-hoo! This is me celebrating."

"That's the spirit." Grey turned his attention back to the notebook. "Feverfew? I'm guessing that's an herb too. Looks like we're just boiling down a bunch of herbs in a pot, adding some of your blood, and bottling it."

"Herbally Grounded. I think that's the place. We can look it up in the phone book." Sage jumped up and hunted around the room. "There has to be one in here. That's another thing. This whole no-technology blackout is driving me insane."

"Just a few more days. You can handle it. We have to do this old-school."

She found the phone book in the second drawer of the bedside table and hefted the heavy tome on the bed.

"Back in my day—"

"You're admitting your age now?" Sage laughed for the first time all evening and began to thumb through the pages.

"We had to carve our information on stone tablets."

"I believe it." She found a listing for Herbally Grounded. "They have a phone number. We can call first thing and get their hours."

"Look at you, using analog technology. I'm so proud." Grey mimed wiping away tears.

The television flashed brightly, red and white. Sage looked up as the words *Breaking News* scrolled across the screen. Aerial images of an apartment complex on fire stole her attention. The news channel shifted focus to a reporter on scene.

"Shit, that's my apartment." Sage dropped the phone book and perched on the edge of the bed.

Grey was on his feet, inching closer to the television as the reporter gave a statement about evacuations. "Zack and Matt are not in there," he said cautiously, but how could he know?

The reporter stood a safe distance from the burning apartment, but the camera showed the fire in all its horror still glowing through the windows. People who had been evacuated from their apartments stood watch as firefighters scurried around manning hoses to combat the remaining flames.

The reporter pulled people from the crowd and began to question them on what they knew, if they had seen anything suspicious.

"My home. Everything I own. Gone!" Sage blinked, hoping to wipe away the vision before her. "Matt's things. Our life!"

Grey put his arm around her. "It's only things. The people are safe."

"The other shoe. This is it. See, I told you!" She fought against her tears. "I knew it."

"It's bad. I won't deny that. But it's not the end of the world. Remember, we have to keep our head in the game."

His words were no comfort. How could he possibly understand? This was definitely the work of the Mystics.

She prayed Matt and Zack had escaped. The fire looked as if it had been raging for a while. What if they hadn't escaped?

She didn't want to watch anymore, and yet even with the remote in her hand, Sage couldn't press the button to make it all stop. The cameraman following the reporter made sure to keep the burning building in the back of every shot.

Neighbors whom Sage knew by sight but never spoke to stood crying and holding each other. The Mystics might have targeted Sage, but they had destroyed innocent lives in the process.

The camera panned to a figure she hadn't thought to see. Luke. He stood out in the open as if wanting to be visible. In his arms, he held a jacket.

"That's mine!" Sage shouted.

Grey jumped back as if she'd bit him. "What?"

"Luke! Right there. You see. He has my jacket. Why would he have my jacket?"

The camera's focus was with the reporter, still talking with distraught neighbors, and just to the side was Luke staring straight into the camera. His face was a stony mask of determination as if he were willing Sage to focus on him.

"Do you think he set the fire?" Grey asked.

"Why would he do something like that?" Sage couldn't think of any reason he would cause such destruction. He'd been stripped of his magic. He had no master guiding him. No. He was innocent of that. But how would he have her coat?

"He just looks guilty."

"He looks like he's trying to give me a message."

"No." Grey waved his hands in the air as if he already knew what Sage was about to suggest.

"Why does he have my jacket?"

"It's a trap."

"It's a message. From Matt."

"You're reaching."

"Why else would Luke of all people have my jacket?"

"You think Matt set the fire and gave Luke your jacket?" Grey scrunched his face in confusion.

"No. The jacket is a message from Matt. It's my trail of breadcrumbs. They got out before the fire, and this is the proof."

"And what if it isn't?"

"The alternative is Matt and Zack were in the apartment when it was set ablaze? If that's true, then game over. I have to know."

"Sage, please. No. This is not a good idea."

"The Mystics set my apartment on fire. They might have killed my friends."

"They are calling you out."

"To what? Survey a burnt-out husk of my former life? No. An act like this demands retaliation. They're expecting me to show up and use my new power publicly."

"You're right, that does sound more like you. I stand corrected. That would be a stupid move."

"But going in, under the cover of dark for a secret meeting with Luke, that would be less likely. He's a known enemy of mine."

"Either way, you're still going into enemy territory," Grey cautioned.

"I'm getting my jacket and finding out what Luke knows." She pointed to the screen with Luke still staring down the camera, her jacket folded neatly over his clasped hands.

"Can't you call him?"

"Don't have a phone number."

"Of course you don't.

"Remember, my intuition hasn't failed us yet. Law of attraction and all. Where's that positivity?"

"I'm positive you're going to be the death of me."

THIRTY

Nerves threatened to paralyze Sage as she approached the night gate of her apartment complex. Lamps dotted the pathways, their dim light protecting only tiny spheres of concrete from the ever-encroaching threat of darkness. The circus of firefighters had long since left, but the air still smelled of damp smoke.

Every shadow could be a lurking enemy. People she passed on the sidewalk could be spies. She couldn't rely on her palm to act as an alarm system. The Mystics operated with complete anonymity, and many in their employ were humans.

The breeze picked up, rustling the leaves of a nearby tree. Sage pulled the dagger Grey had given her, and held it at the ready, wishing she had something a little more powerful. Daggers were her favorite kind of weapon, but in this case, she didn't want to let someone get close enough to use it.

Grey had tried to warn her. He'd told her of the danger, but reason flew out the window when a loved one might be in danger. If it were anyone other than Matt, Sage would have never have attempted this crazy mission. Matt was family. She had to know that he was okay. The jacket was her clue. Surely he'd passed it along as a message for her.

Quick stop to check in with the friendly neighborhood stalker. Simple enough. In, out, and done. Sage repeated the mantra to bolster her failing courage. She had to own this whole new level of exposed vulnerability.

Everything seemed so much creepier at night. Darkness reached out from every angle—a gaping maw, voracious in its pursuit to consume the light, and anything else that dare travel into its depths. Which was exactly the path Grey was leading them down. He worked them along a serpentine pattern weaving around buildings, avoiding the lighted paths, using the walls of each apartment as their shield.

"Which way?" Grey stopped short. He poked his head around the edge of the building, surveying the gap they'd have to cross.

"Directly across from mine. Second story." She looked back the way they'd just come, and ahead, searching for any sign of danger.

The unnerving sensation of unseen eyes had become all too familiar to her in recent days. Hairs on the back of her neck tingled as they darted across the gap, giving a wide berth to the pathway lights. Someone or something was watching. Sage could only hope it was her friendly neighborhood stalker.

Every step they took became a dance. Eyes open, head on a swivel, she scanned every shadow.

They rounded on the building directly across from hers. Sage chanced a quick peek at the burnt-out husk that once had been her apartment. Surrounded in yellow police tape, it was a hideous eyesore. Where her front door should have been sat a gaping hole. She couldn't make out much of what was inside, not that she wanted to. It was clear her apartment had been the start of the blaze.

Grey nudged her back into reality. "I'll keep watch down here." He nodded to the concrete stairs leading to the second-story apartment and disappeared into the darkness, cloaking himself in the shadow of the stairwell. "Be quick about it."

Sage scurried up as fast as her legs could carry her. Light glowed from Luke's apartment window. A good sign that he was home. She turned to look out over the railing toward her apartment. He'd always watched her from this lofty perch, and she could see why. A perfect vantage point, not just to see what remained of her building, but beyond for a full view of the pool.

A cold chill trickled down her neck as she gazed out at the water. Sage stepped backwards, one foot, then the other, retreating into the darkness as she searched for the source of her unease.

On first glance, the pool appeared empty. Then she spotted them. Hiding in plain sight. Two women lying on loungers close to the pool gate. Neither of them dressed for swimming.

Sage turned to the opposite direction, looking out toward a path that cut between the rows of buildings leading to the tenant's parking lot. An elderly couple were walking a tiny black dog. They looked innocent enough, but she added them to her mental tally.

Quick stop to check in with the friendly neighborhood stalker. Simple enough. In, out, and done. Sage repeated her mental checklist.

"Here goes nothing," she whispered to herself as she knocked on the door.

Metal scraped against metal, the sound of a chain lock being undone.

Luke opened the door. Surprise widened his eyes, before realization furrowed his brow. "Inside, quickly," he growled and yanked her by the arm. "What are you doing here?"

"I saw you on the news."

"That was supposed to reassure you that everything was okay, not have you come crawling back here."

"And exactly how was I supposed to know that when you're standing there like a freaking statue taunting me with my jacket in your hand? Which, by the way, I'd like back."

"You do realize whoever firebombed your house could be watching for you to return, right?"

"Yes, we came in silently, and Grey is keeping watch out."

"Got yourself in some pretty bad trouble from what I hear." He dropped her arm as if she'd burned him and looked at his hand. "I still can't get my head around the fact you took all my magic away."

"Not my fault. You know that, right?"

"You did what you had to do. But you should have dropped off the face of the earth. Coming back here… Stupid."

"I know. But I couldn't leave without making sure my roommate was okay."

"Junior? He's not there," Luke answered with surprising speed, using the pet name Zack had given Matt.

"You saw them leave? Alone?" She closed the gap between them, crossing the lines of personal space, eager to absorb all the information he could give her.

"Not exactly." For each step she took, Luke retreated, as if afraid she might still harm him with her touch. "Your apartment has been dark for the last couple of days. I spotted your jacket folded neatly on the doormat and figured it was a sign."

"Yeah, obviously a sign. Was there a letter with it? How long was it out there? Do you know why they left? Did you hear anything?"

"That Zack guy was talking before…something about the coven…his people."

"That doesn't make sense. Grey went down to the club. No one had heard from him."

"That's what I heard." Luke shrugged and looked over to his front door. "The next day, your apartment was dark. The jacket was at the door. Nothing since."

He had to know more than he was letting on. Sage refused to acknowledge his subtle hint to leave. She needed answers. "They wouldn't be stupid enough to walk into a trap. Zack was the one who warned me I had become a hot commodity on the magical black market." She moved in closer, seeing how nervous it made Luke. "Zack would have known his ties to me would have put a mark on his head too."

"Can't argue with that logic. But, like I said, I haven't seen anyone in your apartment for a few days." Luke crossed his arms and stood his ground.

Maybe that was all he knew about Zack, but she wasn't ready to end her interrogation just yet.

"What about stalkers?" Sage stepped back, allowing a little more space between them. "Have you seen anyone strange around the apartment complex lately?"

"You mean did I see the person who set fire to your apartment? Contrary to popular belief, I do require sleep. Especially now that I'm mortal."

"You have to appreciate the pressure I'm under right now. I need to get some answers."

"And you have to appreciate that you're not the sole focus of my life, such as it is now. What do you think I do all day around here?"

She'd never thought to ask him about his life. Definitely a bachelor if his apartment was any indication. Aside from what appeared to be a wall of TV screens, his apartment appeared to be a dumping ground for garbage. Fast food wrappers were crumpled and tossed on nearly every shelf and table surface. Soda cans and beer bottles lined the kitchen counters.

"You've got a serious junk food problem. And you clearly haven't learned how to use a trash can."

"Not exactly the tone one uses when they want to engage someone's help," Luke warned. "I can see now why your partner is so stern with you."

"Stalker. Creeper," Sage shot back at him with all the fierceness she could muster. How dare he try and act superior after all the crap he'd pulled. "You're always here, and as far as I've seen, spying on me. That's what you do around here."

Luke ducked his head shamefully. He blew out a heavy breath and unfolded his arms. "I guess I deserved that, when you were my assignment. But that was when Thalia had me in her thrall. Even though I had no control, I'm man enough to admit that was wrong."

"And now?" She looked past Luke, into his living room. A desk took up the back wall. Four monitors the size of TV screens had been mounted above it. Each of the screens had a different display. One appeared to be a first-person shooter. Another resembled an old DOS screen with lines of code ending in a blinking curser. The third had an internet browser open, mid search for cheat codes, presumably for the game that sat frozen on the first screen. And the fourth had some kind of automated program running, but she stood too far away to read the text.

"Trust me. Its better you don't know." Luke smirked.

Game console controllers randomly blinked for attention on the desk. Next to them sat a specialty keyboard, each key flashing through every color of the rainbow. She was tempted to have a closer look, but she'd already wasted too much time. This was supposed to be a quick in-and-out recon mission.

"Equipment like that, I'm going to go with surveillance being your profession. When you're not trying to cheat your way to a high score."

"A few days on the run and look at you. I'm impressed with this whole covert spy you're turning into." His easy-going tone returned along with a plastered-on smile. He might not have his magic any longer, but he was still very much a djinn at heart. "Very observant. What else do you see?"

She gave the apartment a second look. The computer was the only thing that stood out. The rest was flea-market furniture and the lingering smell of cigarettes.

"What should I see?" she asked.

"Nothing really. I just like to experience the world through other eyes on occasion."

"Don't screw with me. I've had enough stress this week."

"Sorry." He held up his hands in surrender. "I don't have more helpful information."

"There has to be something I'm missing. Are you sure there was no note left when you found my jacket?"

"No."

"You're not worth much without your magic." She regretted her angry comment the moment it left her lips.

"Play nice," he warned.

"I didn't mean it. I'm just..." What could she say? How many times could she apologize to people? "Plan B."

"Did I miss plan A?" Luke tilted his head, his eyes all but begging her for answers.

Her hands found her hips. There were strange people lurking around. They weren't magic either. Her palm alarm had not gone off once since she stepped foot into her apartment complex. "Look out your patio window. What do you see?" She pointed to the sliding glass patio door that faced her apartment and the pool.

"As you wish," he taunted, but did as she had commanded and walked to the sliding glass patio door. He opened it a crack and lit a cigarette.

"You see the two ladies at the pool?"

Luke took a long pull from his cigarette and gazed out beyond the patio. "No." He exhaled a monstrous cloud of smoke. "But I do see Grey fighting with an old man!"

"We gotta go, Sage," Grey shouted.

Sage flew to the front door, dagger at the ready.

"Wait," Luke called out. He threw her jacket.

As she reached out to catch it in the air, Luke blew past her and down the stairs like a knight charging into battle.

She put the jacket on and hit the stairwell. A body dropped in front of her at the bottom of the steps. Sage sidestepped in time to avoid being hit. Definitely an older guy by the looks of him. She couldn't quite make out who he was, but something felt familiar about him.

Grey picked up the crumpled body and dragged him under the concrete steps. "Obviously, the Mystics are still sending humans after us."

"What do we do?" So much for getting in and out without being seen. "Where's Luke?"

Grey set the unconscious man down and checked for a pulse. "Try not to kill the humans. We don't need to leave a body count. Exit strategy now! There will be more coming."

Sage spotted Luke exchanging blows with the pair of ladies she'd seen lounging by the pool moments earlier. She'd expected them to be spies, not ninjas. The effortless way they moved, striking and pushing, effectively backing Luke into a corner, was a clear sign of their training.

The woman to his right, assassin number one, struck low. Luke's knee buckled. Sage cringed and turned away, not wanting to see him go down.

But it wasn't a man's groan that followed. One of the women shrieked. Sage turned to look and saw Luke tumbling on the ground with assassin number two.

A few thousand years as a djinn and he must have learned a few tricks. Still, two on one wasn't a fair fight.

Grey took hold of her arm and pulled her. "We have to get out of here. Now."

She couldn't argue with the urgency in his tone, but she couldn't abandon Luke either. "Not yet." She pulled free of Grey's grip and jabbed her finger towards the fight still raging. "We can't leave him like this."

"You're the one they're after. You leave, they'll follow." Grey pushed her forward.

Sage held her ground. "We're not leaving him."

Grey growled and took out his throwing knife. He moved with practiced efficiency and let it fly through the air.

A shrill cry confirmed it hit his target. The smaller of the two ninja women went down, rolled through the fall, pulled the blade from her thigh, and returned fire.

It happened so fast Sage would have sworn the little ninja was a vampire. With barely a sound, the blade whizzed past Sage's face. She felt the break of air before the blade found its mark with a muffled *thud* into the apartment door behind her.

The small woman was on her feet, eyes locked on her target—Sage.

Grey unsheathed his twin blades. So much for not killing humans. He moved to place himself between the little ninja and Sage.

Pinned in between an apartment door and the battles going on in front of her, Sage had nowhere to go.

Luke finally dropped assassin number one to the ground. He looked up, his left eye swollen shut, his face dripping with blood.

Grey's blades sang as he fought with assassin number two. If there were a better word than ninja, she'd use it. Sage's palm had not awoken. There was no way that woman had magic, but she moved with vampire-like speed, deflecting each slash of Grey's machetes.

Luke stumbled unsteadily toward Sage. Assassin number one lay unconscious in the grass. As he came closer, the truth of his injuries became apparent. His swollen eye wept tears of blood. He opened his mouth to speak, and teeth were missing. "I think we're even now."

She didn't laugh at his attempt at levity.

"We'll get you patched up. I'm sorry." Sage reached out to steady him as he came towards the stairs. "Where's the old lady?"

"What?"

"Old man and lady walking their dog. Grey got the man. Where's his partner?"

Grey and assassin number two had danced their way toward the pool gate. Sage peeked around. The pathways were empty. She caught silhouettes appearing in lighted windows. Neighbors were starting to take notice. Cops would be called. Her apartment complex would make the news twice in one night. They had to be far away before the entire apartment complex turned into a three-ring circus.

"We have to get out of here. And pray the woman isn't following," Sage said. "We have a car parked just outside the night gate."

"No bike today?"

"Too conspicuous. Everyone at ASSET knows Grey's bike."

Grey howled in pain. Sage turned to see him fall to the ground. Assassin number two swung her foot hard and landed a brutal kick. Bones crunched, followed by another cry from her partner.

Sage was in motion, instincts kicking in. She reached into her belt, retrieved her throwing daggers, and launched them as she continued to sprint toward ninja woman.

The nimble little assassin ducked and dodged, avoiding each of the blades Sage threw her way. Exactly what Sage hoped for. She spotted Grey's machete lying within reach and slid like a baseball player, straight into home plate, taking out the assassin's legs.

Sage grabbed the blade and swung blindly, hoping to connect with skin.

The blade made contact, drawing a thin line of red through the assassin's clothes, but not deep enough to spill blood.

The woman stepped out of reach and reset for a fight.

Sage got to her feet and brought the machete up, ready. Grey hadn't fared well with this assassin, and Sage wasn't too sure she'd last long. Only the knowledge that the Mystics would want her alive gave her courage.

A gun went off.

The loud blast sent Sage's ears ringing.

Assassin number two dropped to the ground.

Sage turned, her hands already rising in surrender.

The old woman stood on the stairs leading to Luke's second-story apartment, her gun pointed straight at Sage. "Drop the blade and come with me, and I'll let your boyfriend live."

Sage looked down to her partner lying barely an arm's length away. Sweat poured from his pale face. His shattered leg resembled a lightning bolt, clearly broken in more than one place. Her stomach churned, and she had to turn away or be sick by the sight of it.

"Save me when you can," Sage whispered and dropped the machete. She glared up to the old woman. "I go quietly and he lives?"

"Move." The woman signaled with her weapon.

Sage approached, her hands held high. Luke had all but vanished in the shadows behind her. Even without his magic, he seemed to have that special ability. The throwing dagger had disappeared from the door too.

Sage kept her expression neutral and her approach as slow as possible to keep the old woman's attention on her.

"Faster," Grandma shouted.

"Where are you taking me?" Sage asked loudly.

The old woman answered with her gun, firing a shot toward Grey.

"Fine. Okay." Sage jumped and quickened her pace.

Luke moved within striking distance. As soon as the old lady hit the bottom step, he'd have her.

Sage breathed slow and steady, her hands trembling as she continued to keep them up and out in the open. "Who's paying you? What could they possibly have offered you that would be worth the lives you're ruining? Did you set my apartment on fire too?"

The old woman stepped down. Her feet touched concrete. Luke moved like a viper. Grandma gasped, then her whole body went rigid.

Sage reached for the gun, and missed.

The old woman turned sharply toward Luke. She stumbled and fired another shot as she crumpled down to the ground with Luke under her.

Luke shoved her aside, freeing himself from her weight. Sage spotted the knife he'd buried deep in Grandma's back. The bloom of blood staining her shirt grew rapidly. The old woman sputtered and choked as she struggled for air.

Blood dribbled down Luke's legs.

Sage reached for his face, bringing his eyes in line with hers. "Hold on, buddy. We'll get you fixed. We just need to make it to the car. Okay?"

"This is what death feels like?" Luke asked calmly.

"Don't talk like that. I won't let you." The way his brow beaded with sweat as the color drained away from his cheeks made her wonder how badly he'd been hurt.

"It's okay. I'm not going to die from this." Luke winced as he tested his bloody leg. "But you will if you don't get moving."

Sirens wailed in the distance. The police were on their way.

"I can't leave you." She wasn't exactly sure how she'd manage to keep her word, especially now that the authorities were in earshot.

"He needs help." Luke pointed toward Grey.

She glanced over her shoulder. Grey was struggling to get to his feet. His broken leg wouldn't hold him. He'd cause more damage trying.

Sage struggled with what to do. The sirens were getting louder. She could already see flashes of blue and red lights heading towards the guest parking lot.

"Sage. I'll be fine," Luke assured her. "Help is already on the way for me. I was attacked by a crazy lady with a gun. My ride to the hospital is almost here."

The old woman had stopped sputtering and lay in an ever-growing pool of blood at Sage's feet.

"Thank you. For everything."

"We're even now. Go!" Luke urged.

With no time to argue, Sage jumped to her feet and turned on her heel to help Grey. Acting as his crutch, she took one last look at Luke as they headed into the shadows.

THIRTY-ONE

By the will of the gods alone, she managed to get Grey to the car and leave without being seen. So focused on escape, Sage had hardly given thought to what came next. But once they reached safety, the reality of Grey's injuries reared its ugly head. Not simply broken, his leg looked as if it had been roughly pulled apart and shoved back together. She had never seen his face so pale. In shock and yet somehow still clinging to the edge of consciousness, Grey held up as much of his own weight as he could while she rushed him into the safe house.

"Tell me what to do!" She helped Grey to the bed.

He fell face forward, and cried out into the mattress as his body came to rest. She would have left him as he lay, but despite the pain it caused him, Grey would not be still.

"See…how bad…it is." He struggled in a pitiful attempt to roll onto his back, arms and legs flapping like a dying fish.

"Oh, for the love of…" She added her own weight and leverage, managing to roll him flat on his back. One leg lay straight across the mattress while the other resembled something of a lightning bolt. "It could be worse," she lied and frantically searched around the room for scissors. "We have to get those pants off."

He groaned. "Buy a guy dinner first?"

At least he was still joking. That had to count for something. She dug into her bag and pulled out a knife. "This will have to do."

"You sure about that?" He tried to recoil, gasping with pain, before finally giving up. "I've seen you with a blade. Your aim is terrible."

"If you're referring to the ninja lady, I was distracting her with them. I didn't aim."

"Obviously." He laughed and moaned at the same time. "Because aiming might have worked."

"You really want to piss me off when I have a knife in my hand?" She pointed the tip of her blade towards his balls. "It might affect my aim."

"Be gentle."

Sage cut through his jeans and peeled them away. His leg was clearly broken in a few places, and his kneecap looked like it had been knocked backwards.

"That's…." She fought to hold back the chunks in her throat. "Oh god!"

"I'll heal, remember?" Grey lifted his head in an attempt to see, then dropped it quickly to the mattress. "I need you to be my eyes. Any bones poking out of skin?"

She cringed and forced herself to look down again. His leg was swelling. Purple and black bruising bloomed in three spots. One spot protruded like a knot, but the skin hadn't erupted. "No bleeding out."

"Any bulging?"

"Yep." She slapped a hand over her mouth and turned away.

"That's the first break you want to work on." The calm and control in Grey's voice served to keep Sage grounded to the task. If he could hold it together, so could she. "Gently feel the protrusion and see if you can move any masses below it." He lifted his hand as if trying to reach for it himself, and hissed the moment his fingertips grazed the top of his thigh. "Pull the leg straight if you can…" He panted. Tears leaked from the corners of his eyes. "And put pressure on the…the break…" He pressed his hands against his thigh as if holding on for dear life. "Try to align…"

I can do this. I can do this. Her hands trembled as she reached toward his leg. Gently, she prodded the swollen area. Definitely something hard there.

Grey bit into his bottom lip. His eyes riveted to the ceiling. She fingered the area as gently as she could to assess the shape of it. His whole body stiffened. She had to be quick, but what if she did something wrong?

"Sorry."

"Just do it," he barked at her.

She took hold of his ankle in one hand and pulled back while providing pressure to the bone with her other hand.

Grey howled through gritted teeth as the bone shifted.

"You okay?" She felt it move and struggled to hold on as every instinct inside her demanded she let go.

Grey panted and whimpered but made no attempt to stop her.

A little more pressure and she felt the leg straighten. Hopefully the bone had lined up. She couldn't be too sure.

Grey had the bedsheets balled in his tight fists. "Keep working the rest." He managed to get the words out between breaths.

The sight of his kneecap on sideways sent her stomach churning. This is why she had never considered nursing as a career. The only saving grace was the fact he wasn't bleeding out. Bad enough she was putting the puzzle pieces of his leg together. Add blood or puss or worse… Nope. She couldn't do it. Grey's face had gone so pale she wondered if he might die from his wounds.

"Stay with me," she ordered as she felt his kneecap floating under the skin on the side of his leg and worked fast to manipulate it back in line.

Grey growled through the herculean effort it took to stay still and endure the pain. She couldn't have held it together like that. His strength of will was pretty damn impressive.

"The rest of your leg looks straight, but there are serious areas of bruising up top. If those are breaks, they are as lined up as they're getting." Sage hoped that was all she'd be required to do. "What next? A splint?"

"Yeah…something…stiff."

Sage searched the room for anything she could use. What the hell did someone make a splint with? Tree branches? *Stiff.* That's what Grey had told her. Long and straight. Something that could run the length of his leg, or at least the broken part.

She searched frantically, feeling completely inadequate to the task.

In the bathroom, she spotted the shower curtain hanging from a cheap pressure rod. Long. Straight. A little unorthodox, but it would have to work in a pinch. She grabbed it, separated the two halves, and brought them and the shower curtain into the room.

She sliced up the shower curtain into strips and Mac-Gyvered a splint using some towels, the shower pole halves, and the strips of curtain to secure it all.

"What next?"

"I need sleep," he croaked. Shock or just exhaustion from the pain was kicking in. "I'll heal… Need…rest." He lifted his hand and waved it. "Just leave me be."

Sage paced the room. She felt like she should be doing more. He was a Terra. They healed amazingly fast. Maybe rest was all he needed. They could be back at it in the morning. But what if he wasn't?

She needed sleep, too, but doubted that would come anytime soon. Short of that, she needed distractions. Something to quiet or at least overpower the anxiety and stress. Sage shrugged out of her leather jacket and laid it on the bed. It bulged from the blades in its hidden pockets.

She needed to focus on her assets. That was as good a distraction as any. Step one: assemble assets. She dug through the pockets and pulled knives and daggers from various hiding spots. The inner lining had been specially sewn to maximize space for carrying many weapons comfortably and seamlessly. One of the inner pockets had a piece of paper inside. Sage recognized the handwriting but not the address. Matt had written it.

Better than a distraction. That was something she could work with.

No message came with the address, but it was more than what she'd had before. It wasn't like Matt to dig into her pockets. If he'd meant to simply tell her he was okay, then he'd have said so. *Why send an address?* A trail of breadcrumbs. It had to be clue.

Sage mulled it over, trying to figure out his angle. *They didn't get taken by ASSET, or the Mystics. If they did, they won't know the exact location they're going.* Nothing in the way the address was written gave Sage any idea of Matt's urgency in writing it. *They know where they're going. And they want me to follow.* Probably to a safe house for Zack. One even his vampire buddies weren't aware of.

As soon as she was certain Grey was healing, she'd follow this new lead.

THIRTY-TWO

If not for Grey's occasional moaning and snoring, Sage would have thought him dead. All the color had drained from his face. Sweat clung to his brow, giving his features an odd, waxy sheen in the dim light of the motel room.

Sage fought to stop herself from calling a doctor. Could a Terra develop infections from their wounds? The healing factor in their magical blood had not really been tested. Sage kept a silent vigil through the long hours until the first rays of light pierced the blinds.

Grey shifted, crying out as he tried to move his bad leg. He lifted a hand to shield his eyes.

"I'm here." Sage was at his side in a flash. "Tell me what to do."

"Close the blinds," he ordered hoarsely.

"You look like you're dying. Tell me what to do."

"Just let me rest," he barked at her.

She forgave him the outburst. He could be as grumpy as he wanted. "I'm going to pick up the supplies we need for the Oil of the Ages." The excuse gave her plenty of time for recon.

"There and back only!"

"Sure," she lied. He didn't need to know where she was heading. That would only make him worry. Or worse. Knowing him, he'd probably try to come hobbling after her and damage his leg further.

Recon only. That was what she told herself. He'd be healed by the evening, and then she could take him with her to pay a visit to the vampire boys.

She drove out to the address Matt had left in her jacket. The neighborhood was a remote subdivision on the outskirts of old Henderson, quiet and calm, the house a single-story, ranch-style home. If only the neighbors knew they had vampires right under their noses.

Her palm began to itch as she closed in. No need to verify the address. But she couldn't barge in on them during the day. If this was a safe house, there could be more than just Zack and Matt inside. And she knew better than to barge in on a vampire when they slept.

She took a few more laps around the neighborhood, making herself very familiar with the exits and entrances. After what had happened at her apartment, having an escape route was her first priority.

***

She set the bag of ingredients for the Oil of the Ages on the dresser when she returned. Grey was still sleeping off his injuries. Occasionally moaning between heavy snores, he still appeared to need more time to heal.

Sage followed the recipe, boiling the ingredients needed for the oil of the ages on the hot pad she'd picked up. Seemed simple enough. Not that she was good at cooking or recipes. But, as it basically instructed her to throw everything in a pot and boil for an hour, how could she screw it up?

Grey slept like the dead. And with only her inner monologue for company, she convinced herself that rather than disturb him, she should just take a quick trip to visit the vampire boys herself.

They were her boys after all. No real danger there. And she'd be back in a couple of hours. Easy-peasy.

If Grey had been awake, she knew what he would say. He'd try and stop her. And he would probably be right to do so. But she reasoned that they were in a safe house, so the danger was minimal.

He could yell at her all he wanted when she returned. Yes. That was for the best. It wasn't like he had been awake for any of her science experiment stuff anyway.

She finished with the oil and bottled everything up, leaving it on the dresser to cool. The sun had sunk below the horizon. She gave one last glance at Grey, still snoring, and set off.

Just make sure they are both unharmed and let them know you're still working to clear your name.

She parked the car around the corner from the safe house and took to the street on foot. Eyes wide open, she checked every direction, searching for any signs of surveillance. Anything out of the ordinary. She wouldn't be fooled by a kindly couple walking their dog this time.

Tonight is not going to end in a fight.

Small, uncomfortable tingles quickly grew as the seed awoke in her palm, craving nearby magic. Definitely the right place.

Clenching her blackened hand as tightly as she could, Sage approached the house and peeked in through the front window.

Soft bluish light flickered in the darkness. Probably a television, though she couldn't hear any sounds. One of the few benefits to having vampire roommates—their excellent hearing. Sage had never needed to ask them to turn it down.

Knowing that, she whispered, "Have fun stormin' the castle, boys" and waited to see if they would respond. Zack could never resist a movie quote.

A moment later, the chain lock clattered against the front door. It opened with a creak.

"What the hell are you doing here?" Zack glared at her with utter disbelief.

Not the reception she'd expected. She took a steadying breath and plastered a smile across her face. "I have good news."

"Get in here before someone sees you." Zack ushered her inside, giving Sage a wide berth to avoid her deadly touch.

"I'll admit, I was hoping for a warmer reception." Sage crossed the threshold and spotted Matt.

He stood from the couch where he'd been watching television. Unlike Zack's frosty glare, Matt was all smiles. His relaxed posture a marked improvement on the last time she'd seen him. If she hadn't known better, she might have thought he had already been cured.

"You're wanted by everyone in the magical community." Zack ruined her happy thought with his accusation. "Why did you think we went into hiding? They know we're linked to you."

"Someone is using their big-boy voice," she replied harshly. "I was worried you'd been lost in the apartment fire. I risked everything to come here."

"And what exactly did you think you were going to do if anyone but me had answered that door?" Zack fired back.

"I…uh—"

"Where is Grey?" Anger blackened Zack's irises. "How could he let you do something so stupid?"

"Don't you start with me." She noted the change in his demeanor, his darker half rising to the surface. Her palm throbbed. The seed demanded to be fed. She clenched her fist tight, using the pain to give strength to her words. "And how the hell do you get off being mad at me for following the address you left me? If you wanted me to know you were okay, then why didn't you say it?"

"I told Matt to leave you a note," Zack replied.

"He did." She held up the paper with only an address written on it. "What was I supposed to learn from this?"

His eyes flickered between otherworldly blue and demonic black, their target the small paper in Sage's hand. Proof of what had caused the confusion. "I just can't even with you two." Zack slammed his palm into his forehead and turned on Matt. "Why did you write that?"

"I wanted her to know where to find us." Matt shrugged, unaffected by Zack's anger. "You and I both know Sage doesn't take direction well. Better to deliver messages in person. So here she is."

He knew her so well, she'd forgive Matt for calling her out for being a little too impulsive.

"And if someone followed her?" Zack jabbed a finger at Sage.

"No one is tailing me," she assured them.

"Fine. You've seen us. You know we're okay." Zack pointed to the door. "Please don't take this the wrong way, but go."

"Missed you, too, jerk." Happy as she was to see them alive and well, Zack's cold shoulder was seriously souring her mood. So much for his efforts to get her to like him.

That had clearly gone out the window during the time they'd been separated. "I'll leave in a minute." She rolled her eyes past Zack. Her mission had been Matt. And she still had something to offer him. "How are you doing?"

Matt moved with ease, no signs of the struggle she'd seen days earlier. "I'm getting the hang of this. I'm glad you're okay."

"I was so worried when I saw the apartment on fire. And no one knew where you were." She wanted nothing more than to rush over and give him a hug. He always gave the best hugs, squeezing her tight and lifting her all the way off the ground. She needed that more than she could admit aloud.

"That was kind of the idea. We needed to lay low until it blew over," Matt replied. He came up and stood just out of arm's reach. "How are you? Figure out how to fix the death touch?"

Sage hid her throbbing hand behind her back. "Yes. And it might help you out too."

"Go get yourself fixed, then, and we can kiss and make up when you return safely," Zack urged.

"I was getting to that." It took all she had not to reach out and slap him. Zack was being beyond rude. She breathed through the annoyance and focused on what she needed to say. "There's this ritual thing."

"It's always a ritual," Zack grumbled. "Wait. How are you going to perform a ritual?"

"Yeah, that's the thing. I can't. But we're taking care of that, Grey and I. Everything will be ready tomorrow," she spoke excitedly.

"Why isn't he with you now?" Zack's eagerness to push her out the door shifted as if he had suddenly realized she was alone.

"He got hurt back at the apartment," she replied. "We were ambushed. Grey barely made it out."

"Who sent them?" Zack looked as if he'd seen a ghost. "Your people or—"

"They were all human assassins," Sage said.

"Humans!" Matt's voice turned demonic. "I'd have ripped out their throats."

"Woah there," she snapped at him. "What the hell are you saying?"

"Junior's still new, remember? Urges run high." Zack's was the only calm voice in the room. He glanced over to his charge and held out his hands peacefully. "Bring it down a few notches."

"Have you…?" She couldn't finish the sentence. Matt was not a killer. No. She shook her head. Not possible.

"He's been a good boy, I assure you. Perfect gentleman." Despite the sickeningly sweet voice he used, Zack's words were far from reassuring.

"Matt?" She stared directly into his eyes. They were still blue, thankfully. "Tell me you haven't hurt anyone."

"If I find out someone is hurting the ones I love, I won't be responsible for what I do," Matt replied.

"Dammit. No. This is not you." She stomped her foot. Waiting for another full moon just wasn't an option. She had to convince him to join her now, before he went full demon and could never return.

"I'm a vampire now." Matt puffed his chest proudly and proclaimed, "This is me."

"I can fix you too," she blurted out.

"Fix him?" Zack scoffed.

"I don't mean it like that." Sage struggled for the right words. This was going so much worse than she had imagined. "I just—"

"He's a vampire. Are you implying something about my kind?" Zack argued.

"No. I'm just…" Sage growled in frustration, and turned to Matt, pleading with her eyes for him to see reason. "He never wanted this. I know you've tried hard to help, and I appreciate it. But there is a chance to give him back the life he had."

"No one goes back. It doesn't work like that," Zack said.

"Maybe it does. And shouldn't we try, if there is a way?"

"I am a vampire, and I love it." Matt's tone darkened. He speared her with a look she'd seen so many times before. Between the two of them, he'd been her voice of reason. He'd been the adultier adult in their shared home. "The person who needs fixing is you."

She held up her blackened hand. As badly as it burned, it should have been glowing red, but even without the physical evidence of her pain, he had to see the damage that had been done. "I am going to fix this, and I can put things right with you too. You can be human again."

They stared at each other, locked in a silent battle of wills. Sage kept her hand raised, the reality of all her failures staring Matt in the face. This was her promise. She would make it all better, including him.

Matt's stony expression began to crack. "Sage, this is me. This is my life now. I've more than accepted it. I'm happy. I can never go back to being human. I don't want to."

"You've only been a vampire for a short time. You haven't passed the point of no return. You're just—"

"Don't tell me what I am." Matt crossed his arms, becoming a stone wall she wouldn't be able to break. "You can either accept me as I am, or not. Your choice."

"I do. I love you, Matt. Vampire or human. But what about Josh?" She hated throwing that in his face, but he'd left her with no other option.

"Josh and I will be fine," Matt defended with a quickness that smacked of blind defiance.

"Really?" She let her hand fall to her side and slammed them both on her hips. What had Zack been feeding him? This was his fault. The Matt she knew would never cast aside Josh so easily. "Can you honestly say that?"

"This process takes time. Our relationship is solid." Matt softened his tone.

She wasn't buying it. Especially after Grey's story. Yasmine. Their love didn't work. Blood trumped heart. Sage opened her mouth to say as much but stopped herself as she saw Matt's eyes begin to blacken. She'd lost him. No argument she could make would sink in with his beast rising up to greet her.

"Fine." She sighed.

"Go take care of yourself." Zack nudged, his voice soft. "We'll be waiting for you."

"Don't." She had to remind herself that slapping him might just kill him. Sage turned her back on the vampires and opened the door.

"What?" Zack asked.

"Don't pretend this isn't your doing. Matt didn't want this. I have a real chance at saving him from this life. Why aren't you backing me up on this?"

"It's his life. His decision." Zack rubbed salt in the wounds with his words. "Have you ever stopped to consider he wants this?"

"I can hear you both, you know," Matt said.

"Oh, you'll get an earful when I get back." Sage refused to turn around and look at either of them. Tears stung her eyes, but that pain paled in comparison to her heart, ripping in half. This felt like goodbye.

"Looking forward to it." Matt laughed off her threat, completely oblivious to the reality of what he had chosen.

"Zack… When this is done…." She stopped herself from saying something she'd regret. No good would come from her words this night. She opened the door and crossed the threshold.

"Have fun stormin' the castle," Zack called from the doorway.

THIRTY-THREE

How can Matt choose being a vampire even after I told him there's a cure?

The question plagued her all the way back to the motel. Zack. She blamed him for this. A week earlier, Matt had been a reluctantly converted man. He'd have jumped at the chance to turn back the clock and right the wrong that had been done to him. She should have never left Matt alone with Zack.

More than ever, Sage needed this ritual to work so she could rid herself of the seed. Then she'd come back and tear Zack a new one, making sure he would live long enough to see her give Matt back his life.

She stormed into the motel room, still shaking with rage, and blindly tossed her jacket onto the bed before double checking the locks.

"Where the hell were you?" Grey's sharp tone nearly sent her up the wall.

Sage pawed for her dagger, realizing a moment too late that it was in the pocket of her jacket, which she was no longer wearing. He was lucky she wasn't armed. On edge as she was, a scare like that would have definitely ended in blood.

"I found Matt." Sage turned toward him. Her jacket draped over his bad leg. "Shit, sorry."

The look on his face was enough to do her in. She expected Grey to rail on her.

But when he opened his mouth, all that came out was, "And?" He groaned as he pushed himself up, propping his back against the headboard.

"I don't want to talk about it." She needed something to punch, and short of Zack's face, she found nothing else that would bring her satisfaction. She scooped up her jacket and flopped down on the second bed.

"That good, eh?" Grey abandoned his angry tone. His head cocked to the side curiously.

"No one died."

"Were you followed?"

"I don't think so. I drove around in circles for the last hour. Picked you up something to drink." She pulled out a bottle of pre-mix margarita from her bag.

The beginnings of a smile played across Grey's lips. "What's the point? You know alcohol has no effect on us."

"Never hurts to try." She hadn't tested alcohol since being cursed with the seed. The way her luck had been going, it might actually work. Either way, she wasn't drinking alone.

"I don't do frilly drinks."

"Don't do the alpha male thing. You can enjoy a drink that tastes good."

"Tequila shots done right are very tasty."

"And are a complete waste when you can't enjoy the benefits." She walked over to the dresser and started prepping two cups with ice left over in the bucket. "How's the leg?"

"Still attached." He hissed as he adjusted his posture.

"You going to be ready to make the drive tomorrow?" *Please say yes.* It had been over twenty-four hours and Grey was still bedridden. What would happen if he wasn't healed? She couldn't make the rest of this journey alone. She'd put her trust in Sylvia to help rid her of the seed, but once it was removed, all bets were off. Sage needed backup. The kind of swift swordsmanship Grey specialized in should their truce with the Shade end abruptly.

"Did Sylvia call?" He skirted her question entirely while plucking the frightening Shade's name right out of her mind.

"I was going to ask you the same. I've been out most of the day. Full moon is tomorrow. It's go time." She took a gulp from her cup as she walked over to Grey. "Sorry, fresh out of umbrellas."

This was as good a time as any for alcohol to numb the pain. They'd both had their fill of it. Sage perched on the edge of his bed. Grey accepted the cup and drank from it like a man dying of thirst.

"Last time I spoke with Sylvia, she said she was working on it. She'll call us when she's ready."

"I hate all this uncertainty and waiting." Sage took a slow sip, letting the tangy flavor wash over her tongue before gulping it down.

"Your intuition has been spot-on. Planning, not so much, but as much as I hate to admit it, you have the right read on people. Sylvia will come through for us. Remember the law of attraction."

"You're dying, aren't you?" She nearly choked on her drink. Why was he being so agreeable? Why hadn't he railed on her for sneaking out? Oh Goddess, no. She wouldn't survive it if that were true. "You'd tell me if you were, wouldn't you?"

"Calm down. I'm just trying to keep the faith. Sylvia has been helpful so far. No reason to think she'd double-cross us." He drained the last of his cup and handed it back to her. "How's your hand?"

"Better now that I have pain killers." She set both cups on the bedside table.

"Liar." He reached out and took hold of her blackened hand. "I'm the tough guy here. You don't need to pretend."

"You've got enough pain." She turned her head to avoid looking him in the eye, and ended up staring straight at his broken leg. The makeshift splint looked absolutely ridiculous, but it did its job holding everything straight. No amount of eye bleach would burn away the memory of having to reset his knee cap. How fast could a Terra's bones heal?

Grey smoothed his fingers over the worst parts of her damaged hand. The unexpected softness of his touch stopped her from the downward spiral she'd been heading towards. She sucked in a quick breath, muscles clenching, ready to pull her hand away, but didn't.

"It's okay, Sage. I'll heal," he assured her with confidence. "But you won't until we rid you of this thing." Grey turned her hand over.

She'd never known him to be so gentle. He was the master of combat and cocky words. And yet, here he was, fingertips ghosting over the lines of her palm, drawing circles around the pit in the center where the seed resided.

For all the reasons she should have taken her hand back, she couldn't. She needed this connection more than she was willing to admit.

"Do you really think it will work?" Round and round, her eyes followed Grey's fingertips as he caressed away her aches. His touch worked like some form of magic she couldn't understand.

"It has to. We've come too far to fail." How could he speak so confidently? Death followed them at every turn. His focus was on fixing her hand, but even then, they were still wanted criminals. ASSET would lock them up and throw away the key. The Mystics would do far worse, especially if they were brought in and had no magic worth taking.

"You're doing it again." Grey broke through her dark thoughts, calling her back to the surface again. "No giving up until you're dead, okay?"

His eyes conveyed all the confidence she lacked. They weren't dead yet. On that fact, Grey was one hundred percent correct. They still had plenty more chances to get themselves killed.

"Why go through all of this for me?" she asked.

"We're partners." He pulled away as if she'd burned him, severing their connection. "We made a deal, remember? Honesty. Having each other's backs. Our mission isn't done as far as I am concerned. And I will see you safely to the end of this."

Her palm ached for the connection he'd severed. No. Not only her palm. Another pain she'd tried too hard to bury made itself known. Nobility wasn't exactly the explanation she had hoped he would give her. Every time they touched, she felt it. Tried to ignore it. But couldn't deny it. Grey was more than just a partner to her. Somewhere between the name-calling and one-upping, he'd wormed his way into her heart.

"And when we complete the mission?" she asked.

"You're my partner, Sage. Where is this coming from?"

Her chest felt hollow as if her heart had knocked out all the walls. She picked up her cup from the bedside table and drank deeply, hoping to fill the void.

"Did Matt or Zack say something to you?" Grey asked, oblivious to the true meaning of her question.

Better she not openly admit her feelings. That would just cause drama. And she had her fill of that.

"Matt wants to stay the way he is," she mumbled into her drink, keeping the cup up to her face long enough to hide her emotions.

"I'm sorry."

"No 'I told you so's'." She covered the break in her voice with playful snark.

"I wouldn't dare. I'm already in enough pain."

"Life is pain, or so it seems." She still couldn't wrap her mind around her roommate's decision. It made no sense. "Why would Matt do this?"

"Blood is his master."

"He still thinks he can keep Josh, too, being a vampire," she scoffed.

"Maybe he wants to turn him too," Grey suggested.

Sage set her empty drink on the nightstand. "Why not people the world with vampires?"

"Don't you dare say something like that!" Grey reached out, groaning with the effort, and pulled her down.

She had no strength to fight back. Starved as she was for something positive to hold on to, she needed this connection with Grey. He cradled her head against his chest.

The rhythm of his heart called to her. Muscles in his chest tightened and released with each steady breath.

"You can't carry the weight of the world on your shoulders. Share it with me," he said.

If only she could. "It's hard to let go."

"You have a good heart. It's sweet."

"You mean naïve."

"Stop it."

"Why? You always call me a newbie."

"Because you are. You haven't become jaded by the world. Hold on to that for as long as you can. It's one of your best qualities."

"As is getting people in trouble, or worse."

"Matt must make his own choices," Grey spoke softly. "Who knows? Maybe when he sees you've been cured, he'll come around." His hand found the back of her head, fingertips digging in gently as he raked them through her hair.

That man's touch was magic. She didn't deserve it, but damned if she would tell him to stop. "And you? Your leg?"

"Occupational hazard."

"I made you go there. You warned me not to."

"True. It was a risky mission, but also a successful one."

"How do you figure?"

"You learned where Matt and Zack were, and that they were both safe."

"Luke got hurt too." Everyone she came into contact with ended up injured.

"He kind of owed you one. Call that a draw. And as for me, you want to make it up to me?"

"How?"

"Just be here. Right now. With me."

"How's that supposed to—"

"Shut up and let me have this moment with you."

How could he be so insufferable and endearing at the same time? As much as she wanted to challenge his order, the soothing spell of his heartbeat lulled her into compliance. Tomorrow would bring new drama, but for the moment, she'd allow herself to enjoy this peace.

THIRTY-FOUR

The phone's shrill ringing woke Sage from a deep sleep. At first she thought it came from her dream, but as her eyes opened, the noise continued. She swatted at the nightstand, her hand missing the mark each time, landing with a dull *thud* against the wooden surface.

"Too early," she moaned, even though she hadn't seen the time. Blackout curtains blocked out most of the sunlight, leaving a glowing halo around the window.

The phone continued to ring.

Sage finally pushed herself up and grabbed the receiver. "Yes. What?"

"I'd expect someone so concerned with keeping a low profile to avoid altercations and side-trips around the city." Sylvia's voice came through loud and disapprovingly clear on the line.

"Good morning to you too," Sage grumped back.

"Afternoon. We have a schedule to keep. I expect you to be ready for pickup in one hour."

Sage glanced at the clock. *Just past noon.* Her head ached, punishment for a night of drinking that she had not been able to enjoy. "Yes. We'll be ready. Thanks for the heads-up."

"See that you are. I'm doing you a huge favor, Ms. Cyn-wrig. Don't make me regret it." Sylvia disconnected the line.

Sage stood and went to the sink to splash some water on her face. In the mirror, she watched Grey shift under the covers in the bed behind her. Pain etched across his face with each slow stiff movement. He didn't look any better than the previous night.

She didn't want to ask, fearing the answer would confirm her fears, but they only had an hour to prepare. "You going to be okay?"

He untied the splint and threw his good leg over the side of the bed. "Only one way to find out."

Sage held her breath and turned to face him.

Grey put his weight on his good leg and shifted his other, wincing as he let his foot touch the ground. "I've got this." He pushed off the mattress. "Nope!" he yelped, and fell back on the bed. "Nope. No, I don't."

Sage was at his side in a heartbeat. "Easy now." She helped reposition him back on the bed. Her worst fear confirmed. He'd gone as far as he could on this mission with her. "You're not going anywhere like this."

"I can't let you go off alone. I'm supposed to protect you." Grey sounded angry, but she understood it was not aimed at her.

"You're going to have to stay behind." She put on a brave face, more for herself than for Grey. She'd been counting on him being at her side. Alone, she wasn't sure she could handle Sylvia. If that woman did decide to dou-ble-cross her, she'd be alone. What could she do? No. She couldn't think like that. She had to stay the course. She had to keep positive. She had to get this damn thing out of her hand before it killed her. If Sylvia tried anything, at least she had the stone to protect her. "Sylvia will be here in one hour. And it's another four or five to Sedona."

"I don't like this."

"I know you want to be with me, but you can't even stand. How are you going to protect me?" She turned away, afraid he'd see her tears.

Grey let out a growl of frustration loud enough to shake the walls. His anger matched the intensity of her fear, but they just didn't have the time to argue over this. She walked back toward the bathroom and finished prepping herself for travel.

"At least take my blades," Grey said when she returned fresh from the bathroom.

"What does that leave you with?" she asked.

"You're the target. With you gone, no one will care about me. If ASSET brings me in, at least I know I'll get medical attention." He folded his arms behind his head. "I could use a spa day anyway."

His false smirk looked more convincing than the flimsy mask of bravery she wore. He was lying, obviously, but she wouldn't call him on it. Better he feel he had convinced her to go without additional worry.

Time was ticking away, and whether she liked it or not, this was the way it had to be. She picked up his weapons belt and wrapped it around her waist. "Thanks. I'll be sure to bring them back to you."

"Remember to stick your enemies with the pointy end," he teased. "And don't cut yourself."

He was good. Even as she could see the quiver of his lips, Grey was still trying to play his part to keep her calm.

The phone rang again.

Sage grabbed it. "Yes."

"I'm waiting, Ms. Cynwrig," Sylvia said. "Blue SUV in the parking lot." She disconnected the call.

"Time to go. You sure you will be okay here?" Leaving him felt like the worst kind of betrayal. Sage grabbed her bag of supplies and the oil.

"Go! Hurry, before there's still time," Grey teased as he waved her off.

THIRTY-FIVE

Sage's hand throbbed as she approached the large blue vehicle.

Sylvia rolled down the window of the passenger seat. "You're in the back. We're not taking any chances."

She didn't need to be told twice. Sage opened up the rear door and climbed in.

Sitting next to Sylvia in the driver's seat was a woman Sage hadn't seen since her first meeting with Devon. Nyx. She'd enlarged herself to appear as if she were driving, but Sage could see through the glamour to the tiny pixie fluttering behind the wheel, waving her hands to magic the car into motion.

"Where is your partner?" Sylvia asked.

"He's coming up later. Had some loose ends to tie up."

"I take it the leg hasn't healed?"

Sylvia knew. But how did she know? How long had she been spying?

Sage kept her face neutral, making a mental note. No need to lie. Clearly, Sylvia knew all. "Almost healed."

"I seriously doubt that," Sylvia countered. "Injuries like his… Should be laid up for at least a week."

Sage certainly hoped not. She winced as the seed made its demands known, and sat on her hands, hoping to mute the throbbing. Four hours of it would be the death of her. No. She could last. Only a few more hours of this torture, and she would be free.

"As long as we are not being followed, you shouldn't have to worry much," Sylvia said. "You've been reckless with the safe house and your time. You should have been lying low. Instead, I hear you went to Quarn, your apartment, and had a little tête-à-tête with your vampire friends."

"I was gathering information," Sage offered in defense. "And ingredients."

"You were making your presence much known in the city. I expected a little more intelligence from you," Sylvia reprimanded.

"What did you expect?" Nyx replied before Sage had the chance to say exactly the same words. Her voice floated innocently on the air, much as she did in the driver's seat. A clever deception. Nyx was anything but innocent or sweet despite the clever disguise. She laughed like the ringing of a bell as she continued to speak to Sylvia as if Sage wasn't sitting right there. "She's so young. You'd have been better off locking her up yourself."

"If this spell was not in service to the greater good, I would not help you with it." Sylvia, however, addressed Sage directly with all of her annoyance.

If this was how the entire drive was going to go, Sage would not be able to maintain her composure. Her pain level already inching upward to a ten, it would be a short trip for her attitude to match.

"Your help had nothing to do with the greater good when we talked in your office." Sage reminded herself that she needed Sylvia's help and bit her tongue before saying anything more damaging.

"Shall I have Nyx pull over, then, and let you out?" Sylvia replied.

"No." Sage slunk down into the seat. *Play nice until this is all over.*

"I expect you to do exactly as I say when we get there. To the letter. Do you understand?" Sylvia asked.

"Of course," Sage said, her voice saccharine.

"You may look, but do not touch the supplies I have assembled for your spell," Sylvia instructed.

Behind her seat sat a large cast iron Dutch oven, two jugs of water, and a sword. She could only make out the hilt because the rest was sheathed in a leather scabbard and wrapped in leather cording. Next to all that was a cooler bag, the contents she could only guess.

"Will it be just us three?" Sage asked.

"It's best to keep the guest list small, don't you think?" Nyx giggled.

Her laughter bothered Sage more than the obvious disdain Sylvia was doling out from the front seat. Either she was that excited to be participating, or something very bad was going to happen, and Sage had not been let in on that plan.

"Who else knows about this?" Sage asked.

"I'm sensing a bit of distrust here, Ms. Cynwrig." Sylvia said.

She had hit the nail right on the head. If Sage didn't know better, she'd swear the Shade was psychic. Even so, Sage was Terra. That kind of magic shouldn't work on her.

"You were the one to visit with the Elemental," Sylvia reminded her, referring to Quarn. "Took his blood, as I hear."

"How long have you been following me?" Sage asked.

"That one I'm afraid he revealed to me. The Elemental was quite interested in knowing what you were on about with this spell. He was under the impression this was an ASSET sanctioned mission, and to that end, I did not correct his belief. However, he seemed very adamant that we find a way to follow you there."

"Did you tell him where we were going?"

"Secrets are like underwear, my dear," Nyx teased. "Be careful who you reveal them to. Even your closest ally might embarrass you with them later."

"You know how I feel about your secrets," Sylvia said.

"I just thought you guys had like a trust circle or something. You know. Devon and all."

"The only one you chose not to include in this," Sylvia was quick to point out.

"He has a reputation to maintain."

"And we do not?" Sylvia asked.

"I didn't mean it like that. He was tied to Devon. I couldn't involve him." Sage needed to just shut her mouth. The more she spoke, the bigger the hole she dug herself into.

"She was right to leave Devon out of it. Imagine the position she'd put him in, with ASSET actively searching for her." Nyx surprised her with the seriousness of her tone. Sage had begun to wonder if the pixie could speak without giggling.

"You do as you're told," Sylvia ordered. "We get that thing out of your palm and back into a safe vessel, and everyone goes home. I have meetings in the morning I do not plan to miss, so there will be no screwups."

THIRTY-SIX

Sedona was as beautiful as any desert could be. The red rocks were a nice contrast to the browns and occasional greens surrounding them. They drove into Boynton Canyon, a place that felt as magical as it looked. If Sage's hand had not been in flames the whole ride down there, it would have certainly ignited the minute they entered into the glorious canyon. Nyx bypassed the parking area and took the SUV off-road and down a trail she seemed to know.

When they finally came to a clear spot, far from prying eyes, Nyx and Sylvia went to work.

"Sit here in the dirt and don't touch anything," Sylvia ordered and began placing stones in a circular pattern around Sage.

Nyx sent out her magical confetti as she flitted around in all directions. "This should cause any humans to turn away, but won't negate magic. We still need that to work here."

The last time she'd seen the pixie do something similar, it was to stop anyone spying on Devon's gym. Grey had broken through that easily being a Terra.

She wished he were here now. Sylvia and Nyx had not given her a reason to distrust, but she couldn't help the sinking feeling in the pit of her stomach. The spell had no guarantee of working. And that weighed heavy on her mind. If this was all for naught, what would she do?

Grey would tell her to stop worrying, to deal if it happened. Devon would tell her no good came from worrying. It wouldn't change the outcome.

She sighed and watched as the two women worked. Sylvia drew patterns in the sand with salt. The white on red made a striking contrast. The random squiggles and lines could be words. Maybe some ancient language. She wanted to ask but, interrupting the Shade when she looked so deep in concentration would only result in her getting another earful of how rotten and impudent a child she was. At least Grey used small words, calling her a newbie. Sylvia preferred to insult with pomposity.

Nyx retrieved the cauldron, floating it to a spot a few inches in front of Sage before conjuring a fire for it to sit upon. "Careful, it gets hot very quickly, and will stay that way for a long time after the fire dies."

"Is there anything I can do?" Sage felt all but useless sitting there.

"You can't touch anything until we remove that." Nyx pointed to her hand.

Sage sighed and let her head drop between her knees.

"Rather than sulk, Ms. Cynwrig, why not prepare your mind and body?" Sylvia called out as she began to place crystal pillars at points around Sage. "A great deal of whether or not magic works comes from your own belief. How can you think to call forth the Great Mother to assist you if you don't believe she will?"

"Law of attraction. Even the humans know of this," Nyx added.

That had been the theme of all Grey's pep talks over the past few days. Maybe it was time she really adopted it.

"I have hope," Sage replied.

"Hope gets you nothing. Believe it with all your heart." Nyx sounded as if she were singing the words. "The Mother will have no choice but to come and channel her energy through our talismans."

"Believe. Believe. Believe," Sage chanted to herself, silly as it sounded, but it didn't change the way she felt or the sick feeling in her stomach. So much could go wrong. So much rode on the need for it not to.

"What are you afraid of?" Sylvia broke through her inner monologue, sounding surprisingly concerned.

"What if it doesn't work?" Sage answered truthfully.

"What if the Mother chooses to strike you dead?" Sylvia replied. "Or in working the spell, we are all killed for daring to invoke her power?"

Nyx hovered for a moment, looking as equally shocked as Sage.

"That would be terrible," Sage admitted.

"Exactly." Sylvia began to fade into black smoke. "Which is why you need to banish those thoughts from your mind. They serve no good purpose."

"I don't mean to be a pessimist." Sage tamped down on her anxiety. Seeing Sylvia shifting between forms was never a good sign. "I'm just being real."

"We're dealing with magic, child. What humans call fantasy. I hear you're something of an expert in that." Sylvia disappeared into black smoke and reappeared right in front of Sage.

Sage jumped backwards. "I guess you could say that."

"And what would the fantasy version of you do when going up against the big, bad adversary?" Sylvia surprised her with such an accurate question.

Sage had never thought about it before. Sylvia's analogy made sense. Free of reality, Sage played her game characters with a confidence that often bordered on recklessness. And it was fun. If the spell worked, she'd win. If she lost, she'd probably die, and that was an inevitability anyway so she'd only be speeding up the timeline. The only difference was her refusing to let go of the worry.

"Well, Ms. Cynwrig? Has that thing in your hand somehow stolen your voice?"

"You're right. I believe this will work." Sage smiled and closed her eyes. She imagined herself as the cleric high priest she had last played during game night. Powerful. Brave. Filled with magic. Sage turned her face up to the sky and called to the Mother.

I believe you want more from me than to shrivel up and die as my magic is devoured. I made an oath to serve magic. I am your servant, and I trust that you will take this curse from me.

When she opened her eyes, twilight cast the desert in its Ethereal glow. Reds turned to orange in the fading light. Greens became turquoise. The sky shifted between purples and pinks. What few clouds dared to float overhead burned in bright oranges and yellows.

"It's time." Sylvia brandished the old sword Sage had seen sheathed in the SUV. She dipped the blade into the cauldron bubbling with water.

Nyx floated with a jug of water and dumped it over the top of Sage's head. "Ritual cleansing. Sorry for the quick shower. Can't really scrub you down."

"You could have let me do it." Sage shook herself and pulled strands of wet hair from her face.

"You're tainted. No, I couldn't." Nyx stuck her tongue out. She flitted off to the SUV and returned with a burning stick of sage. "Stand very still." Nyx flew circles around Sage, wrapping her in heavy white smoke.

When the haze cleared, Sage saw Sylvia performing a similar bathing on the sword. She pulled the bottle of oil Sage had brewed and stroked the blade, anointing it with the oil while she chanted something under her breath.

Sage whispered a prayer to the Mother that the oil would work.

"Now the blood," Sylvia called to Nyx.

With the tip of the sword, Sylvia pierced Nyx's hand, and let her blood fall into the bubbling cauldron. She repeated the same process with her own hand. "You have obtained Quarn's blood?"

Sage nodded. "In my bag."

Nyx flew off and returned with Sage's bag. She up-ended it, pouring all the contents into the sand before finding the vial. She popped it open and poured it into the cauldron.

The smoke billowing from it turned black and rose up to the sky. Moments before, there had been but a few wisps burning away in the twilight. They had all but disappeared as the sky darkened above them. Sage couldn't quite make out clouds in the sudden void. Only black, empty space.

A chill ran down her spine, and that all too familiar feeling of unseen eyes settled on her.

The Mother is listening. Sage gasped with the realization. *This might actually work. No. It will work!*

"Down here, Ms. Cynwrig," Sylvia commanded. "Look to me."

She did as ordered and let out another shocked gasp, seeing Sylvia pull the sword from the cauldron. It had to be a trick of her vision. The sword gave off a strange glow as Sylvia lifted it high overhead.

"Blood of the families created by the Mother and Father," Sylvia shouted and pointed the sword above her head, towards the black void that had settled above her. "Lend me your power."

A flash of light blinded them. Sage blinked and refocused on Sylvia, just in time to see the sword slip from the Shade's grasp. Sylvia looked as if she'd been frozen in time. Then suddenly, she crumpled to the ground.

"What the hell just happened?" Sage held her breath. They couldn't have failed already. They'd only just started. Was it the oil? Why had she brewed the oil herself?

Nyx's glowing form turned red hot. She flew up above them, her head turning this way and that. "Someone is here."

The unseen eyes. Not the Mother. Sage reached for Grey's machetes belted at her waist and pulled them out.

Sylvia lay motionless on the ground. The sword, no longer glowing, had embedded itself into the dirt next to her, sticking straight up like a fabled weapon of old.

Another flash of light and Nyx fell from the sky, her glowing body shifting from red to a dim white when she landed a few feet from Sylvia.

Sage turned around, trying to locate whoever it was that had attacked. She hadn't heard a gunshot. No sounds of weaponry of any kind. Magic was definitely at play. Her hand had been burning for so long she'd gotten used to the pain. As long as that seed remained in her hand, no magic would harm her.

"Enough with the games." She dropped her grip on the machete handles and held her hand out in front of her. "Show yourself, now!"

"Give an old man a moment. The terrain is a bit treacherous." Quarn hobbled slowly out from behind a large shrub. "Easy now." He held his webbed hands out peacefully. "I'm here to save you."

"How the hell did you know where we were?" Sage wasn't sure what to make of his sudden appearance. The desert wasn't his element, so he couldn't possibly be comfortable here. It had to count for something that he'd come all this way. And based on how he'd dressed, robes covering every inch of his skin, she guessed he was more than just a little uncomfortable.

"I was concerned when you would not reveal your intentions for a practitioner of this level of magic. You couldn't possibly be working under ASSET sanctions." He smiled, those shark-like teeth on display. His coal black eyes reflected the light of the fire as he approached. "I went to my dear friends here with my concerns."

"What did you do to them?" Sage demanded.

"Stopped them from making a very big mistake. One that could have killed you. I warned you this was dangerous magic, did I not?"

"Are they dead?" She couldn't tell if they were breathing. Nyx was too tiny, and Sylvia had fallen on the opposite side of the cauldron, out of sight.

"Stunned only. I assure you." Quarn stopped just out of Sage's reach.

"You should have come to me. Or at the very least, ASSET if you really felt concern." She stalled for time, trying to get a read on him. Her intuition had been spot-on up to this point, but she just couldn't figure him out.

"Indeed I did go to ASSET and learned quite surprisingly that you were wanted for misuse of magic." Neither

Quarn's tone nor his expression betrayed anything of his intentions.

Could he be telling the truth? If so, he might have spared her life. But why? If his purpose was so noble, why hadn't he joined with Nyx and Sylvia? For that matter, why had they not asked him to join them? Too many questions. ASSET too. He said he had inquired.

"Where are they, then?" she asked. "If you were so concerned, why not tell my bosses? They are, after all, the law."

"You wouldn't be attempting such a spell if you didn't want to be reinstated. Consider it a favor that I kept your secret from them. Imagine what that would look like." He clicked his teeth disapprovingly.

That was enough to set off warning bells. "Get to the part where you tell me what you're really up to," Sage demanded.

"Isn't that obvious?" Quarn smiled.

"How long have you been with the Mystics?" Sage asked.

A twig snapped behind her. He had been stalling the whole time. Dammit. She clenched her good hand tight around one of Grey's machetes and held her damaged hand out as a shield, ready for what was to come.

"Very sad to see Grey was not able to make it," Quarn said.

"No you're not."

"Well. Seeing as how I cannot touch you in the current state, why don't we finish what they started?"

"You're not getting the—"

"It will kill you eventually." Quarn spoke the warning calmly. "I can have my people hold you until that happens, or you can go through with this now and walk away with your life."

She had another option. Sage turned to run and crashed into a brick wall of a man. Human. Another appeared before she could move. Everything happened in a blink. She was disarmed, restrained, and turned to face Quarn.

"Let me go!" Sage shrieked.

Arms like cannons wrapped around Sage in a bear hug that threatened to squash all the breath from her lungs. She tried to head butt him, but she bounced against the taut muscles of his massive chest. When that didn't work, she bared her teeth and bit at any flesh she could reach.

The man roared but didn't let her go. A second man, one unseen, made himself known with a hard strike to the side of her head.

Stars danced in her vision. Someone was speaking to her, a shapeless blob, maybe a man. It didn't matter. She couldn't understand what they were saying. Everything sounded as if it were underwater.

He ripped the locket from her neck and pressed it into her damaged palm.

Vision fuzzy, twinkling stars still blinking in and out of her line of sight, she didn't register at first. But after a moment, sounds became words. Quarn was giving orders to someone. The shapeless blob came into focus. A man. Military by the looks of him. Armed to the teeth. He was dragging something. A body bag.

"Put it there." Quarn gave the order.

The mercenary was joined by another. Together, they dragged the bag to Quarn's feet, dropped it, and unzipped.

"Grey," she shouted. It was him. Unconscious, she hoped. Still wearing the ridiculous leg splint. "What did you do to him?" She struggled, trying to free herself from the iron grip of the giant holding her.

"No harm will come to either of you if you cooperate. I quite like you and your partner here." Quarn bent down and shuffled through the items left next to the cauldron. He sniffed at the bottle of oil Sage had brewed. "But if you continue to be a problem for me and my organization, you will be removed."

The man holding her pushed her forward, toward the fire and cauldron. If not for Grey lying there unconscious, she'd have tried again to make a break for it. Damn him. Quarn had played her well. Checkmate.

"Why?" she asked.

"I don't think so." Quarn bent down and pulled the sword from the ground. He rubbed away the sand and dirt from the blade and dipped it into the bubbling cauldron for a quick moment. "My offer is all you need to be concerned with. Do as I say, and you and Agent Maddox here are free to walk away."

Just as Sylvia and Nyx had done before, Quarn pierced his hand and let his blood run into the pot. He bent down a second time and grabbed Grey's limp hand and repeated the process, letting blood dribble down into the pot. Quarn smiled as smoke began to billow again from the cauldron, thick and white. It crawled out over the sides and down to the ground like a thick fog, reaching out in all directions around them.

"This spell requires blood of all the classes. Terra too. Not tainted as yours has become." Quarn plunged the sword into the bubbling pot. "Ethereal, Elemental, Shade, and Terra. Blood of the families wrought by the Mother and Father. Givers of the magic." He pushed the sword down farther, its blade disappearing completely into the pot. "What you have created we call upon you to destroy." He stopped as the handle neared the smoke, turning his coal black eyes on Sage. "Hold out your hand."

Sage clenched her fist tight around the locket. The man at her side yanked her hand out.

"Open your palm, please," Quarn requested. "Or I will cut the whole appendage off."

Sage closed her eyes, trying to conjure the image of white light. *Mother, if you are there, please, send help.*

"Do not try my patience." Quarn held the handle of the sword deep within the depths of the bubbling liquid.

Sage opened her eyes and gazed into the dark void that had settled overhead. She thought she heard a rumbling. Thunder perhaps. Maybe the Great Mother had listened.

"Please listen." Sage's voice cracked. "You are a scholarly man. You preach on the Great Mother's blessing. You know you cannot abuse the power she has sent to earth. That is why it must be kept in neutral hands."

The rumbling was getting louder. A constant sound like thunder but without a beginning or end.

"You are too young to understand what is happening. And yours are far from neutral hands. If that were true, I would not have to employ mortals to help me," Quarn replied.

"Has he promised you magic?" she whispered to the man holding her. "He can't bestow magic on a human, no matter what he says. You have to help me."

Quarn lifted the sword from the bubbling pot. It glowed white hot. "Enough. The hand or the arm. Your choice!"

Sage winced as she opened her hand, fearing the pain that was to come.

A spotlight blasted their circle. The thunder growled overhead in a roaring crescendo. Sage turned to look. A helicopter, the source of the sound, was speeding toward them, its spotlight having found the mark.

Searing heat sliced through her open hand. Sage let out a scream loud enough to wake the dead. Quarn had run her through the center of her palm. The white-hot blade burned with a fire unlike anything she had ever felt before. It was as if her entire body had gone up in flames but was never consumed by them. She dared a glimpse at her skewered hand, but tears washed away her vision.

Helicopter blades whirled above. Sand blasted them all as the helicopter landed nearby.

Quarn glanced around suspiciously. "You told ASSET?"

Mark! He'd told her to come here. It had to be him bringing the cavalry.

Sage couldn't form the words. The blade embedded in her palm. The pain. The electric shocks of magic. It all short-circuited her brain. She could not summon her voice for anything but the scream that continued to pour from her throat.

Grey stirred at Quarn's feet. His eyes fluttered open and closed again.

Black-uniformed soldiers descended on their circle.

A hood came over Sage's head, throwing the world into darkness. A hand clasped around her wrist. She felt the sword come free, but pain remained.

All around her, Sage heard sounds of fighting. Quarn bellowed a scream of his own, almost as terrifying as the one that had come from her own mouth. But before the sounds had died out, Sage found herself being shoved toward the thundering blades of the helicopter.

It was bound to happen at some point. She'd have to face the music, and her fate with ASSET. Another sharp blow to the head silenced her pain as she fell into the abyss of unconsciousness.

THIRTY-SEVEN

An electric shock jolted Sage back into the world. The hood came off, and she found herself in a dark room she'd never been in before. The disapproving face glaring down at her, however, she was very familiar with.

"You've had quite the run, Ms. Cynwrig." Ava's tone matched the anger in her eyes. So much for a happy reunion.

"I was trying—"

"I don't need your excuses or crybaby explanations. You have caused more trouble than you're worth. And skipping town like that... I should have you locked away for the rest of your days. You and Mr. Maddox, wherever he is."

"Why don't you do it, then, and spare me the lecture." Sage clutched her hand. Somewhere between the desert and the prison she had found herself in, it had been wrapped up tight. The bandages were near soaked through with blood, but she still managed to wiggle her fingers, so there was hope of healing.

"You are in no position to make demands." Ava stood. She crossed her arms and took a loud breath. "Your fate is no longer in my hands. Can you stand?"

What did that mean? Sage regretted her snarky tone. If she hadn't been so quick to snap, maybe Ava would have explained herself. No way was she getting that now.

"I can try." Sage tested her muscles. Everything hurt, but she managed to work her way slowly to her feet.

Ava turned on her heels and headed toward the door. "Follow me."

Sage followed behind, down a long, sterile hallway. They had to be back at ASSET, but she'd never seen this on the tour.

Ava pushed open a set of double doors, and light flooded her vision, blinding Sage as she entered. It opened wide like an amphitheater. Magical creatures had been assembled in seats all around. The Magical Confederacy. She remembered Grey mentioning this before, the governing body with powers above even ASSET.

Sage gulped as she gazed down. In the center of the room, a full flight of stairs below where she stood, a single seat sat in the middle.

This was a trial.

Ava led Sage down to that seat. "Sit here and don't say a word until I tell you. Do you understand?"

She was on trial. No, more like a firing squad. Where was her lawyer? Did magical law provide her with one? Panic sent her heart racing. Sage collapsed in the seat. Her hand ached as she rested it on the arm of the wooden chair.

In front of her, four chairs sat behind a wooden desk. Ava took her place in the farthest seat. Sage had never met the other beings occupying the remaining chairs, but it was clear they were representatives of their classes of magic.

Shades were represented by a gaunt-looking man, his balding head partially ringed in shaggy white hair. Ethereals were represented by a woman in gold. Her body glowed with an inner light that gave her the appearance of an angel. At any moment, Sage expected wings to sprout from her back. The Elemental representative was the scariest of the bunch, even more sinister-looking than the Shades. Hair of flames danced from the top of a tiny red man's head, the only one not sitting. He stood maybe two feet tall, on top of the desk. Small as he was, the vibe Sage got from him was nothing short of terror. Magic or not, fire was never something to mess with.

"Shall we begin?" the Elemental asked.

"We are ready," Ava said.

The attending crowd above them, a mix of all varieties of magical families, murmured with interest.

"It has been reported that a dangerous weapon," the Elemental man read from a paper in front of him, "one with the potential to destroy anything magical it touches, has gone missing."

Gasps of shock echoed around the large room.

"No such weapon exists in ASSET databases," Ava replied loudly.

"With respect, Mrs. Masters." The gaunt man unfolded his hands and turned to address Ava. "This isn't the first time ASSET has hidden the truth from the magical community."

The Elemental man spoke again. "We have reports that a vampire coven in North Town was decimated with exactly that weapon."

"Let the record show, ASSET headquarters came under attack not a week after that reported vampire coven was unfortunately destroyed," Ava replied, calm as ever.

"Noted." The Ethereal woman picked up a pen and scribbled something on the paper in front of her. "We also have reports of a Brownie, Shadowrunner, and Gemini Twins taken captive soon after."

"Yes." Ava made a show of shuffling her papers, as if looking for the right case. "Our agents apprehended a kitsune attempting to create the Amulet of Emmuri."

"Where is the amulet now?" the Ethereal asked.

Sage held her breath.

"Destroyed," Ava answered.

"How is this possible?" Fire flickered on top of the Elemental man's head. He turned and stared at Ava, eager for her answer.

That woman had the best poker face Sage had ever seen. Ava had the attention of the entire room, but not a bead of sweat formed on her brow. "Our agents located and shattered it before it was complete. All the magical beings were recovered and returned to their families, safely."

The Ethereal's focus shifted curiously from Ava to Sage. "Who was the agent who did this?"

"That would be Agent Cynwrig," Ava answered without hesitation.

"Can you point her out?"

Ava pointed to Sage.

She gulped, feeling as if a noose had just been tied around her neck. Her hand throbbed with each thundering beat of her racing heart.

"How is it that a low level agent was able to destroy something so powerful?"

"As I just said, she shattered the amulet before it was complete," Ava replied.

"Impossible," the Elemental roared. "Even incomplete, that amulet would have had immense power."

"Power a Terra is not affected by," Ava reminded him.

"Smashing it would do little to it," the Elemental replied.

"It's what I have here in her report." Ava held up a piece of paper. "I believe you all have copies."

The crowd above rumbled, a mix of horror and dissent. They weren't buying it, despite Ava's convincing performance. They were going to make her reveal her hand. That would be it. Soon as they saw it, she'd be executed for the good of all magic or whatever nonsense they decreed.

"I have another report from a pair of Ethereals who visited this agent of yours." The Ethereal woman held up a paper of her own. "She claims to have the power to remove magic. Called it the Terra's special gift."

Ava shuffled papers around and retrieved another from the pile. "According to my agent's report, they were abusing their magic in public, and she did not feel safe to apprehend on her own. She embellished in order to remove them from the premises."

"You have an answer for everything, don't you, Mrs. Masters?" The Elemental man seemed to have it out for Ava. His hair ignited with every answer she came up with to their accusations.

"ASSET runs a tight ship. I expect my agents to not only do their job well, but safely." Ava stared the little red man down. "She was not in a position, being a new agent, so she performed a little theatrical damage control. I have placed those two Elementals on a watch list, as they have been rumored to belong to the Order of the Mystics."

The crowd above gasped all at once at the mention of the Mystics.

"Rather than halt our ability to execute the law and track down those who are actively breaking it, why don't we end this charade of a trial?" Ava continued.

"ASSET has repeatedly broken the very laws they were meant to uphold using the execution of law as their excuse." The Elemental's flames flickered. "We will not allow that to happen when a weapon of such magnitude, as to extinguish the very flame of magic, is running wild under the cloak of your organization."

"If a weapon like that existed, do you think we would dare allow it out of our sights?" Ava replied.

"It does and you have," the Elemental shouted. "And we're here to prove it."

"By hauling my agent down here like some common criminal?" Ava replied.

"According to our records, you have her listed as unfit for duty. And as of a few days ago, she was listed on your magical most wanted list." Flames shot up two feet above the Elemental's head.

"You do realize that our organization works in secret, do you not?" Ava fired back. "Agents, especially undercover ones, must appear to be working outside of our jurisdiction."

"A junior agent. Barely through training," he scoffed. "What undercover mission could she have possibly been assigned to?"

Ava nodded to the top of the amphitheater. Sage looked up and spotted Devon. He opened the door, and two more agents dragged an unconscious Quarn into the room. Chains circled his body, and wrapped around his webbed hands like cuffs.

Ava smiled as she turned to address the Elemental man. "Agents Cynwrig and Maddox have been ferreting out members of the Mystics."

Murmurs from the crowd seemed to hush as Quarn was carried on his way down to where Sage sat.

The three representatives put their heads together and whispered quietly.

Sage tried to make eye contact with Ava, but her former boss refused to look at her. She really regretted smarting off now. Her only hope lay in Ava's ability to keep them from looking at her hand.

"This council has a hard time believing that a junior agent has been so successful," the Elemental said. "We return to the accusation that she is in possession of a weapon of magical destruction."

Quarn began to wake, no longer hanging limply from the arms of the guards holding him.

"You have brought charges against my organization as well as one of my agents based on nothing more than rumor," Ava answered with outrage. "ASSET has been serving and protecting magic since the dawn of time. You do realize that in doing this, you are revealing the very need of our organization? Power corrupts. At the mere mention of a weapon that could destroy magic, you are all clamoring to destroy the one organization that could safeguard it. What if that weapon were to be real? What if it were to fall into any of your hands? Read your histories. Before the Mother created us, you were all at each other's throats. Your lust for power and control nearly destroyed the world. And here you are at it again, salivating at the mere mention of it, ready to destroy what has kept the peace."

"If you are so keen to prove this weapon does not exist, then humor us," the Shade said, his voice the calmest of all the representatives.

Ava stepped down and joined Sage. "Where is this supposed weapon?"

Quarn lifted his head. "Her hand," he rasped.

Ava motioned for Sage to stand. As she did, Ava took her uninjured hand. "This one? Bring forth the accused. Let her touch him and see what happens."

Quarn jerked back. Chains rattled as he struggled against the two agents holding him.

"What about the bandaged hand? What is it hiding?" the Ethereal asked.

"She's badly injured," Ava replied. "The accused man here attempted to remove it."

"We'd like to see, if you don't mind." The Ethereal looked on eagerly. "Why would such a man be driven to remove a Terra's hand?"

Sage winced. "It hurts."

"She has not yet healed," Ava replied.

"We need proof."

The guards positioned Quarn within Sage's reach.

"Apologies, dear. This might hurt a bit." Ava took a knife and made quick work of slicing the bandages open. They fell to the ground bloody.

Her hand was still black and blue, topped with a fresh coating of crusted blood. A clean line from the gap between her ring and middle finger ran all the way to her wrist. The sword had nearly cleaved her hand in two. Exposed to the air and without the bandages keeping it together, the wound gaped, oozing fresh blood. Sage held back the chunks threatening to burst from her throat as she looked at her ruined hand.

Ava held it up. "You see what he did to her, all because of a rumored weapon of death? He and others in the order of the Mystics were willing to butcher my agent for this fantasy weapon."

"It was said her touch would destroy magic. She had the weapon in her body," Quarn called out in his defense.

Ava brought Sages hand down to touch Quarn's shoulder.

Sage hissed in pain. Her hand felt as if it were splitting in two. Blood belched out from the wound, painting Quarn's shoulder.

"Please, stop," she screamed. Her knees went slack.

Quarn sucked in a breath and jerked away. He didn't make it but a step sideways before the guards had him back in place.

Ava released Sage's hand. Her knees buckled, sending her crashing to the floor.

"You see? Nothing happened other than my agent being tortured to assuage your bloodlust," Ava addressed the room. "ASSET is not in the business of furthering any magical family's desires for power. What you have done here today is prove that we are the only reason peace exists. Not a one of you had any concern for the repercussions of what you have forced us to do here today. But rest assured that we are aware of the order of the Mystics. We will be ferreting out each and every one of you, and when we do, you will wish we had this weapon you've accused us of having. Because your punishment will be far worse." Ava turned to Sage. "Get up and let's get that hand taken care of."

"Mrs. Masters, we are not done here," the Elemental said.

"Oh yes we are," Ava replied. "You know the way out. And if you don't, my agents will be happy to show you."

Sage limped up the stairs behind Ava.

Devon came down and lent her his strength, acting as her crutch. "You look like you're on death's door."

"If she loses too much more blood, she will be," Ava replied. "Hurry now."

THIRTY-EIGHT

Ava moved swiftly toward the infirmary. Sage's legs gave way, and Devon was forced to carry her the rest of the way.

Inside, Grey was already laid out across one of the medical beds, his leg wrapped properly. He looked a lot better than he had back in the desert.

Devon set Sage on top of the other medical bed. He and Ava worked quickly, pouring stinging liquid over the top of her bleeding hand.

"I do apologize for all of the theatrics. It was necessary." Ava talked as she stitched Sage's hand closed. "The Mystics have a reach far greater than we had originally anticipated. They are like a cancer on the magical community. All the families are vying for power again just like before, and frankly, we just don't have enough agents to control them."

"My hand." Sage could barely speak.

"The seed is gone," Ava replied. She worked quickly, finishing her stitching, and snipped the thread.

Devon took over and began wrapping it tightly.

"Where?" Sage turned away, not wanting to look at her hand. Grey came into view, unconscious, but breathing.

"Agent Maddox was instrumental in helping us locate it. It appears the spell worked." Ava held up the locket for Sage. She pressed the button on it, and a dark pebble fell out.

Devon set Sage's hand gently across her chest.

Ava held the seed out. "A demonstration." She offered it to Devon.

He picked it up without hesitation.

Sage held her breath, but nothing happened.

"See, just a rock now," Ava confirmed.

"It worked!" Sage released her breath in a loud sigh of relief. "Matt has to know."

"The vampire?" Devon asked. "Your roommate?"

"Yes."

"Absolutely not," Ava replied. "It will kill him, not save him."

"But how?"

"You invoked the power of the Mother to destroy the magic. Imbued in the sword, it gave it the power to slice through your hand and push out the seed." Ava took back the seed and replaced it into the locket. "It killed the magic it touched. The seed is void of any magic now. If you were to do that to a vampire, it would kill the magic animating them. His body is dead. He cannot change."

If she had any tears left, Sage would have wept for Matt. She'd held out hope for him after seeing herself fixed. But now there was nothing. She had to accept him as a vampire and all that entailed. At least he had accepted it. Or so he'd said the last time they were together.

"Sylvia and Nyx?" she asked, remembering they had been laid out in the desert.

"They are both fine. Quarn only stunned them," Devon said. "I have to say I am very disappointed in him.

I've known that man most of my life. To think he was part of the Order…"

"Why?" Sage asked.

"Power corrupts. He would have claimed it and used it to dole out his own justice. Fanatics are often born of zealots." Devon sighed. "Speaking of, I need to see to our special guest." He gave Sage a nod of approval before seeing himself out of the infirmary.

Ava set the locket down on top of Sage's hand. "You're going to need a few days to heal."

"I will, right?" Sage asked.

"Of course you will. And then we will talk about your next assignment." Ava moved between Sage and Grey's beds. "Since the two of you work so well off the grid, I am going to assign you to our Shadow Ops division."

Sage sat up, clutching her hand to her chest. Would it ever stop hurting? "So we're not fired?"

"You never were. Didn't you hear what I said back there? We had to make it look legit. And as poor as you have been at keeping secrets, you had to be made to feel it was real."

"But now that I know…"

"I trust you've learned enough to be able to handle working undercover." Ava stared down her nose at Sage.

She nodded, not quite sure how else to respond.

"Congratulations on your promotion, Agent Cynwrig. You and Agent Maddox may take the rest of the week to heal. Once you're both cleared for duty, I will give you your first assignment."

Sage turned to Grey, wishing he were awake to hear the good news. "Yes, ma'am," she mumbled.

"I trust you two will take full advantage of your time off. See that you are ready to work upon your return." Ava walked to the doorway. "Dismissed."

334

BOOKS BY KATIE SALIDAS

Agents of A.S.S.E.T.
A Weapon of Magical Destruction
A Taste of Your Own Magic
Magic in Disguise

Chronicles of the Uprising
Dissension
Complication
Revolution
Transition
Retribution
Annihilation

Little Werewolf
Pretty Little Werewolf
Curious Little Werewolf
Fearless Little Werewolf

Immortalis
Carpe Noctem
Hunters & Prey
Pandora's Box
Soustone
Dark Salvation

Olde Town Pack
Moonlight
Mated
Being Alpha

Autographed Editions of all Katie Salidas books may be purchased at www.KatieSalidas.com

Book 5: Retribution

Former gladiator turned freedom fighter, Mira has carved a trail from New Haven to Caldera Grove and back, freeing her people, the vampires, from enslavement by the humans. But with victory almost within reach, a new and powerful enemy emerges. One who'll be satisfied with nothing less than complete subjugation--or destruction--of all supernatural beings.

Book 6: Annihilation

2017 RONE award Finalist

Still clinging rabidly to power, the Elites spin lies of prejudice and hatred, stoking the flames of war between humanity and otherkin. Mira, had sacrificed everything. But it will take more than even she can give to end this war or face annihilation.

THE IMMORTALIS SERIES

"Becoming a vampire is easy. Living with the condition, that's the hard part."

Book 1: Carpe Noctem

Bloodlust, fanatical vampire hunters, thousand-year old vendettas, and a pair of sharp, new fangs. Newly-turned vampire, Alyssa got a lot more than she bargained for when Lysander gave her the dark gift of immortality.

Book 2: Hunters & Prey

Rule number one: humans and vampires don't co-exist. One is the hunter and one is the prey. Simple, right? Not for newly-turned vampire Alyssa.

Book 3: Pandora's Box

When the box is opened, the sinister creature within is released, and only supernatural blood will satiate its thirst. Alyssa and the Peregrinus clan soon learns how it feels when the hunter becomes the hunted.

Book 4: Soulstone

Save her mate, or save her clan? Alyssa's choices could doom more than just the vampires living in Boston.

Book 5: Dark Salvation

Targeted, and marked for death, Kitara's only hope lies with the lethally seductive yet emotionally scarred vampire warrior, Nicholas.

If you like Shifters

Both the Olde Town Pack (Adult) and the Little Werewolf (Young Adult) series belong in the Immortalis Series world.

Little Werewolf Series
(YA Wolf-Shifters)

Book 1: Pretty Little Werewolf
2016 RONE award Runner Up: Best YA Paranormal
All Giselle ever wanted was a family... who can accept her for what she is, a werewolf.

Book 2: Curious Little Werewolf
Just when she thought she found the fur-ever home she's always wanted a witch blows into town promising to reveal the bloody past of Giselle's birth, and the circumstances that led the little werewolf to end up in the foster care system to begin with.

Book 3: Fearless Little Werewolf
In the game of Alphas, claiming the title is the greatest prize, one which most would kill to achieve. But for Giselle to win, she'll have to risk her pack, her family... and her life.

THE OLDE TOWN PACK
(Adult Wolf-Shifters)

Book 1: Moonlight
Good girls don't wear fur, fight over men, or run around naked, howling at the moon. Good thing no-one ever called Fallon a good girl.

Book 2: Mated
All the man-candy you can take, with none of the calories, because this one's off limits. The ultimate forbidden fruit. Confirmed bachelor, serial womanizer, and self-proclaimed sex god.

Boyfriend or mate... No way! He'd never let a woman tie him down... like that.

But Rachel Marsden might give him a reason to change his ways.

Book 3: Being Alpha
Newly minted Regional Alpha, Aeson Silverman hit the jackpot. Power, prestige, and wealth, he's got everything a wolf-shifter could ask for.

Except love.

About the Author

Katie Salidas is a best-selling author known for her unique genre-bending style.

Host of the Indie Youtube Talkshow, Spilling Ink, nerd, Doctor Who fangirl, Las Vegas Native, and SuperMom to three awesome kids, Katie gives new meaning to the term sleep-deprived.

Since 2010 she's penned four bestselling book series: the Immortalis, Olde Town Pack, Little Werewolf, and the RONE award-winning Chronicles of the Uprising. And as her not-so-secret alter ego, Rozlyn Sparks, she is a USA Today bestselling author of romance with a naughty side.

Facebook
http://www.facebook.com/pages/Katie-Salidas-Author/214780936916

Web
http://www.katiesalidas.com/

Twitter
http://twitter.com/QuixoticKatie

Email
KatieSalidas@gmail.com

SpillingInk
https://www.youtube.com/c/spillinginkshow

Join the Paranormal Posse
Connect directly with Katie and get exclusives and updates.
https://www.facebook.com/groups/ParanormalPosse/

Please Review

Your opinion matters! When people first look at a book, beyond the description and the cover, they pay close attention to what others **like you** have to say.

If the book is getting overwhelmingly good or bad reviews, it can weigh heavily on that readers decision whether or not to click that purchase button.

It does not have to be a book report.
It does not have to be 5 stars. *I would never ask for any special favoritism.*

A book review is simply sharing what you thought of the book. It answers two very simple questions:

Did you like it?
Would you recommend it to someone else?

That's it. Your opinion matters. Most importantly to me, because I want to ensure you are enjoying the books I write. But beyond my hope for your satisfaction, the review you write caries great weight in the publishing realm as well. It can quite literally make or break a book.

So, here I am, groveling at your feet.

If you have read one (or more) of my books, would you do me the greatest of honors and leave a review?